I0633298

SPIRIT RANCH

Prequel to *The New Witch*
First book in the Broussard Court Series

Nancy Smith Gibson
and
William J. (Bill) Schuler

Moonshine Cove Publishing, LLC
Abbeville, South Carolina U.S.A.
First Moonshine Cove Edition November
2021

ISBN: 9781952439216

Library of Congress LCCN: 2021921779

SPIRITS SURROUND US ALL, AND IT'S UP TO US TO LISTEN TO WHAT THEY ARE TELLING US—WHERE TO GO AND WHAT TO DO...

From the bayous of south Louisiana to the arid hills of Arizona, they follow us. Or maybe they beat us there. We can do nothing except listen and obey.

Deep in the swamps of south Louisiana, a young girl is guided by the spirits of her ancestors. When she is older, she is trained in the mystical arts by Madame, whose powers are known to all of New Orleans. She will need it all when she is called to work at Spirit Ranch, especially when young Bill arrives. The spirits have a job for him, working with a survivor of childhood abuse trying to fit into today's world.

With a college degree and not much else, young Bill sets out to see the country, hopping onto boxcars headed south and west. The challenges are many and the danger real, but the spirits have a job for him to do, and he squeaks by harrowing situations on the way to where he ought to be. When he is arrested and thrown in jail for being a vagrant, he learns of a ranch that often has job openings. "You'll get the job," Maxine tells him at the gate. And she ought to know. She knows everything. Before it happens.

What Others are Saying about Spirit Ranch

What happens when you take an ordinary sort of guy and drop him into a mystical ranch in the Southwest? These authors have been able to take that unlikely scenario and turn it into a compelling story—interesting plot, compelling characters. —**Carole Katchen, Author,** *I Was a Lonely Teenager, Murder by the Book*

The dot on the horizon was a man, a black man, who was running to catch the train. He had been away from his family, working, but at the end of the time only had a

i

comic book to show for it. The 'company store' had kept all his wages to pay for cokes and such. Bill pulled him onto the boxcar, and they talked as they made their journey. Yes, I think that chapter was the very first chapter, the one that persuaded Bill he could write a book, and he then went back and told the whole story. That chapter was brilliant, as is the whole book. —**Charles (Chap) Harper, Author of** *Once Upon a Reef* **and** *Beer, Bait and Ammo.*

Excerpt

Now that I was actually there, I felt stupid.

When I confess to never actually riding a horse, they're going to think I'm retarded.

I tapped Juan, the cabbie, on the shoulder. "I think I'd better go back to town."

He turned around and grinned. "Hey, you're here. You might as well ask them for a job. What are they going to do, shoot you?"

I sighed. "I was hoping it wouldn't come to that."

We drove down the long dusty road, past the stables, up to the ranch house. I paid Juan. "If I give you three extra bucks, will you wait five minutes? I'll either come to get my duffle bag or leave with it."

"Sure, I need a siesta."

"Thanks, Juan, you've been a big help!"

I looked up and saw a lady standing in front of the taxi, wearing a tan blouse and a peasant skirt. She was small, perhaps five-two, shiny black hair, olive complexion, thirty-five. Smiling. I assumed she knew Juan. I got out of the cab and walked toward her.

She said, "Don't worry, you'll get the job."

I was about to say, "What job?" when she took my arm.

"Come on, I'll take you to the office. The owner's name is Danny. He'll be sure glad to see you."

"I think you've made a mistake. I'm not the person Danny's looking for."

"Of course, you are."

About the Authors

Nancy Smith Gibson has been a voracious reader since early childhood, but she needed two things to become a writer: an empty house and computers.

Mother of four, grandmother of four, and great grandmother of two, she believes in ghosts, divine order, UFOs, the power of gemstones, and that things happen in threes.

Up until a few years ago the work of raising a family along with careers as a telephone operator (reaching as far back as the 'number please' days), supervisor with the Census Bureau in two states, and selling real estate kept her too busy to write, but the stories were there, buzzing around in her head, waiting for her to slow down.

She now lives in the country near Hot Springs, Arkansas, where she is interrupted in her writing by a dog and two cats who demand her attention. When not writing novels, she enjoys genealogy research and lunching with friends.

She is author of several series: Tales from the Brazos (Historical Romance), Imagickation (contemporary witches), Sissy and Miss Boo (cozy mysteries) and, of course, this Broussard Court Series, which consists of: *Spirit Ranch, The New Witch* and third in the series, *True Memories,* forthcoming in May 2022.

http://www.nancysmithgibson.com

William J. (Bill) Schuler had always planned to have a career in theater. As a young man in New York, he studied acting, voice and dancing and he performed in many plays, often touring the country with a production. Later, with a family to support, he became a radio broadcaster, specializing in weather reporting. For several years he also had a late-night radio show out of Chicago that specialized in mystical and supernatural ideas, some of which found their way into this book. For the last years of his life, he performed with a local theater group in Arkansas and developed his skill as a writer. Bill and Nancy met as members of a writer's critique group in Hot Springs, Arkansas, and in the mystical way life works, Nancy remembered listening to his late-night radio program about ghosts and spirits and things that go bump in the night.

Author's Note

I had just finished writing *THE NEW WITCH when fellow writer's* group member, Bill Schuler, said, "I'm through with **SPIRIT RANCH,** but it's not long enough for a book."

"Write some more," I suggested.

"I wrote everything that happened," he said. "There is no more."

"Make it up."

"I can't," replied the veteran stage actor. "I have no imagination."

Thus began this strange collaboration of truth and fiction.

Bill swore that everything he wrote was true.

I swear that everything I wrote was made up.

We met and melded it into one story.

Bill was an active member of our local little theater group. He was a superb actor. He tried, with some success, to put fictional short stories onto paper. It was hard to do, sometimes, since he didn't type.

Before the pandemic, Bill moved 'back East' to be close to his daughters, Lara and Alesa. He was very proud of both of them.

Then came the pandemic.

RIP Bill. We miss you.

Introduction

SPIRIT RANCH exists in the desert north of Tucson, Arizona, but only when needed. Like Brigadoon, it disappears into the mists of time, hidden from the sight and mind of man until the time arrives for it to reappear. Its purpose is to help those whose lives stray from their destined paths, those who fail to grasp the meaning intended for their lives and have fallen into despair. It doesn't have to be in the desert, of course. It could exist anywhere: in the Pacific Northwest, the plains of the Midwest, upstate New York, or sunny California. Its purpose is the important thing.

SPIRIT RANCH is Touched by an Angel with a touch of Quantum Leap, set on a ranch, with no angels. Or at least not what we think of as angels. Maxine is no Roma Downy, and Bill is no Michael Landon. Instead we have:

New Orleans

Bayou, spirits, ranch, precognition

Nazi concentration camp

The next time SPIRIT RANCH appears, it may be in the 1800s, the 1920s, or present day. Maxine, Shallah, Bill, Miss Emily, Grandfather, and the ranch-hands may be called on to help all sorts of people: an athlete whose self-image is tied to his sports ability, until he is injured and can no longer play: a couple whose marriage falls apart when their child is convicted of a crime: a dance-hall girl who wants to change her profession: a cowboy with a secret that haunts him. The list of people needing the spirits' help is endless, and can be plucked from today's headlines or from history books.

Next time, Bill may arrive on a stagecoach, or hitch a ride on a big-rig, or ride the rails and be arrested yet again, wondering why it seems like Déjà Vu. Will he ever catch on to what is happening?

So, for your enjoyment, here is *Spirit Ranch,* the first book in the Broussard Court Series,

List of Characters

MAXINE: a Cajun mystic, who knows things before they happen, goes 'spirit-walking' (out of body experiences) and communicates with spirits, both seen and unseen. She really runs the ranch, but she lets the owner think he does. She keeps everything in line.

SHALLAH: Maxine's daughter, who has inherited some of Maxine's talents. She cooks for the ranch.

BILL: he is new to this spirit stuff. He doesn't realize the spirits have sent him to **SPIRIT RANCH,** and the mystical events puzzle him. He is finding his own faith and path as he helps others find theirs.

MISS EMILY: an elderly lady who is a permanent resident of the ranch. She's the grandmother everyone needs. Does she know who she really is?

GREAT-GRANDFATHER: a Cherokee Indian, in his time the oracle and shaman for his tribe. His spirit drops in on his great-granddaughter, Maxine, from time to time to give her information.

SPIRIT
RANCH

PROLOGUE

The pink and gold sky on the Arizona horizon announced the arrival of day, spreading a soft light across the desert floor. Barren and lifeless, it offered no comfort to man or beast. A large mound sat in the middle of the desolate valley, waiting, as it had for centuries. Perhaps millennia. Waiting for what? Whatever the spirits brought.

As the velvety night sky lightened and the stars winked out, a mist began to form. It thickened and spread, covering the arid wasteland, deeper and deeper, until the cloud obliterated everything, even the mound. Stillness. The very air was as dense as the vapor, thick and tangible.

Then a breeze came. Slowly at first, it caught the corner of the cloud and pushed it up and away. Then another. Soon, wisps of white were swirling like small dust devils, blowing into nothingness with ever-quickening speed.

A water tower pushed its way through the top of the white layer, breaking the veil that hid...what? A barn appeared, then a large house, welcoming and serene. Buildings dotted the mound, with paths leading between them. Below the mound, the mist evaporated slowly, revealing more buildings and barns. Inside fences forming paddocks and corrals, horses tossed their manes, welcoming a new day.

All was ready for the new adventure.

MAXINE

Chapter One
1922. Bayous of south Louisiana.

I know things.

What things, you ask?

Hmm. That's a hard question to answer.

Good things. Bad things. Whatever the spirits tell me, I know.

Some people would call this a curse; others would call it a blessing. Me, I don't call it anything, it just is.

My name is Maxine Thibodeaux. When I was four, an old Indian man came to me one night before I fell asleep. His skin was dark, darker than Maman or me, and his hair was in two long braids, like a girl would wear. He was dressed in clothing made of skins and adorned with feathers and beads, and he had feathers woven into the braids. He was quite an interesting sight and I still remember it today, over thirty years later. I knew right off he was an Indian because of a picture in my storybook, but he didn't frighten me at all. My father was an Indian too, and he wasn't a bit scary. The old man's form was all shimmery and I could see right through him, but that didn't upset me either. Living in the bayou I was used to seeing strange things.

"You have a gift, little one," he said to me. "But you must learn to use it wisely."

"A gift?" I asked. The only gifts I knew anything about were given at Christmas and birthdays. I had gotten a doll as a gift and I treasured her beyond measure. So, I was happy to hear the old man's pronouncement.

"Yes, but not the kind you are thinking about," he replied.

I pondered that for a minute, then asked, "How do you know what I'm thinking?"

"Because I know things, and that is your gift; you will know things."

The next day I told Maman about the Indian man in my room.

"That must have been your great-grandfather," she said. "Your father has told me about him. He was a legendary wise man in his tribe and told the elders where to camp and what crops to grow and where the best hunting was. This is good, that he came to see you. Did he speak to you?"

"He told me I had a gift."

My mother became excited, and pulled up a kitchen chair to sit in front of me.

"Did he tell you what the gift is?" Her dark eyes sparkled as she asked me.

"He said I would know things,"

"Know things?" She drew back in the chair. "Know what things?"

I shrugged, having lost interest in the subject.

Later I overheard her telling my Tante Louise about it, and Tante Louise said, "Oh chère, your girl's gonna have some kinda power, getting it from both sides like that."

At the time I didn't understand what she meant by both sides. It was several years before I heard the story of my mother's mother, who had been a *traiteur*, a healer of no small renown. She had helped the people like us, people who lived in the bayou and had no doctors to turn to and no money to pay if there had been. Indeed, they had no need of one with Grandmère in the vicinity. She would hop into a pirogue before word could even be sent that she was needed, and one of her many children, grandchildren, nieces or nephews would paddle through the bayous and swamps to take her where the spirits told her she was to go.

That's what she told everyone—the spirits told her where she was needed.

So here I am, many years later, and the spirits tell me things. I didn't become a healer like my mother had hoped, but I have my own gifts. I know things.

Know what, you ask?

Whatever the spirits want me to know.

Chapter Two
1934. Bayous of south Louisiana.

When I was twelve years old, the spirits sent me a very bad feeling. For several days I knew something bad was on the way...something bad indeed. Each night I tossed and turned in my sweat-soaked bed. On the third day I woke up earlier than usual, filled with a foreboding beyond explaining. I padded to the window and looked out, hoping to find some reason for my feelings.

A silver white mist covered the bayou so solidly it appeared to be a roadway. A whippoorwill asked its question in soulful repetition. An owl wondered who. We all had our questions.

I heard the sounds of someone moving in our little house, and I hurried to the kitchen, where Maman was filling a thermos with coffee for my father to take out on the boat with him.

"Don't go," I said as I threw my arms around him. "Stay home today. Please don't go."

"What is this?" he asked in amazement, looking toward my mother.

"What is it? What's going to happen, Maxine?" my mother asked.

I shook my head. I didn't know what was going to happen, I only knew I didn't want him to leave.

"Maybe you ought to stay home this time, cher," my mother said to my father. "After all, she has the gift."

"Well gift or no gift, that won't get the fish caught, and without the fish caught we'll have no money." He turned to me and kissed me on the cheek and hugged me. "I'll be extra careful, I promise."

He pulled me from him and started for the back door, lunch and thermos in hand.

"I'll see you in a few days," he said as he kissed my mother on the way out.

I watched my father disappear into the morning mist, and suddenly I knew what was going to happen.

We never saw him again, except in his coffin. The storm that came up on the unpredictable Gulf washed him overboard and into the hands of God.

It was raining the day we placed the body of my father in the family vault. The little cemetery on high ground a few miles from our house was crowded with mourners. I counted twenty-six pirogues pulled up along the bayou. All the umbrellas wore black, as did my heart.

Maman tried to stop my crying, but I loved my father and he deserved my tears. All the trees in the cemetery wept in sympathy.

The whispers went round and round at the funeral. "Maxine, la petite fille, warned him...told him not to go...but he wouldn't listen." "She has the gift, you know." "The spirits come to her, tell her things." "She was born during a hurricane, she was, and she knew this one was coming before anyone else." "Oui, and she knew it would take her papa, too."

But I didn't understand how this knowing came to me. It just did, and I couldn't believe my gift hadn't saved my father. It would be years before I learned how to access any information the spirit world would be willing to share with me.

We lived another few years on the bayou, but without a man to care for us it became increasingly hard to survive. My aunts and uncles helped us, but my two older brothers left home—headed for the promised land of California—and weren't around to share the proceeds from their catch with us.

Then there was my shame...my fall from grace. After that, no one would help us.

Chapter Three
1937. Bayous of South Louisiana.

Strangers didn't often come to our part of the world, and when they did, they generally weren't welcome. Usually, it was someone trying to get us to do something we didn't agree with. Occasionally there were federal marshals looking for stills hidden away on hummocks in remote areas of the swamp. During one particularly unhappy period there were workers who wanted to take away the children and put them in boarding schools where the Cajun tongue and lifestyle could be wiped from their mouths and minds.

But in the fall of 1937 a stranger came who was, if not exactly welcomed, at least tolerated. His hair gleamed gold in the sunlight, an oddity among us dark-headed people. His skin was a golden color also, instead of the plain brownish tint of ours, which made me think he had been burnished with precious metal. Our heritage came from many cultures—French, Spanish, and Indian—and we were generally brown headed and darker skinned. I was fifteen and he looked like a golden god who walked among us. I was enthralled from the time I set eyes on him.

He came with several cameras and a duffle bag full of film and said he wanted to "capture the beauty of the swamp in pictures." To prove his goodwill, he took a picture of everyone who would let him and sent the film off to some far-away place to be made into pictures. When those were returned to him, he picked them up at the post office and gave them out. Everyone flocked to get their picture, probably the only one they would ever have of themselves, and admire everyone else's.

This act guaranteed cooperation among the people who lived in the bayou, at least most of them. He showed us the pictures he had taken in other places, and we marveled at the scenes of deserts and mountains and strange animals we had never known existed. He told us he wanted to photograph the bayou, as he had these other places. He said a famous magazine wanted the pictures to show what the 'gators and herons and muskrats, and all the other creatures living in the swamps were like.

The elders said as long as he didn't disturb anything, didn't interrupt the fishing or trapping, it was OK by them. This meant keeping the peaceful quiet of the bayou and not bothering anybody. They let him use the abandoned cabin that had belonged to Etienne Ballew before he had died. It was just a half-mile from our home.

When it came time for him to go into the heart of the swamp he asked if someone would be his guide. He would pay a little, he said, for someone to go with him so he wouldn't get lost, and to keep him from accidentally stumbling into danger.

The men thought that was smart of him, but all the men and older boys were busy with fishing, trapping, and hunting 'gators. The younger tads were all saying, "pick me, pick me," when I stepped forward and said, "I know every inch of the bayou. I'll guide you."

The next day he came to meet Maman, showed her his pictures, and asked respectfully if I could be his guide. He quoted a sum of money that amounted to several weeks of living without worry for us, and then brought out letters of recommendation from publishers he'd worked for.

Staring intently into Maman's eyes, he took her hand into his and said, "M'am, I don't want you to worry. I promise you I'll take good care of your little girl. This will be an educational experience she'll long remember."

Maman snorted. "Don't worry about taking care of *her*. This is the bayou. She'll be taking care of *you*."

His words held a lot of knowing in them, if I had only understood what they would come to mean. But I didn't. Not then. I did know something else, though. From the moment I saw him, I knew how smooth his skin would feel against mine. I knew how sweet his kisses would be and how soft his lips would feel as they suckled at my breast. I knew the feel of his hands, of the calluses, as he ran them over me.

And even though I had never experienced it before, I knew how it would feel when he slid his body into mine.

What I didn't have a knowing of was what would come after that. The spirits told me about the pleasure; they didn't tell me about the shame and pain that would come later.

Chapter Four
December, 1937-August, 1938.

The Bayou

I sat by my bedroom window, watching the rain making splats in the water of the bayou. It looked like little fish, coming to the surface and snatching a gnat or mosquito that had foolishly landed there. The weather matched my mood: dismal and dreary.

I had begged my lover to stay, but he had refused, saying he had to get home before Christmas.

"I have to be there for my children," he said. "My wife expects me."

Wife? Children?

With all my gift of knowing, which had told me he was the man I was waiting for, why hadn't I known he was married? If my gift had told me how perfect he felt in my arms and in my body, why was this important information held back? It would be many years before I came to understand the perfectness of situations that appear to be disastrous at the time.

My mother, seeing the tears that sometimes escaped and rolled down my cheeks, tried to console me. "Ah, Maxine, chère, it was not meant to be. He was from another world—a world where you would never fit in. This is your home, and his is someplace else."

That rainy day as I was moping in my room, I sensed movement and turned away from the window. There, in the old ladder-back chair by the door, sat an old woman. She wore a long-sleeved blue dress and had a red shawl around her shoulders. Her gray hair was in two braids, which were coiled over her ears, as if to keep them warm. She smiled at me, and then faded, like the Indian man had done many years before.

I puzzled over it a while, and then went in search of my mother. I found her in the kitchen, stirring a pot of beans for our supper.

"Maman, there was a spirit in my room, the spirit of an old woman."

She turned from the stove and reached for a stick of wood to build the fire higher. "What did she look like, chère?"

As I described the fantôme, she immediately stood up straight and stared at me, crossing herself.

"Ah, that is my maman! She has come to you for some reason. You have no cause to fear her. She was a good woman, a traiteur, a healer and midwife to all who needed her. She must have come for a purpose—perhaps to tell you something, something important. You will tell me if she comes again, oui?"

A few mornings later, as I was vomiting into the chamber pot, she was there again. She held my hair back from my face, and I felt her hands as surely as if she were there in solid form. I immediately felt better as she stroked my hair and smiled at me, and then disappeared like a mist dissolving in the sunlight.

"This is good news, chère. You have the gift of knowing and you have my maman watching over you. Some day when you learn to use these gifts wisely you will be a great help to those who are in need," my maman said when I told her the spirit had appeared again.

It only took a couple more times of emptying my stomach into the pot and my grandmère's visits for me to realize the reason for my maladie; I was enceinte. With no man with whom to march to the altar.

My shame was not so much that I was with child. There were many babes who were born along the bayou whose parents had been married only a few months. When the necessity of a quick marriage arose, a priest had to be located and the banns posted, and by that time it might be only a few short months before the child arrived. No one thought anything about it.

But me? I didn't have a man who would, whether willing or not, marry me to give the child a name. One might have been found if my family had been wealthy enough to give a substantial dowry to ensure a prosperous start to married life, but my father's death and my brothers' departure had left us almost destitute, depending on the kindness of others.

Everyone knew, of course, who the father must be. The stranger. A man from the outside. *A man who had paid me for my services.* And so, I was branded a whore. Ostracized.

I stayed in my home and helped my mother as best I could. A few kind people saw to it that we did not starve.

* * *

August 9, 1938. The Bayou.

The days pressed heavy on me. Not only was my child nearing the time to be born, I knew there was a storm coming. All the inhabitants of the swamps know the feeling in the air when a storm is on the way. The smart ones pack up and leave before it hits.

My mother and the mid-wife had several whispered conferences about me. I wondered what they were discussing, but I was too lethargic to care. I could only sit and stare at the bayou and listen to the distress among the birds that inhabited the swamp.

"We have decided," my mother said, "Angelina and I, that we will stay here throughout the storm. You are too far along to start out in a pirogue for higher ground, and we have no relatives or friends upstate that would take us in. This house has survived many a storm and it will survive another one. That is better than taking a chance of your giving birth out in the open, in a boat somewhere along the bayou."

Our house was built of thick cypress and oak planks and sat atop ten-foot-tall stilts on our particular hummock, which was four-feet above the water line. I don't know if I felt safe there, or if I just didn't care if I survived, but I didn't worry about the storm.

And so we hunkered down, closed the shutters over all the windows, and waited.

The pain was intense. At the height of my labor, the spirit of my grandmère wiped my brow and held my hand. Her smile convinced me I would survive this ordeal, and she whispered words in Cajun French I did not understand, but comforted me nonetheless.

When the child was born, I cried out a mighty yell, and the mid-wife wrapped it in a blanket and took it from the room while the brunt of the hurricane battered us. My mother came and took my other hand.

"My baby," I asked. "It's a girl, isn't it?" I had known from the beginning it would be.

There was a long pause before she answered, "Yes."

"Her name is Shallah," I told her. "It means peaceful one."

"Oh, my poor chère, she did not survive the birth. She was born dead."

For the second time in my sixteen years my heart was broken. I threw myself into the scream of the hurricane and became one with it. Its tears were mine. Its pain was part of me. By the time it left, I was at peace.

Chapter Five
September, 1938. New Orleans.

We moved to New Orleans so my mother and I could find work. I knew I would miss the peacefulness of the only home I had ever known, but in another way, I was excited to see new places, experience new things. And there was no other answer for us, of course. We needed to find jobs in order to eat.

On the first day, we looked for an apartment we could afford with the small cache of money my mother had accumulated from the few relatives who did not shun us. We saw an *Apartment For Rent* sign in a shop window and although my mother was hesitant, I felt confident as we entered the unusual premises. I was agog from the moment we walked in. There was the pungent smell of herbs and other unknown exotic mixtures in the air, and the shelves were filled with all sorts of things: candles, small dolls, crucifixes, bottles, and boxes. Strings of beads hung from nails on the edges of the shelves. There was a magnificent light hanging above us glittering with hundreds of crystals.

I had never seen such a place in my life, and I knew immediately it held many mysteries and secrets. The place was fascinating to me, but my mother took a step back and made the sign of the cross. I thought she was frightened.

"It's OK, Maman," I reassured her, and she stepped forward again.

A beautiful woman stepped through the door from the back room of the shop. She was tall and slim, with smooth skin the color of café au lait. Her black hair wasn't the usual tight ringlets of a black woman, but was gathered atop her head and spilled down the sides. Her black eyes saw right through us, and in that moment I thought she could read every secret I ever had. Later, when I knew her better, I was sure of it.

"Can I help you?" she asked with a slight French accent.

"Oui. My name is Marie Thibodeaux. The sign in the window—about the apartment." My mother stuttered, which I thought strange. My mother was a brave woman, sure of herself, a woman who was never at a loss for words. "How...how much are you asking?"

The beautiful woman didn't answer Maman's question, but instead asked one of her own. "You are looking for a place to live?" she asked, coming out from behind the counter. It was hard for me to stand my ground as she approached me.

"Oui," my mother responded.

"This is your daughter?" she asked as she stood in front of me.

"Yes. This is my daughter, Maxine."

The woman circled me, looking me up and down as she did so.

"Where are you from, that you are looking for a place to live?" She asked this of me, not my mother.

"We lived down in the bayou, but we have moved to New Orleans," I answered.

"Why you do that?"

"My father drowned when the hurricane struck four years ago. The fishing was ruined and my brothers gave up and moved west to California. We can't keep ourselves any longer. We moved here to find work."

She was silent for a few moments. Her eyes narrowed as she studied me. My mother seemed entranced by the place as she glanced here and there at the objects around the room.

Finally, the woman spoke to me. "This is part of it, but not all."

I hung my head. There was no doubt in my mind that she knew all about me.

"You have a gift. Do you know this?"

My mother came out of her trance to answer. "Yes, my daughter does have a gift. She has inherited the power from both sides of the family."

"But you are not so blessed," the woman said, turning at last to look at Maman.

"No, I'm not, more's the pity, but my mother was a great healer until her death. And Maxine has been visited by her spirit, as well as the spirit of her father's grandfather, who was a seer of his tribe."

"Ahh," voiced the woman in a long, low breath.

"But I don't understand it," I said. "Sometimes I know when things are going to happen, but I don't know exactly what. If my father had listened to me, he would still be alive. Of other things, I know nothing."

"That is the way of the world," she said and turned abruptly back toward the counter. "I'll rent you the apartment. It is above this shop, and has two bedrooms. You will find it satisfactory."

"I'm sure we will, having come from a home on stilts in the middle of a swamp," my mother answered smartly, "But how much is it? I can't afford much."

"You can afford it," came the answer. "You will soon have a job that pays very well."

"You know this?" Maman asked. "And how?"

A lazy smile came across the beautiful face. "I know things," came the reply.

Chapter Six
1938. New Orleans.

Life changed entirely for me in New Orleans. I was used to the slow, quiet life along the bayou. Days were lazy there, with nothing much to do but visit with friends and neighbors or sit on the dock and watch gators sunning themselves on the bank, or perhaps dangle a line into the bayou and catch some perch for supper. The men were away all day, either trapping for furs or out on the larger boats in the Gulf. The mink, muskrat, and gators were skinned and the pelts put to dry on wooden boards. When the men had enough, they would pile a pirogue full and paddle inland to the fur trader, where they would haggle over the prices until both sides thought they were the winner and be satisfied.

When I was young one of my brothers would paddle the pirogue, with me in it, a couple of miles up the bayou to the neighborhood school, where a woman from the outside taught us to read and write and know something of the world. The school was fairly well attended until the word came down from the state that the children would no longer be allowed to speak any language except proper English. No French; no Cajun dialect; nothing but proper English. Suddenly, there were no students coming to class.

They sent officers in boats out into the swamp to find the truants. They threatened to take children from their parents and send them away to school. When the men in our community put up blinds made of brush and cane to direct the boats away from our area, the officers became hopelessly lost in the swamp and needed assistance in finding their way back to civilization. They more or less gave up after that. I was sixteen when my mother and I moved to New Orleans. On the bayou, that was old enough to be married, had I a sweetheart and we had wished to do so. As it was, I was expected to find a job and help support Maman and myself.

Our landlady, Madame Badeaux, was right when she predicted Maman would find employment. Within three days she was hired into the wealthy LaCroix home, as maid, assistant cook, and general household help. From what I later learned of the power and scope of Madame Badeaux's reach, I have no doubt it was her doing. Perhaps she suggested to Madame or Monsieur LaCroix they should hire this woman recently up from the bayous with absolutely no experience in a grand household. Or maybe it was some sort of spell or charm that did the trick. Whatever it was, Maman was happy with her employment, and from the first she was so enthralled with the prosperous life-style she learned everything she could about how to manage such a home.

Two weeks later Maman, Madame Badeaux and I were having tea in Madame's kitchen.

"Now, Maxine, you must find a job," Maman told me.

"Non," Madame countered. "There will be times she will help you at your employment, but until then I need her help here. Consider it part of your rent. What I charge you is reasonable, *n'est pas?*" Our flat consisted of a living room overlooking the courtyard, a kitchen and two bedrooms. The furniture was old but a much better quality than we were use to.

"Indeed it is, Madame Badeaux. It is a beautiful flat, and you are charging us far less than it is worth."

"It is because I took one look at your daughter and saw that she has a gift, a special talent. I knew the spirits had sent her to me."

Madame Badeaux took over my education and work habits.

"We will see what you can learn with your gift," she said. "I will teach you about the spirits. You will be able to do things even you have never dreamt of, and ordinary people would believe to be impossible."

I shivered, when she said this, and she saw.

"Are you afraid?"

"I don't think so, Madame. Only excited."

"That is good. It would not do for you to be frightened. You must be sure of yourself else evil spirits might intrude. We cannot allow that to happen, understand?"

"Yes."

"And you must listen carefully to what I tell you, and follow my instructions to the letter."

"Yes, Madame. I will."

"Your gift, it is meant for helping others, not for your own pleasure alone. Although you may use it for your amusement, at times, the main purpose of you being so gifted is to help others."

"But my papa, he didn't listen." Tears came into my eyes as I thought about my beloved Papa, and I turned away from her so she would not see my grief.

"That was a lesson for you, too. Not everyone will listen to you and believe."

The elegant woman walked to the window and looked out, sadness covering her face. "If you become famous for what you can do, as I am, people will begin to believe you. But until then, they will scoff and turn away."

She turned back toward me. "I have much to teach you. Not only about the spirit world, but also in preparation for making a living, for it is in that manner you will meet the people who need your help. You must be ready on both accounts.

"First, you will help in my apartment. Your maman, she is a superb cleaner of houses, *n'est pas?*"

"Oui...I mean yes," I was trying to do as I was taught in those few years of school and erase the French from my tongue.

"You, too, will have need in knowing how to manage an establishment."

"But how do you know this?"

She smiled that lazy smile that implied much more than what was spoken.

This is when she began to teach me about the spirit world. It was my first lesson.

Chapter Seven
1938. New Orleans

The first thing Madame Badeau taught me was that everyone, no matter who they are, no matter rich or poor, high or low, has some sort of gift from God.

"If they did not, they wouldn't be here on earth," she said. "This life, she is a classroom, and all the people, they are supposed to learn what is their gift."

We were setting the dining table in her apartment in preparation for a small dinner party she was giving that evening. It was my job to learn the correct way to lay everything just so. At my old home, in the bayou, we just put the plates and utensils down. I was surprised to find out there was a proper way to place each piece. The table was always to be set properly, at least in Madame Badeaux's establishment.

Along with the household lessons, Madame tutored me in more arcane matters.

"You will do well to learn to recognize these gifts in others," she continued. "They will not be the special gifts such as you and I have, but they are gifts, nevertheless. Perhaps it will be the gift of music, or painting beautiful pictures, or healing." She gave me a sharp glance. "They may have the ability to take superb photographs."

I stared at her, marveling at how much she knew, and wondering how she knew it.

"Some people may not even know they have a gift, but you will be able to see what they cannot." She went back to polishing wine glasses and placing them on the table. "You may help them see what they are capable of, to make them aware of their potential, their gift."

"How, Madame? How will I know?" I asked as I folded the linen napkins into fans and placed one on each plate.

"Because that is *your* gift, the gift of knowing. And that gift comes in many ways. You already recognize that you know things that are going to come to happen. Is that not so?"

"Well, I knew something bad was going to happen to my papa, and sometimes I know other things, too."

"You will learn to listen to the spirits as they whisper to you. Then you will know more."

As time went on, she talked more about the spirit world, and she cautioned me to always listen to what the spirits were telling me. As if I wouldn't.

"Chère, you must learn to hear what is inside you. You must learn to never doubt what you know, even if it doesn't make sense to you at the time. And you must learn to recognize what other people call 'coincidences' as what they really are, signs."

Often, she took me to a sidewalk café, where we sat and drank coffee and observed the people passing.

"Tell me about her," Madame would say, indicating a nicely dressed woman passing.

"I know nothing about her, Madame."

"Then make up something."

Within a few months, I came to realize if I made a wrong appraisal of the person, Madame said nothing. But if I were correct, she would ask additional questions.

"You say she is very unhappy? Tell me, Maxine, why is this so?"

"Because she thinks her lover is unfaithful to her."

"And is he?"

"Yes, he is."

"And who is the other woman with whom he consorts?"

"That woman's niece."

I also came to realize many of the people who sat at the other tables, the people passing in the street, recognized Madame. Some looked frightened when they saw her, while others would smile and nod in a subservient way, as if giving homage to a queen. And indeed, she was a queen in the neighborhood, the Queen of Hoodoo.

I finally worked up enough courage to ask her about it.

"That is my gift, little one. My grandmother was a master of the craft of Hoodoo. Like you, it skipped a generation, and then came to me. My father had no facilité in anything mystical, but he helped my grandmother, who had been a slave and could not read or write, put the spells and potions into a journal, so they could be passed down to me."

"The people, the ones who come to your shop, is that what they come for?"

"Oui. The ones who are not too frightened of me, and the ones who have such a need that even fear does not keep them away, they come to me for help."

"And you charge them for this? This is how you make your living?"

"Yes. That is what supports this household."

"Will I be able to do that someday?" I asked.

"Non. This I do know. Your gift is in knowing things, and in helping people through that knowing. You are blessed to be able to see through the veil, to see the spirit world as others, even myself, cannot. And this will grow as you practice."

"Veil?"

"Oui, the veil that was torn asunder when the Lord Jesus Christ was crucified and rose from the dead."

"I don't understand."

"The spirits, the ones who have passed through this world and those not yet born, are here around us, as alive in their world as we are in ours. Most people know nothing of this, and want to know nothing. The veil acts as a separation between their world and ours. Most people of this world cannot see or hear them, but the spirits can see us, if they wish to.

I was silent as I pondered what she was telling me.

"Chère, you must always use this gift to help, not harm. Terrible things happen to people who use their gifts for evil. Remember, whatever you put out into the world, whether good or bad, comes back to you tenfold.

"Me, I do not charge the people of the neighborhood when they come for help. Sometimes they bring me gifts, jars of jelly or fresh tomatoes from the vine in their backyard. Peaches from the tree by their door. I never ask them for anything, but I cannot insult them by refusing the token they give me. They, too, will receive tenfold for what they give from the goodness of their heart.

"The rich people, though, the people who come for help in business, or to avoid an enemy they have made by their choice, those people I charge dearly. They can afford it. The cost is their punishment for getting into the trouble they are in, for behaving badly."

"Will I support myself with my gift, the way you do?"

"Non. Not in the way you are thinking, although your knowing will lead you to where you need to be in order to support yourself. You need never fear for a place to lay your head or food to eat. Your gift will provide for you, and more importantly, it will lead you to where you are needed, and that is your true blessing.

I have thought of that conversation often, when I puzzled about why I found myself in a new place. Eventually, I came to accept the purpose would soon make itself clear.

Chapter Eight
1938-1941. New Orleans.

My days were spent, in the most part, with Madame Badeaux. That is, when she was not dealing with a client or accompanied by one of her lovers. She had several lovers, of varying races, and all were handsome and wealthy. I had overheard talk about her husband, gone now for several years. It seems he made the mistake of thinking he could be unfaithful to her. The talk around the neighborhood was that she had turned him into a dog, which then cowered about her, licking her hand. The dog finally went mad, and the police came and shot it and hauled the body off to the dump.

My mother liked her job at the LaCroix household, and soon she was a valued part of the staff. When there was to be a special event, she saw to it I was hired as extra help. Madame, of course, had to approve of this, but she said my lessons were progressing nicely and I could be spared for a few hours or a few days.

"Indeed, it is where the spirits wish you to be," she said, but would not comment further about it.

So sometimes I worked in the LaCroix kitchen, helping the cook prepare for a large dinner, and other times I helped clean the enormous house, polishing every inch to a high shine in preparation for guests.

Madame Badeaux gave me lessons in much of this in her own flat: the proper way to put sheets on a bed: the placement of guest towels, special soaps, fingerbowls, wine glasses. The list went on and on. I had never dreamed, back in the bayou, there was such a rigid plan for each and every item in one's life.

When I asked why I needed to know all this, I half expected Madame to be angry that I was questioning her lessons, but she took it in the way I meant it; what was going to occur in my future that made it necessary to know these things?

"Chère, the spirits may take you in many different ways, from a fine establishment to a horse ranch, and you must be ready to meet whatever comes. You will be able to take over the running of a home or a business, no matter the kind or size. In this way, you will be able to help those who need you, whoever and wherever they are."

Now I understand, of course, that she knew exactly where I would be going, and why. But the spirits hadn't told me that, and wouldn't for several more years.

We continued my lessons on 'knowing', and it became increasingly obvious I could look at a person and know much more about them than they knew themselves. Madame stressed that I shouldn't let people know this. They would be uncomfortable around me, which would defeat the purpose of my gift.

"It is best kept secret," she said, "Unless it is necessary to tell them for their safety."

One day, news came over the radio that Japan had bombed America's ships that were at Pearl Harbor, in Hawaii.

"Why, Madame, did we not know this was going to happen?"

"Because it would have only distressed us. We could have done nothing to change it."

Soon, the whole town was involved in the war effort. Maman decided to leave her job at the LaCroix household and go to work at a defense plant, as so many women were doing. She would be building amphibious landing craft at the Higgins facility. After checking with Madame Badeaux, she recommended me to Mrs. LaCroix as her replacement. So, I went to work and learned more about what it took to run a large household. I set schedules, did ordering, made sure there were all sorts of supplies on hand. When rationing came, I sought out the places that had hard to find items: sugar, butter, nylon stockings. My gift enabled me to do this, of course; I knew where to go to find what we needed, and got there just as the truck was being unloaded and before everything sold out. Mrs. LaCroix marveled at my competence in keeping everything running smoothly. While her friends were decrying the absence of the things they needed, the LaCroix household was always well supplied.

It was during this time spirits started visiting me. Often, I would turn and there would be an unknown person standing there, looking at me. They seldom spoke, only smiled and faded away.

"They just want you to know they are there, chère. Perhaps they want you to be more aware of them," Madame said.

"But who are they? Why me?"

She shrugged her shoulders. "Who knows? They just want you to pay attention, *n'est pas?*"

Soon, I became accustomed to this, the appearance of people I didn't know. I would smile and nod my head, and then go about my work. I often couldn't speak, at least when I was at work, for fear the household would think me off in the head. After a while, when it was safe, these apparitions and I would talk.

The spirits were often helpful to me, pointing out something I was looking for or warning me of some unexpected happening in the future. I considered them my friends. They would become even more so in the future.

MARY KATE

Chapter Nine
1942—Denver, Colorado

Patrolman Peter Mallory checked his watch. It was 10:15 on a warm June night. His next call-in was due in five minutes.

He was a six-foot-two towhead. A rookie, working the three to midnight shift in the downtown precinct. Not exactly wet behind the ears, but there was dampness there. He was still having trouble twirling his nightstick without hitting his elbow. He was feeling especially sharp tonight. Jan, his newlywed wife had cleaned and pressed his uniform this morning. Even shined his badge. He passed closed shops, vacant lots, the First National Bank, and the Tyler Hotel, which had a few cars parked in front of it. Otherwise, the town was getting ready for bed. Restaurants had shut down at ten. This was the quiet time Peter looked forward to all day. He was walking along Harrison Avenue. After crossing Second Street, he could see a line of cars on the left. *Kitty Foyle* with Ginger Rogers was playing at the Grenada. The cars should be gone in a few minutes. The call box was a block down on the First Street corner.

He passed the movie house. Nickie's, a beer joint on his right, sat sullenly silent. By now, the patrons had run out of words and were staring into their beers, wondering if this was all there was.

As he walked by, Peter heard glass breaking down the block. In the First Street lamplight, two figures were wrestling with a large box and losing. A man and a woman. They were in front of McGrew's appliance Store. Peter quickened his pace. He could hear the couple shouting at each other, yanking the box to and fro. Suddenly, the male fell on his back. The box was now lying on top of him like a great square tumor. The woman was kicking him in the ribs and in a voice as flat as the concrete he was laying on, encouraging him to get his lazy butt off the sidewalk and help her.

The twenty-two-year-old patrolman had only been on the force six months, but this story told itself. McGrew's plate glass window was on the sidewalk in small pieces. The big box was a brand new Philco AM-FM console radio and phonograph with the price tag still hanging from a knob, and the lovely couple was drunk out of their skulls. It was now 10:20 and the call box was eight feet away.

Sometimes, thought Peter, *life is good*. He called for a paddy wagon.

The man wearing the radio was now snoring belligerently. Peter never realized a person's snore could sound drunk. The lady, sensing the jig was up, swore for ten seconds and then lost interest. She slowly slid down next to her sweetie and cried.

Peter squatted to get a better look at her. She was somewhere between twenty-five and forty. Chubby, with fat cheeks and tightly curled red hair. Her makeup looked old and dirty. Mascara flowed down her face in muddy tears. Rouge, stamped in clearly defined circles covered her cheeks. Lipstick, applied while dreaming of an insane clown, made her mouth look like an open wound. She sat, legs splayed out, head back, crying like a grotesque baby.

"Can you tell me your name, Miss?" He'd seen her many times, always drunk, sidling down the sidewalk, clinging to the buildings in an attempt to stay upright. She was usually with her equally plastered, skinny boyfriend, his straight brown hair hanging over his eyes. He always wore a filthy wrinkled tuxedo, implying better times. Now, implying a lifelong binge.

"Your name, Miss?"

She stopped crying, slowly lowered her head and tried to focus her eyes. The intense effort caused her to vomit. The green bile, in sharp contrast to her red dress, plunged from her mouth, ran down her stomach to her lap.

Her boyfriend stirred. Tried to get up. Flailed his arms like a newborn, not realizing he had a large radio on his tummy. Then gave up. Mumbling various vowels, he fell back to sleep as the paddy wagon pulled up.

An hour later, Peter called in. The sergeant on duty told him to go to the Castaway Hotel on Adams and check the room of Mr. and Mrs. Gleason for stolen goods.

"Who are the Gleasons?" asked Peter.

"The two lushes you arrested."

Peter knew the Castaway. Every cop in Denver knew it. At one time the Castaway was posh. Built around a Hawaiian theme, it was the Plaza of Denver. The place to meet the best the West had to offer.

It had long since descended into Hotel Hell. The damnation was official when a sign reading "Transients Welcome" was hung in the filthy front window.

As he stepped into the ancient lobby, Peter was welcomed by the smell of insecticides, body odor, booze, urine and dust. The old wood floor was soft and spongy. The lobby itself was mercifully dark. It felt like a permanent condition no sunlight could penetrate.

On the left, a bare bulb hung over the check-in counter, a silver teacher's bell sat on the counter with a card reading, "Ring For Service." Peter tapped it three times and waited. He hit it again.

"Hello? Anyone awake?" he called.

Shuffling feet moved in the darkness behind the counter. Bedroom slippers being pushed across the floor. A little old man with stringy gray hair and thick glasses appeared out of the gloom. He looked up at Peter with a face too tired to show expression.

"What can I do for you?" Without a hint of hope. He's seen it all and no longer cared.

"I'm Patrolman Mallory and we're investigating the Gleasons. They're charged with possession of stolen goods among other things."

The old man turned, reached into a mail slot, pulled out a key.

"Room 203. They never let anyone in their room, so I have no idea what you'll find. If you take anything, please let me know."

"Of course. How do I find it?"

"Stairway on the left. Second door on the right."

Peter took out his little flash light and made his way up the creaking staircase. The hallway seemed to stretch on forever. Bare 60-watt bulbs hung from the ceiling every twenty feet. Noisy. Coughs, thumps, wailing, sobbing, someone shouting about the awfulness of life. No laughter. The smell from the lobby followed him. Odors of burnt food joined in the mix.

He quickly went to the second door on the right, unlocked it and pushed it open. A great stench attacked him; feces, vomit, sweat, mold, sour milk and rotting food. He gagged. His eyes watered. Alarm bells rang in his stomach and he fled back to the stairway where he stood gasping, waiting for his body to settle down.

I've got to go back there. It's my job. OK, I'm fine. I can do this.

He went back to the room. Held his breath, stepped through the door. Found the light switch, flipped it on and dove across the room to the window, opened it and leaning out as far as he could, inhaled the sweet night air.

"Well, so far so good," he said. Then ducked back into the room. With the door and window open the smell was tolerable. He sat down on the bed, covered with dirty clothes, surveying the room. Something walked across his hand. He swatted at it. A cockroach casually sauntered away.

Besides the bed, there was a straight chair with a loaf of moldy white bread on it. A tall dresser stood next to it. The walls were covered with cracked peeling yellow dirt. The floor was made of newspapers, beer bottles, milk bottles, rotting fruit and empty bean cans. A pile of dirty underwear sat in a corner. There were two doors: closet and bathroom. He stood up.

That's when he heard the noise. Something in the room was making a bumping sound. Like an elbow hitting wood. The only light was a bulb covered with fly specks, hanging from an electrical cord.

There's that sound again. Only this time it was softer, more like the rustle of leaves. Or something shifting position. Then a deep sigh.

The Gleason's were keeping a dog. Had to be. But where was it? He looked under the bed. More papers and bottles. No dog. He waded through the trash to the closet. A ball of clothes, old shoes, hats. No dog. The bathroom was as expected, filthy. Piled high with everything but a dog.

There was that sigh again! It was coming from behind him. He turned, checked the possibilities. Bed...chair...dresser. It had to be in the bed, beneath the clothes. He grabbed arms full of dresses, underwear, men's pants, shirts, slips, bras and a milk bottle He was now down to the sheets. Still no dog. That left the dresser. The drawers across the top were too small. Beneath, were three large drawers. A hole had been drilled into the face of the middle drawer.

For air! Of course!

He gripped the knobs and pulled. He screamed then threw himself backwards onto the bed

It wasn't a dog. But it was alive and it was moving. He slipped off the bed and turned on his flashlight. He carefully peered into its nest. At first, his mind rejected what he saw. But then...he knew.

Dear Mother of God! It was a baby. Completely covered by its' own feces. It was dark brown, some of its waste hardened to a thick crust

That's why they never let anyone in their room.

Peter ran into the bathroom, took all the trash out of the tub and started running water. When it was lukewarm, he went back to the dresser and bent over to pick up the baby, ran back into the bathroom and threw up in the toilet. He stripped down to his underwear and tried again. This time, he was able to hold back his gag reflex. He knew he should call this in. The sergeant would send an ambulance. But he couldn't let anyone see it like this. It was a human being. It deserved a little dignity. He put his hands under its' arms and lifted it out of the drawer. It weighed twenty pounds or so. Holding it at arm's length, he rushed it into the bathroom. The water was now about four inches deep.

He sat it down in the tub and using only his hands began scraping the feces away, a little at a time. There were spots where the skin shown through—behind its knees, the armpits. The water was now up to its chest. He lifted it out and set it on the floor. It appeared to be emaciated. It looked completely unnatural with its ribs visible. Its skin was fiery red and peppered with cuts, bruises, and open sores. It must have been extremely painful, but the baby never made a sound. Not a cry or a whimper. It must have been trained to be silent. How would you do that?

He drained the water, cleaned the tub and started over again, with clean warm water. As he worked, it slowly became human. The hardest part was the head. He placed the baby under the faucet, and gently ran warm water over it, cupping his hand over its' eyes, nose and mouth. It had curly red hair, like its mother. And it was female.

Suddenly, Peter was crying. He could see it now. No longer an *it*, a thing, but a baby girl, and his heart was breaking.

Someday, he and Jan would have a baby. Perhaps a girl. Bitter anger surged through his body. Hatred at the ignorant meanness of what he was seeing.

"Look kid, I'm sorry." The baby stared at the wall.

He placed her on the bed, went into the bathroom, cleaned the tub and took a shower. Watching her all the time.

Dressed, he looked for a clean towel to wrap the baby in. He finally found a white pillowcase, set the baby in it and carried her down the stairs. The little girl showed no interest in her new journey. It was as if, whatever happened, it was none of her business. He knew instinctively the child had removed herself and escaped into her mind. But where did she go? All she knew was the drawer.

When he reached the check-in counter, he rang the bell. The old man came out.

"Did you find anything?"

"Yes. A baby girl. They were keeping her in a dresser drawer." Peter pulled down the edge of the pillow case.

The old man peered in. "Pretty little thing. She's got her mother's hair."

Peter smiled at the baby. "Can I use your phone? We've got to get this little lady some help."

MAXINE

Chapter Ten
1942-1948. New Orleans.

I began to see what Madame Badeaux meant about my gift helping others. I could see what others could not, and I could give help and reassurance to those who trusted what I told them. More help than keeping a household well supplied during wartime.

My mother started going out with a man who worked alongside her at Higgins. He seemed like a nice man, very industrious, as my father had been. He had not been drafted, as most men were, because he had a lame leg. Like us, he was Cajun, and he and Maman got along well. After some months he asked her to marry him.

"Oh, I don't know what to do, chère. I don't know," she said, as she wrung her hands.

"Why not? Do you love him? Do you want to be married to him?"

"Yes, I do. But his place is small, and there would not be a room for you."

"Never mind me. I am content here with Madame Badeaux. I'm sure I could stay. And I make my own way now, as you very well know."

"But what if his dead wife objects? What if she comes to make our lives miserable?"

Maman claimed to have seen this happen in the bayou where we had lived. The jealous spirit of Antoine LeClerque's wife had made the new wife's life a hell. Milk soured, dishes broke, the fire wouldn't stay lit, anything that could go wrong, did. Finally, the second wife left.

"Antoine's first wife was always jealous when she was alive and she wouldn't share him with anyone after she was dead. What if Ed's dead wife is like that?"

"She's not."

Maman looked at me. "Are you sure? Do you know?"

"Yes. Yes, I know. Marry him, Maman, and be happy."

And I *had* known. After months of working with Madame, I became even surer of the things I knew without knowing how. Often, I would not know until I heard myself saying the words. From time to time, even Madame consulted with me.

"See the woman across the street? That is Mona Breaux. What can you tell me about her?"

"That she is very ill. She will be dead before long. Is there nothing you can do?"

"Non. I will give her herbs to take away the pain." She turned away from the front window of her shop. "I had hoped I was wrong, but you have told me true."

It was about this time that spirits started visiting me at home as well as at work. Spirits I did not know, spirits that didn't have any message for me as my great-grandfather and grandmother had, or the spirits at work, who seemed to want to help me with my job. I might be ironing my dress or making my bed, or even sitting in the courtyard, when a movement to the side would catch my eye, and there would be a strange person standing there. It might be an old person, bent with their years, or a younger spirit, looking happy and gay. They might just stare at me solemnly, or smile before they faded away.

I formed the opinion that on the other side of the veil someone was saying, "Look! There is a girl who can see me! Go see if she can see you!" And so they did.

"Good morning," I said to an old man in farmer's overalls. He looked startled, nodded his head, and faded into nothing.

"Beautiful day, isn't it?" I said to a young woman in a long gown from the previous century. She smiled, put her hand over her mouth and turned into mist.

After I started speaking to them, it seemed like the timbre and appearance of my guests changed, and after a year or so I began seeing not only more spirits, but well-dressed, prosperous looking people. *What could they want?*

I talked to Madame about it, of course, she being the expert on all things mystical, in my opinion.

"They have heard you can see them, and so they want to see if the phenomenon is true. If they get to be a nuisance, just tell them so. And never put up with an evil spirit. Tell me, *tout de suite,* if that happens."

"How will I know if they are evil?"

"You'll know."

It was in this manner I started conversing with the spirits who visited me. Eventually, I guess the novelty was over and most of them stopped coming, but there were two or three that came regularly.

One was a painter. I could tell because he was holding a paintbrush in his hand and had streaks of color on the smock he wore. His clothes were quite old-fashioned, and he had a beard. I tried to speak with him, but when I asked, "Are you painting a picture?" he replied in some language I didn't understand, then disappeared. A few minutes later he would reappear, study me intently, and then disappear again. I got the idea he was painting my portrait.

"Do they paint pictures in the spirit world?" I asked Madame. "Do they paint portraits and landscapes and still-lifes?"

"This I do not know, chère. Perhaps it is someone who is alive in his own time who has discovered he can leave his body and visit you in your time."

"What? Isn't that impossible?"

"Nothing is impossible, chère."

"Then I could do that? Leave my body and visit other places? Other times?"

"Perhaps. Some can do it, others cannot."

The thought frightened me, and I left the idea alone for a long time, years in fact, but I finally questioned Madame about how to do this amazing thing.

"It is called 'spirit walking,'" she told me. "And many people do it without trying, usually when they lay down to go to sleep. As they drift off, they find themselves outside their body, above it, perhaps, or beside it. They can go anywhere they wish and observe what is happening there, and then, when they wish to return to their body, they just think it, and it is so."

I started practicing this, but it took many months, and more instruction, before I could succeed. I would lie quietly in my bed, and... I cannot tell you exactly what I did, but I found myself above my body, looking down at my still form on the bed. It frightened me so much the first few times I did it I quickly hopped back into that immobile part of me and went to sleep. Gradually I began to venture farther and farther away: down into the courtyard, down the block, to the LaCroix's sleeping household.

I was testing what Madame had said—that all I had to do was wish myself back into my body and it would happen. It was so, and having proved it to be true, I ventured farther and farther away from Broussard Court.

It was during this time that I started having visits from a child—a little girl. When she first came to me, she appeared to be about five or six years of age. It would always be evening, and she would be dressed in a white nightgown of the finest cloth and design, sometimes with delicate embroidered flowers on the bodice. Her hair was long and brown, and her skin a golden hue. She was very pretty. Sometimes I would be at my toilette, and other times I would be climbing into bed. She would look at me, and look around the room, but she didn't speak. A few weeks would pass, and there she would be again, studying my room as if she were trying to determine where she was.

"Good evening," I said to her on her fourth or fifth visit. She looked at me shyly, but did not respond.

I mentioned it to Madame, who grilled me as to her appearance, then said, "I believe she is not a spirit from the other side. She is someone who is spirit walking."

I accepted this, and wondered why this child came to me.

MARY KATE

Chapter Eleven
June 12, 1948. Fort Collins, Colorado.

The ever-curious sun gently peeked into the Hanson's cozy kitchen. The aroma of coffee, eggs and toast filled the room where Hilda and Carl Hanson were reading the *Denver Post*. They had two copies delivered every morning. They were both professors at Colorado State, where she taught piano in the Music Department. He, the newly appointed head of the Physics Department.

Last week, they celebrated Carl's promotion by turning in his '34 Plymouth coupe and buying a brand-new black Packard.

Hilda had been talking to Carl for months about adopting a baby. She felt if they waited any longer it would be too late. In their mid-fifties, financially secure, their sharing instincts were making noises. Carl had settled on the Packard. He'd share that with Hilda. She was undeterred. Though Hilda was fifty-two, she looked ten years younger: smooth, unlined skin, even, well proportioned features, golden yellow hair. Not beautiful, but a face that implied lazy days on the farm, warm sun and robust health. Naturally taciturn, much of her life was spent deeply imbedded in music.

Carl was her opposite. While he was short for a man, she was tall for a woman, at five seven. He was an inch below that, with dark skin, brown eyes, black hair. More comfortable in the world of words, he was, at heart, introverted.

What they shared was a past: a past that contained many secrets. They were German Jews. In 1935, Carl and Hilda were teaching in a small private college in Wiesbaden, overlooking the Rhine. As a career move, Carl had his nose straightened and they officially changed their names to Hanson. He had a number of articles published in scientific journals as part of his doctoral program. Articles that created a bit of a stir in the physics community.

The atmosphere in the country was becoming increasingly anti-Semitic. So, protected by their new identities, Carl and Hilda applied for positions at Berlin University. They wanted to go as high as they could as fast as they could. They were accepted as associate professors and began their climb. There was safety at the top.

"Would you like another cup of coffee, Carl?"

"No thank you, my dear. I have had quite enough."

They spoke only English—the English they'd heard the announcers use on Armed Forces Radio during the war. However, they had no way of knowing Americans no longer spoke the King's English. As a matter of fact, it marked them as immigrants.

"Carl," Hilda said, as she folded the *Post,* "Here is an article in the paper, a follow- up on a headline story from 1942. It's concerning an eight-year-old girl kept in a dresser drawer for the first eighteen months of her life. She was discovered in a hotel by the police and put into an orphanage where she's been ever since.

"She's very bright and speaks well, but rarely. Withdrawn and moody, she has trouble making eye contact and is given to fits of crying, going through her days without close relationships with staff or schoolmates, it says. According to the writer, she's unadoptable and will probably be institutionalized for the rest of her life." Hilda laid the paper down and walked to the sink. She stared out the window and tried to stop the tears.

This may be the one child I can save, she thought.

Carl went over to her and put his hand on her shoulder. Hilda hadn't cried since before the war. She pulled away and ran outside into the garden. He walked quickly after her. She was standing next to the square of rose bushes. Head up, eyes tightly shut, fists clenched, her body rigid. He could see her arms trembling, as though she were straining to lift a tremendous weight. He reached out to touch her, paused, then pulled away and walked quietly back to the house, with a feeling that the life they had struggled and fought for, sacrificed for, way beyond human reason, the life for which they endured the basest primal cruelties, was now coming to an end.

* * *

Their new black Packard carried the silent couple down Route Twenty-five on a brilliant, sunny June day. The spectacular Colorado scenery flew by, seen, but unnoticed. Carl and Hilda were deep inside themselves. If an observer were riding in the back seat, he'd see two relaxed, self-assured professionals, enjoying a ride through the Rockies. He'd be wrong. Inside them was a constant tension caused by a lack of trust in the next moment. They hardly spoke; like taut pieces of piano wire, they silently vibrated. They were comfortable with silence. Silence created no situation to be believed or disbelieved. Agreed to or not. No words that cut to the bone. No flash of violence that opened veins. Or killed.

Carl and Hilda stayed safely inside.

They arrived at the Colorado State Children's Hospital and Orphanage at three. Their appointment with a Mrs. Bridges was for three-fifteen.

The large limestone building sat proudly behind a well cared for lawn, with walkways and green benches beneath a stand of oak trees. They walked up the steps of the Administration Building, across polished marble floors to the island desk sitting in the middle of the lobby. The elderly lady in horn rimmed glasses looked up. Carl stepped to the desk.

"We are the Hansons from Fort Collins. We have an appointment with Mrs. Bridges."

She smiled and checked her ledger.

"Yes, here it is. I'll call her. She'll be down to pick you up shortly. Meanwhile, you can relax. There are sofas along the wall."

"Thank you. You are very kind," said Hilda.

The Hansons sat down and seemed relaxed. Hilda, in a blue-gray dress and navy-blue jacket, a string of small pearls embracing her neck and Carl in his official uniform: a dark blue double breasted pin stripe suit, paisley tie, and ox-blood wing tips.

49

A few minutes passed and Mrs. Bridges appeared. Tall, perhaps five-nine, she was wearing a severely cut black dress suit and tie, close cut gray hair and an institutional smile, designed to assure them nothing in the meeting will be personal. She managed adoptions at the orphanage.

They followed her into an elevator, rode to the fourth floor in silence. Stepped out.

"My office is just down the hall."

She was right, of course. They entered behind her.

There was a large desk in front of two tall windows. The sun streaming in should have created a warm atmosphere, but failed. The room was too sparse. Two filing cabinets, three straight chairs made up the décor.

Mrs. Bridges sat in her chair behind her desk. Her steel-gray hair matched her steel-gray eyes.

"Thank you for your interest in Mary Kate. I have the information you gave me over the phone, Mrs. Hanson. But it might be a good idea if we talk for a while, before we call her in. What made you decide adopting Mary Kate, was the right thing to explore at this time in your life?"

"We're German, as I told you on the phone." Hilda said, in a calm nicely modulated voice. "We spent the first half of our married life, building our professional careers.

"We finally became part of Berlin University's faculty and we felt free to discuss adopting a child. Soon afterwards, Germany liberated Poland, so we decided to put off having a family until Europe stabilized. You, of course, know how that turned out. Mr. Hanson is now head of the Physics Department at Colorado State. We are financially able to give a child the finer things and—"

Mrs. Bridges cut her off. "How about you, Mr. Hanson, do you have anything to add?"

"I think Mrs. Hanson covered the points she and I discussed very well. I look forward to meeting Mary Kate. But, before we go further, you should know we came to America from Auschwitz. We are Jews."

The phone rang. Mrs. Bridges frowned, picked it up. Listened. Hung up.

"We have an incident I have to monitor. I should be back in a little while."

With that, she stood up and walked out.

The Hansons sat staring out the window. Hilda began plans for redecorating her office and turning it into Mary Kate's room. She'd ask Mary Kate her favorite color. In her mind, she also created a music program for the girl. She'd teach her the piano. Hilda had to decide the best regimen to begin with, and then a lesson plan.

When Mrs. Bridges left the room, Carl relaxed. He hadn't been aware of it, but he'd felt stressed. Something about Mrs. Bridges' attitude bothered him. A subtle, bureaucratic arrogance that he's seen before, somewhere. Sitting in the warm sunlight, he dozed, his head on his chest.

When the office door finally flew open with a bang, his head snapped up. Camp Commander Fritz Korbach marched in, followed by two uniformed armed guards. Korbach was in full Nazi regalia, medals flashing. His black boots gleaming in the sun. Carl and Hilda both stood when he entered.

"Sit, sit. You must be tired. Those cattle cars make traveling tedious. I've complained many times about it," he said, chuckling to himself while he wheeled around his desk. He deftly removed his black leather gloves and placed them carefully on a small table. He stared at the Hansons as he would at huge body lice infesting his office. Still, ever the warm congenial host, he smiled.

"So," he said. "You're Dr, Carl Hanson. A genius of modern physics." He could have added. "As short as you are, you're still taller than me."

This was Korbach's obsession. Everyone was taller than him. Legless dachshunds who had to roll down the street, were secretly taller than little Fritzy Korbach.

"An honor, I assure you," he continued. "I hope you're not insulted when I say, you don't look Jewish." Again, he chuckled at his own cleverness. Korbach dropped his pudgy body into his tall leather chair, took off his hat and laid it on the desk. Bald, with close-set eyes, his bloated face unremarkable, except for a weak chin.

Carl nodded toward Hilda. "Have you met my wife, Commander Korbach?" He smiled evenly. "Hilda's only fault is she's smarter than I. And taller, of course." There was an electric silence when violence could have erupted. It passed.

"I've been ordered to make your stay here at Auschwitz as pleasant as possible. I'm sure you're used to a hectic schedule and your international travel may be a problem, of course, but I have a plan to keep you busy. Naturally, you'll be looked up to by your fellow Jews as a figure of authority and strength. Your presence should do wonders for their morale. To help you with that, I'm appointing you to the position of 'Official Commander's Liaison Officer'. I've posted a notice in all the barracks that you are under my personal protection. You'll be my go-between. You'll have authority to adjudicate disputes and you'll be my eyes and ears in the barracks. For instance, if there's an escape plot, I want to know about it first. In the morning, at what we call "round up time," you'll be given a list of people who will be, shall we say, processed that morning and you will be responsible for their appearance. If you fail, you will unfortunately, have to fill in for them."

"Nooo!" screamed Hilda, as she launched herself across the desk...

"Are you all right, Mr. Hanson?" asked Mrs. Bridges. Carl opened his eyes and blinked himself awake. Hilda had her hand on his arm.

"It looked as though you were having a bad dream," she said.

Carl shook his head as though that could erase it from his mind. "I'm sorry if I upset you. It was a reoccurring dream left over from the war." He pulled out a handkerchief and dabbed his forehead. "It's like a piece of film that starts and stops at exactly the same spot each time."

Mrs. Bridges nodded sadly. "That's interesting. Mary Kate also has a dream that reoccurs on a regular basis, but she dreams of darkness. That's all. Black. Nothing is chasing her, she's not falling through the air and she isn't being threatened by anything but the color black. When she closes her eyes at night, she also sees darkness. That darkness doesn't frighten her at all, but the darkness in her dream seems to be a particular kind that panics her. She wakes up screaming. Yet, according to her, they're both pure black."

Mrs. Bridges face softened and became more personal.

"Let me be honest with you. We've had three other couples respond to the article in the paper. The interviews did not end on a positive note. Mary Kate is a project. She'll take years of work before she's anywhere near normal. You're the last couple we're going to interview. If you want to walk away, now is the time. Mary Kate is a special needs child. Please, I ask you to look past the special needs and see the child. If you can't do that, walk away. It's simply too painful for Mary Kate to face rejection after rejection. To be stared at like a side show freak. This is a good human being. How much pain must we inflict on her before we destroy her with good intentions?" A single tear squeezed out of her left eye. She angrily wiped it away.

"Mrs. Bridges." said Hilda, quietly. "My husband and I have just been through a horrendous, totally unnecessary war, with millions killed. After the war, the streets were clogged with Mary Kates. Wandering aimlessly. Completely lost. No parents, No future. No hope. Mr. Hanson has his nightmare. That's mine. I am standing on a street in a small village. Hundreds of homeless children are there. Perfectly still. All staring at me. Their eyes begging me to help. I rush to a child, who dissolves as I am about to reach her. I try again and again and again. I finally scream in frustration and then the street is littered with dead children. The sad truth is, we wanted to go where death and destruction was not as common as a cup of coffee. Yes, we ran to America. I recognize the guilt that created in us, but I am glad we ran. There comes a time to run, just as there's a time to stay. To Fight. To Die. I feel I know Mary Kate. My husband and I are survivors. I think we can teach Mary Kate to be, also."

Mrs. Bridges actually smiled. "Mr. Hanson?"

"I think that's the longest string of words I have ever heard from Mrs. Hanson. I agree with every one of them. However, we cannot promise to make Mary Kate happy. No one can make that promise for another, but we will try to give her the ability to find her own happiness."

Mrs. Bridges looked at a paper on her desk. "I'm afraid Mary Kate is not available for an interview today. However, if you'd like to make another appointment?" She watched the Hansons intently.

"Yes, of course." said Mr. Hanson. "Same time tomorrow?"

"If you can make it, could you be here at 10 a.m.?"

"Ten tomorrow will be fine," he said.

For the first time Mrs. Bridges smiled broadly.

"That way, Mary Kate won't have time to work up an anxiety attack

Chapter Twelve
June 13, 1948. Denver, Colorado.

A gray day dawned. The light through the hotel window was tentative, unsure of its welcome. "You might be happier if I came back later, when I can bring sunshine with me," it muttered.

Carl and Hilda did not notice. They were sitting on the bed, fully clothed, silently staring at the beige wall. Their emotions, in a liquid state, flowing from fear to hope and back to fear. Always back to fear. Fear for themselves and for Mary Kate, and behind fear sat despair. As soon as they sensed despair, they turned back to hope—the very hope that brought them to America. Hope was the emotion they would ride till the very end of their lives. Hope and fear.

* * *

Mrs. Bridges walked briskly across the lobby of the Colorado State Children's Hospital and Orphanage, right hand eagerly reaching toward Carl and Hilda Hanson. Wearing a maroon dress and a tan jacket, her whole demeanor had changed from the day before. She seemed lighter, almost buoyant. She clasped their hands and greeted them as she would old friends.

"Did you manage to sleep last night?"

"Yes." answered Carl. "Off and on. Let us say it was as expected."

"The problems yesterday were entirely my fault." She explained, as they rode the elevator up to her office. "The children live a very regimented life. Routine is paramount. It helps control stress. With four couples inquiring, I thought two interviews a day would not be too stressful for Mary Kate. What I didn't count on was, after reading the article in the paper, the couples saw it as a fast track to adoption. In other words, since you have this damaged child you'd like to unload, we'll do you a favor and take her home, today. That couldn't be farther from the truth. It's just the opposite. We'll be taking more time and care to create the best possible match. Mary Kate is too vulnerable to throw to the first passing wolf. She would never survive."

"How did the couples react?" asked Hilda.

"Badly. As soon as I spoke of a process lasting months, they were ready to leave. When Mary Kate came in at the end of each interview, they'd already decided against her. She sensed the negativity, and wanted no more of it. It's always good to remind ourselves that a brilliant mind lies just behind her indifferent eyes. Right now, that indifference, that numbing of her emotions, is all that protects her from re-experiencing the cruelties of the past. It's a pretty thin defense line. No General in the war would have depended on it."

"All this trauma because of what happened before she was two years old?" asked Carl.

"No" Mrs. Bridges moved a few papers around and lined up the stapler with the edge of the desk. She sighed. "How serious are you about seeing this adoption go through?" she asked quietly.

"This is not a whim. This began before the war. We need this just as much as Mary Kate. Perhaps more. If we are able to do this, we will be forever grateful to you and Mary Kate," said Carl.

Mrs. Bridges nodded. "First allow me to apologize. Yesterday was a disaster. I'm afraid I projected my stress onto you. You're good people. You deserved better. You've read the article in the paper. What's missing from it is locked in our files. When Mary Kate was five, she had progressed very nicely from the child in the dresser drawer. Every skill we were able to test was now within the normal range. She was improving her interpersonal skills and was on the verge of adoptability. Some people here remember her laughing.

A couple signed up for our foster care program. It was fairly new and since it was considered to be a temporary emergency solution, we did not scrutinize the couples to the depth we do today. They chose Mary Kate. It was a mistake. A glitch in our visitation schedule allowed it to be a four-month mistake and Mary Kate was returned severely damaged. In a way, by hope. Shattered hope. She's come a long way in three years. But, the residue is there." She tapped her pencil on her desk.

"Let's bring Mary Kate in and you can meet her. The longer she waits, the more time her fears have to grow." Energized by her decision, Mrs. Bridges jumped up, moved swiftly to the door and opened it.

"Mary Kate, would you come in here, please?" Mary Kate walked in, wearing brown oxfords and a blue plaid pinafore over a white cotton blouse. "Thank you, dear." Mrs. Bridges walked over to the chair to the left of her desk. The Hansons stood.

Mary Kate came into the Hanson's view. A small child. Though rail thin, she moved heavier, slightly stooped as though she carried a heavy backpack. If birds had hands, they'd be as small and delicate as Mary Kate's. Mrs. Hanson's heart skipped a beat when she saw Mary Kate's tiny hands. The spread wasn't there to play the piano. Perhaps someday.

She was a pretty girl. Her little face was framed by a soft cap of red curls. When she reached her chair, she dutifully turned toward the Hansons, and tried to lengthen herself, as if she knew there should be more. A flimsy, yet pretty, smile inhabited its proper place, unbeknownst to the rest of her face, unreflected in her eyes. Eyes that were used to seeing what's out there rather than exposing what's inside.

Someday, she would, if all went well, be a beautiful girl.

Mary Kate Gleason, this is Mrs. And Mrs. Hanson."

Mary Kate's smile brightened by half a watt. "Hello," she said simply, her heart frantically searching for a way out of her chest.

"Hello, Mary Kate. We are very happy to meet you, at last. You are quite beautiful," said Hilda, smiling broadly, tears of joy trickling down her cheeks. Mr. Hanson was smiling without the tears.

Mary Kate had never been told she was beautiful. She assumed that was a good thing--being beautiful. But why was Mrs. Hanson crying? Crying was a bad thing. She was confused. When that happened, fear leaped in to save her. *Run! Hide!* it shouted. Most of Mary Kate scurried away from her eyeholes to hide in the darkness of her skull. She left the smile out there. Something to hide behind.

"Why don't we all sit down," said Mrs. Bridges. The adults sat. Mary Kate continued standing, her smile fading like an old tattoo. "Mary Kate?" Mrs. Bridges said a bit louder than she intended. Mary Kate jumped to her eyeholes, peered out. "Won't you sit down?" she heard. She sat, her hands clasped in her lap, legs together, feet flat on the floor.

"It's question and answer time," announced Mrs. Bridges. "You first, Mary Kate. What do you want to ask the Hansons? What would you like to know?"

Mary Kate assumed there was a right thing to ask and a wrong thing. But what was it? Mrs. Bridges had given her a list, but she lost it yesterday in the confusion. Putting her forefinger to her temple, so they'd see she was thinking, she checked her smile, brightened it a little bit, and desperately tried to relax. She heard herself ask. "Do you have any other children?" She watched the Hansons intently. But for some reason, they were blurry. She kept blinking to clear her vision. It didn't help. They both continued to smile.

"No, we don't." answered Mr. Hanson. "Would you rather have a brother and sister?"

Mary Kate didn't understand the question. She panicked, forgot her smile and stuttered, "N-n-n-no. I'd rather have a mother and father."

Everyone laughed except Mary Kate, who still didn't understand the question. But, they were laughing, and that was a good thing. Wasn't it? She desperately tried to concentrate.

"Perfect answer, Mary Kate," said Mrs. Bridges "Can you think of anything else you'd like to know?"

Mary Kate took a chance. "Do you have a dog?" She held her breath.

"No." answered Mrs. Hanson. "But I did have, when I was your age. We got him when he was a puppy. He was black, and we called him Robespierre Poodle. The whole family loved Robespierre. My brother and sister, Hansel and Gretel, who were named after a famous opera, used to play with him so violently, he'd become over excited and throw up on the carpet and Papa would be furious. We'd run out of the house and hide. I was the youngest and the slowest so Papa always caught me and made me sit in a corner for an hour. That was my punishment for being seven years old. Would you like to have a puppy some day?"

"Yes."

"What kind?"

"A little puppy."

"And what would you name him?" asked the lady.

Mary Kate thought and thought, then heard herself say. "Robespierre Also."

"Robespierre Also. Isn't that clever?" shouted the man, beaming at her as though she'd discovered God. Actually, Mary Kate had given up trying to think of a name, so she'd settled on the lady's dog. She was becoming confused again. Voices in the room were receding.

"Mary Kate. What's your favorite color?" asked the lady.

Mary Kate didn't have one. She tried to think of something. She was staring out the window when she heard someone say, "Blue?"

"Wonderful," said the lady, as she wrote 'blue' in a little notebook. "Would you like your bedroom to be blue?"

Mary Kate nodded.

"Light blue or dark blue?"

Mary Kate twisted her fingers in her lap. She didn't know. She was still trying to absorb the fact she'd have her own bedroom. She was becoming overwhelmed.

"Which would you like, Mary Kate? Light or dark blue?" asked the still smiling lady.

Mary Kate heard the voice from a faraway place, say "Both." She was watching the lady intently. Then the darkness came. Just round the edges. She could see only the lady's face.

"Of course. Both. Light blue on the bottom, representing day, and gradually becoming dark blue as we move up the wall till it's midnight blue on the ceiling, and we will paint stars and a moon on it."

That's when Mary Kate fainted. She pitched forward from her chair, head leading the way in a sort of dreamlike slow motion. Arms akimbo like the wings of a baby bird falling from its nest. The painted smile still on her face, eyes closed, as if she was too young to see such a sight. Her forehead hit the edge of the desk with a sad little thunk, and she crumpled down between the chair and desk in a pile of pinafore and oxfords.

Fifteen minutes later, Mrs. Bridges came back into the office. The Hansons jumped up. Their faces creased in concern. Immediately Mrs. Bridges' oversized smile wiped the concern away.

"She's fine! A little dizzy, very embarrassed. She has a bump on her forehead. She became over stimulated and fainted; it's as simple as that. She wants to apologize to you. Sit. I'll get her." She rushed out the door.

Almost instantly Mrs. Bridges and Mary Kate were back, holding hands like old school chums.

Mary Kate looked at them through tear filled eyes. Very slowly, working to make every word perfect, she said, "I...apologize...to you...Mr. and Mrs. Hanson."

They smiled and in an amazing feat of self control, did not jump from their seats and sweep her up into their arms. Their faces did that for them.

Chapter Thirteen
July 26, 1948. Denver, Colorado.

Mrs. Bridges and the Hansons met for the fifth and last time in the meager office with the two large windows. If all went well, Hilda and Carl would be taking Mary Kate home that day.

In the six weeks since the adoption process began, they'd met with two psychologists, three lawyers, Mary Kate's housemother, the chief clerk and Mary Kate. Always Mary Kate.

They'd meet her in a small interview room, with a sofa and two easy chairs. Mary Kate had answered their questions with a smile, but offered little on her own.

This morning, they'd met with the Board of Directors and signed their names to a bewildering array of documents and it became a fact; Mr. and Mrs. Hanson had a daughter, Mary Katherine Hanson.

"Well, it's finally over." Mrs. Bridges leaned back in her chair. Her satisfied smile told volumes.

"Any questions, comments, reservations?"

"A comment," said Mr. Hanson. "We want you to know how much we appreciate everything you have done to make today a reality. Thank you."

"You're welcome. I have a few thoughts before you and your daughter leave. Always remember, Mary Kate is somewhat of a miracle child.

"Few children who are abused so early in life develop into a normal functioning adult. Because it began at birth, she had no tools, no intellectual platform to help her understand what was happening to her. She had nothing but her instinct and her innate intelligence.

"She's progressed a long way. Our staff feels she was nurtured at some minimal level. It was probably sporadic. But it was a hint that life was not all pain and solitude. Because she spent the vast majority of her time in the dresser drawer, Mary Kate's internal life may always be more dense, more real to her than her external environment.

"When she's frightened, she'll have a tendency to dive back into herself and find her safety there. After you've been with her a while, you'll recognize the look; Mary Kate is no longer with us.

"Under the best circumstances there will be ups and downs; you can expect them. Often, an adoptive parent will experience regret when there isn't immediate bonding, so remember, it will take time. Just be kind to each other and it will happen.

"As long as you don't expect more from Mary Kate than she's capable of giving, you should be fine. She'll tend to be standoffish. Most people will see her as a quiet, shy girl. It's best you acknowledge that image and not disclose her background. People are not always understanding.

"We feel Mary Kate is at a level where she'll benefit a great deal by being surrounded by normal, loving people in a non-institutional setting. Try to treat her as an average eight-year-old. That's the identity you'll want to implant.

"Hopefully, there won't be any more newspaper coverage of the Dresser Drawer Baby. We think you can provide her with all the tools she'll need to prosper.

"If we hadn't found you, she would have probably spent her youth here. This is the best we can make it, but it's no substitute for a normal loving family. We're counting on you. We'll always be just a phone call away. If Mary Kate finds herself in emotional trouble, our psychologists are here for her. However, within a very short time, you'll be the best judge of what's right for Mary Kate.

"OK! Are you ready to start your new family?"

The Hansons looked at each other, nodded and quietly said, "Yes."

"Good! Now let's go pick up Mary Kate and start her on a brand-new life."

* * *

The big black Packard flowed easily up Route 25, toward Ft. Collins and home. Traffic was light; the sun was shining. Even the flinty, cold Rocky Mountains seemed cheerful today.

The Hanson family was at ease. Relaxed. Why not? They'd gone ninety miles with no problems so far. True, Hilda was a tad anxious.

When they'd bought the house last year, they'd had an addition put on. It was to be Hilda's music room. Next to that was her office. They'd built the music room large enough to house her grand piano. They discovered there was room left over for a desk and shelves for her sheet music and an easy chair. The office was rarely used.

It was the obvious choice for Mary Kate's bedroom. A bathroom sat next to it. Perfect. But, at night with she and Carl upstairs, would Mary Kate be upset, downstairs all by herself?

Mary Kate was also worried. Sheila was alone in the house. What if it caught fire? She wouldn't know how to escape the flames.

"Mrs. Hanson?"

"Yes, Mary Kate."

"How long before we get home?"

"A half hour at the most. Are you eager to see our new home?"

"Yes. I'm worried about Sheila"

"Sheila?"

"My wolf."

"Oh, yes. Well, she asked about you before we left. She was worried about you, too."

The Hansons had originally discussed buying Mary Kate a puppy. Mrs. Bridges felt it might be too soon to bring another new element into the family equation. So, the Hansons commissioned a young artist from Colorado State art department to paint a life-sized wolf on Mary Kate's blue wall.

Mary Kate insisted it had to be a wolf. No painting of a pretty little poodle for her. So, there it was. Just as you stepped into the room, on the wall facing the door, a magnificent gray and white she-wolf greeted you. Sitting on her haunches, tongue lolling out. Beautiful grey and black feathering, blue eyes, big and gentle, but with more than a hint of danger. An animal demanding instant respect. Hilda and Carl were amazed when they saw it. A guardian for Mary Kate and it would never soil their new bedroom carpet.

"We'll be home in just a moment, Mary Kate. Are you excited?" ask Mrs. Hanson, peering into the back seat.

"Yes," she said, thinking about it.

Inside, her stomach was churning away like a little acid factory. She looked out the window at the houses as they moved slowly by. Big houses. Big trees. Long driveways.

All the little tweaky fears she'd had since the adoption began were now roaring monsters, bouncing around her tummy, making a mess. She'd made a promise to herself; she'd be as quiet as a ladybug. She'd be as careful as a cat burglar. The Hansons wouldn't even know she was in the house. She wouldn't drop anything or ask too many questions.

She could feel herself begin to vibrate. What if she...what if she...oh dear, oh no! She could feel the warm pee between her legs. No! No! No! It couldn't be! She began to cry. Ruined! It was all ruined! They'd send her back, back to the orphanage. There'd be no Sheila, no room of her own. No Mother and Father. She let out a wail as the car slowed.

"Mary Kate! What's the matter?"

"I...I...I went to the bathroom!"

Hilda looked at her for a moment, and then smiled her new motherly smile.

"I remember doing that when I was your age. I would get too excited and it would happen. I could not stop it. Don't be upset. We have two bathrooms and one is next to your room. You will simply go in and clean yourself up, put on fresh underwear and you will be as good as new."

"You're not sending me back?"

"Oh Sweetie, send you back because you had an accident? You're our daughter. You'll always be our daughter. We don't believe in going back. We believe in going forward." Hilda had read that recently. It seemed apropos.

The Packard turned onto the red brick driveway and made its way slowly up the hill to the house. The lawn was cut perfectly and seemed to glow a magical green, deep and inviting. The house was a white brick, two story Georgian with a red roof and dark green shutters, matching the lawn. Huge pine trees dotted the perimeter of the property. The feeling was solid and inviting. The front door was up three steps from the lawn and was the same red as the roof.

Mary Kate got out of the car and looked at her new world. She turned around slowly trying to absorb it all: the houses, the trees, the winding road in front of the house. It filled her with pride and slightly behind that, the fear it wouldn't last. It was too big, too grand for little Mary Kate.

"You are not going to faint again, are you, Mary Kate?" Hilda asked quietly. "Look all you want and when you're ready, we'll go in and we'll introduce you to your new home."

"It looks big, now," said Carl, who was standing next to the car, trying to see it from Mary Kate's point of view. "But, by this time next week, it will feel just right. You will have the great luxury of taking it for granted." He sighed. "Unless, you have to pay the mortgage."

Hilda held out her hand to Mary Kate. "Come, child, Let's get you cleaned up and..."

Mary Kate's hand snapped back to her chest as if she'd been burned. "No," she mumbled. "I'm a big girl now."

Hilda was hurt. She'd looked forward to this moment, she and her daughter walking up to the house, hand in hand. She could tell from the flat look in Mary Kate's eyes that this was non-negotiable.

"Fine, Mary Kate. But you will go into the house with us, yes?"

"Yes."

"Good, because it becomes awfully dark out here at night"

Mary Kate had no way to translate sarcasm. Hilda's statement was just that; it becomes dark at night. She followed the Hansons up the steps and into the foyer. A huge multifaceted crystal chandelier, like an airborne Christmas tree, hung over her head. The black and white tiles gleamed under foot. Full-length mirrors stood on each wall. A grand staircase swept up and to the right. She was transfixed.

"Mary Kate?"

The little girl stepped out of her amazement. "Yes?"

Hilda smiled at her. Mr. Hanson had left Mary Kate's cardboard suitcase by the hall tree. "Why don't we go to your bathroom and you can clean up, and change clothes."

Mary Kate picked up her suitcase and tagged along behind Hilda through the living room with its thick oriental carpets, fireplace and heavily brocaded furniture.

Padded. Soft, thought Mary Kate, remembering the hard, shiny surfaces of the orphanage. Easy to clean, difficult to damage. Smelling of disinfectant. She stepped into the dining room with its heavy oak table, hunter green walls with white trim and smaller chandelier.

They turned right and walked down a hall to the bathroom. "Will you be all right or do you need help?" asked Hilda, cautiously.

Mary Kate answered by walking into the bathroom and gently closing the door. *She's a big girl now*, thought Hilda, a little sadly.

After a few moments, Carl came by. "Is she all right?"

"I'm not sure." She chuckled. "She has no social consciousness." They stepped away from the door. "She's an odd combination of sensitivity and insensitivity. She has no concept of other people's needs. She's not cruel or nasty, she just feels it's none of her business." said Hilda.

"She's lived a difficult life. She had to think of herself, if she planned on surviving,"

"Well, we have our work cut out for us," said Carl. "Remember, we'll be all right as long as we don't expect more than she can give."

The door opened. Mary Kate stood looking at them without expression. Waiting. She couldn't react without something to react to, so she waited and watched.

She was wearing a blue plaid jumper, white blouse and black Mary Janes.

"Now," said Carl. "Don't you look nice." She waited.

"Do you want to meet Sheila?" asked Hilda.

Mary Kate's eyes lit up. Her face came alive, as if a switch had been thrown. "Could I?" she asked. It was almost too good to be true. Even though she'd thought of little else all day, she had steeled herself for disappointment. She'd made up her mind that there would be no Sheila. She would survive anyway. But, still...next to the fear, was hope. Small. Feeble. Barely there at all, hope.

"Of course, you can see her. She's your wolf," said Carl. "Open the door to your left. That's your room. It's Sheila's too."

Mary Kate paused, her heart thumping. She turned the knob and pushed the door. Peeked inside.

She let out a squeal and ran in.

Hilda and Carl watched as she launched herself at the big gray wolf with the kind eyes. She was down on her knees. Touching Sheila's fur.

"Oh, Sheila. I was afraid you wouldn't be here. But you are and you're the most beautiful wolf in the world. I'll always be your friend. I'll read you stories every night. You'll never be lonely again."

Like a seven-day clock after a week of work, Mary Kate began to rapidly run down.

"We'll always have each other...and...you'll always be here...we'll sleep together...play." She slipped down to the carpet and curled up at Sheila's paws, one arm touching the big wolf's side, and slept.

Chapter Fourteen

Afternoon, July 26, 1948. Fort Collins, Colorado.

A hundred feet from Mary Kate's room, past a row of tall pines, stood a large Victorian house, painted beige with green and maroon trim; full porch, two turrets. Laying in front of the house in the shade of a row of blue hydrangeas, Robbie, the golden retriever, planned.

To the three black squirrels standing at attention forty feet away, the dog was asleep. Not a threat. They finally dismissed him. Good. Robbie was seven. He'd lost a step or two somewhere in those years, but what the honey blond lacked in speed, he made up for in doggy guile. A fly landed on his ear, which twitched automatically. A mistake, but the squirrels were now leisurely browsing. Nicely ignoring him. Robbie opened his eyes far enough to peek through his lashes. He was waiting for all three to have their backs to the giant oak, twenty feet behind them. They'd have to turn before they could run to safety.

Black squirrels are larger than the red or gray, well muscled and a tad brighter than their cousins, but still no match for a seventy-pound Goldie. Then it happened, all three turned their backs on the oak, their noses buried deep in the lush green grass.

Robbie lunged; the squirrels turned and scampered toward the oak. Robbie closed the gap, his legs churning, his neck stretched out, his jaws agape. A squirrel's tail twitched, an inch from his nose. Then, they were up the tree and safe. Robbie almost crashed into the oak, but slid off to the side at the last moment. He turned and tried to leap up the tree as he always did. The squirrels, now into the game, grabbed leaves and twigs and hurled them down on Robbie, chattering with excitement. Furious, the defeated dog barked and growled in protest long after the game was over.

Mary Kate, deep into her nap, woke to the sound of a dog barking. *There are no dogs at the orphanage.* Curled at the feet of Sheila, her view was of the two windows directly ahead of her. Where was she? Nothing looked familiar. Why wasn't she in her dormitory? Sweat broke out on her forehead. Her stomach clenched in panic. She rushed to the window. Green lawn, pine trees and that awful dog, barking and growling. She opened her mouth to scream.

The teakettle whistled, making an ear-piercing screech. Hilda took it off the burner and poured two cups of tea. She and Carl had recently adopted tea as their noon drink and on this most important afternoon they sat in the kitchen, waiting for Mary Kate to wake from her nap.

"She was exhausted, poor thing." Said Hilda.

"Yes, she is so easily over-stimulated." Carl dropped two cubes of sugar into his Earl Grey. "Do you think she is really ready for the give and take of a public school? Or even a private school?"

"Oh, no. Not close to ready. Mrs. Bridges said it was our decision. I was thinking about it on the drive home. We don't want her education put on hold for a year. The only answer is home schooling until she's ready. I am not only speaking about academics, but social interaction. We can give her a grounding in how to meet people, uphold her part in a conversation, establish eye contact, play well with other children, even table manners. Have you noticed how she holds her silverware? In her fist, as though she were wielding an ax. She chews with her mouth open. And that vacant stare when she's unsure of herself. Tsk, tsk, tsk." Hilda took a sip of tea.

"If she were called upon in class for an answer, she would panic," said Carl. "And if she didn't know the correct answer, there could be tears. Possibly hysteria."

"You know how cruel children can be. They would sense her difference almost immediately. See her as a perfect victim to pounce on," said Hilda.

She thought for a few moments. "We could team teach. I could rearrange my lessons at school around your schedule, so there would always be one of us with her."

"Let's look at the pros and cons of having her tested."

Hilda shook her head. "No matter how well the tests are put together, there is always stress, even for a normal child. Why don't we hold off, till she feels comfortable with us? I would have liked to start her on piano, but she's so frail and her hands are tiny. It would be extremely difficult for her. I can see it creating nothing but frustration. Perhaps, in the future."

"Do you think we should wake her?"

That's when they heard a piercing scream. They jumped from their chairs and ran toward Mary Kate's bedroom. They heard it again. Not a scream this time, but a high-pitched howl that reached a zenith, held it and then spiraled down till it disappeared.

Carl grabbed Hilda's arm. They stopped in mid run.

"It's Mary Kate. She's imitating a wolf, baying at the moon."

"Why would she do such a thing?" asked Hilda, obviously upset.

"Calm down. It may simply be her way of bonding with Sheila. Becoming more like a wolf."

A light twinkled in Hilda's eyes. "Carl, remember the story of the Pied Piper?"

She pulled Carl into the music studio, next to Mary Kate's room, sat down at the baby grand and began to play Mozart's Twelve Variations on the melody known as "Twinkle, Twinkle Little Star."

Mary Kate buried her head in her arms and sobbed. She lay at the feet of Sheila. Suddenly she remembered. She was in her new home! Had they locked her in? She jumped up and cautiously tried to turn the doorknob. It worked easily, and she opened the door. She heard the tinkling sound of a song her housemother had taught the kids years ago. She couldn't remember the name, but it calmed her, wiped away some of the fear. It was coming from the room next to hers. She tiptoed over to the door and peeked in. There was Mrs. Hanson playing the piano and smiling at her. Mr. Hanson was sitting in an easy chair smoking a pipe, his back to the door. When he saw Hilda smile, he turned to Mary Kate, grinned and pointed to a chair.

Mary Kate became very self-conscious and simply slid down to the thick carpet and remained there, half in, half out of the room. The sprightly, soothing sound washed over her. Mary Kate was enjoying herself.

The studio was white. Two side-by-side windows brought warmth into what could have been an austere room. The walls were covered by black and white photographs of Hilda's students, many of them sitting at a piano. Some of them standing next to Hilda, smiling. The effect was reassuring. Mary Kate closed her eyes and listened to the piano. She felt the tension ooze away. A few moments later the music pulled her through the door to a night filled with twinkling stars. A gentle moon seemed to smile at her. For a moment, her ongoing fear of what's to come was put aside and Mary Kate felt peace flow into her. It was as if she were part of the sky, itself, serene and clear and untroubled.

The music stopped. The moon and stars faded away, and Mary Kate opened her eyes.

Hilda was sitting on the floor next to her, leaning against the wall, her knees tucked up almost to her chin.

"What did you see, Mary Kate?"

Startled by the question, Mary Kate felt the fear rush back in. What did Mrs. Hanson want to hear? People ask questions to hear a specific answer. Something they want you to say. Mary Kate couldn't think of what it could be. Sometimes, when her back was against the wall, she tried the truth. "I...I...saw the moon and the stars."

"How did that make you feel?"

"Ah...good?" There was silence for a moment.

"I don't know about you two, but I am starving," said Hilda. "Mary Kate, why don't you wander around the house and become acquainted. I'll call you when dinner is ready."

Mary Kate went on a tour of her new home. She made her way to the front door and stood once again under the huge chandelier. Now that she had time to look at it, she was more amazed than before. It was as if the stars she'd seen in her head had fallen to earth and were nesting in the Hanson's foyer. She looked up the stairway to the second floor. The upstairs was dimly lit and felt private. An exploration for another day. To her left were two richly carved double doors with brass handles. She went over and pulled the one on her right. It didn't open, but the door separated an inch or two. She pushed it sideways and the door slid magically into the wall. She peeked into the room; it was a library, every bit as big as the one at the orphanage. To the left were two large windows overlooking the driveway. Floor to ceiling shelves covered the walls, filled with books. Comfortable looking leather chairs, each with a small table and a standing lamp were scattered around the room in no particular order. All because of books. Mary Kate was learning to read and didn't know a great deal about books, but she could tell these were very different from what she'd seen at the orphanage. They even smelled different. Heavier, more permanent. To her right were two more doors, identical to the ones behind her. Mary Kate guessed they would lead her to the back of the house. She walked to them and slid open the one on the right.

It was a smaller room, with one little window. In front of the window was a large desk with piles of papers stacked on it. The walls had more books. Books and papers were on the floor. The wall on the right was actually a huge backboard. Numbers, symbols, exes, lines and equal, plus and minus signs in wild profusion, created a dense nonsensical pattern that Mary Kate knew must mean something. It was as though she was staring at a great secret that only the Hansons knew, a secret of great importance. There it was, staring back at her, close enough to touch, and yet that blackboard might as well be on the moon.

Mary Kate became upset. She wanted to know what the mysterious markings meant. A chair stood in front of the desk; she turned it around so it faced the blackboard. She sat and stared at it with an eight-year-old's belief that if she looked at it long enough, it would reveal its secret.

"Dinner is ready, Carl. You had better go find Mary Kate."

Carl walked out of the kitchen and headed toward the front of the house.

At the orphanage, they'd been given a list of the foods Mary Kate would have eaten on a regular basis. There was a star by macaroni and cheese with hamburger meat. Hilda had baked it into a casserole with buttered breadcrumbs on top. She turned off the heat and sat down to finish her tea.

Carl walked to the foyer. He noticed the door to the library was open. He went in and saw his office door also open. Peeking in, he saw Mary Kate sitting, looking at the formula on the blackboard. She was staring so intently, he was reluctant to disturb her. Her forehead was creased from the effort. She couldn't possibly be making any sense out of it, and yet he could see her frantically searching the board for clues. Some hint as to what it was all about.

It was at that moment, Doctor Carl Hanson, head of the Physics Department at Colorado State University, fell hopelessly and completely in love with his new little daughter.

Chapter Fifteen
July 27, 1948 - Fort Collins

It was six-thirty on the second day of Mary Kate's occupation of the Hanson house. Carl and Hilda were sitting at the kitchen table, nursing their first cup of coffee. Mary Kate was still asleep.

"What do you think we learned from Mary Kate's first day?" asked Carl.

"Well, I think we realize now how fragile she is, and how isolated," said Hilda.

"School will be starting in a month. Do you think we will have enough time to acclimate her to us? To make some sort of connection?"

"I don't know, but why not start by showing her the town, the area, and of course the neighborhood?" Hilda nodded. "Start from the outside and assume that the steady interaction will eventually become normal and non-threatening.

"Of course, we could start here and work outward," she continued. "I can walk her through the house after she's had her breakfast, and then give her a tour of the yard. I could introduce her to Robbie next door and the neighbors on both sides.

"I'll tell her all she has to do is smile and nod. That way she won't feel any pressure. Then she and I can walk through the neighborhood."

Carl smiled. "Good. It is a logical progression. You may accidentally stumble on some children her age. I would not make a fuss about it. Let it evolve naturally. If she shows any discomfort, just move on.

"By the way, I told you I found our little girl in my office yesterday. Did I tell you what she was doing?"

"No, I don't think so."

"She was studying the formula on the blackboard. I don't mean she was merely looking at it. She had moved the chair around and was sitting, studying it with an intensity I've rarely seen. Most children would glance at it and move on."

"That is extraordinary."

"Yes, Mary Kate sensed that it had meaning and was determined to discover what it was. I walked into the room and stood eight feet from her and she was so focused, she didn't notice me. I cleared my throat; she jumped and I apologized for frightening her, told her dinner was ready."

"What was her reaction?"

"At first, she glared at me. If she'd had a gun, I would have missed dinner. Then she calmed down and nodded. I walked into the sunroom and she followed."

"Ah. I thought she looked angry when she came in, but as soon as she smelled the casserole, she brightened up." Hilda sighed. "I do wish she would talk more. Sometimes she makes me uncomfortable. It's as though I were being watched."

"And evaluated."

"I know she doesn't love us yet, but I do wonder if she even likes us," Hilda said.

"Hmmm. I think it's too early for that. Really. She's still waiting for the hammer to fall. She's a little castle, with thick walls and battlements, who's lived in a constant state of siege. In her mind she's just catching her breath between assaults." Carl drained his cup. "And I'm afraid that's an accurate analogy."

"I was going to begin teaching her table manners this morning, but perhaps I'll put it off until I sense she at least accepts us as the household staff."

Carl laughed as he poured himself a second cup. "Do you ever feel we're in over our heads here?"

"Not recently. I did when we were standing in front of the board of directors. Now, I think we'll do what every couple does when they have a new child—the very best we can."

Mary Kate appeared at the kitchen door. She was still in her pink pajamas. Her red hair was mashed on one side, her eyelids droopy.

Hilda noticed her. "Good morning. Mary Kate. Did you sleep well?"

Mary Kate thought for a moment. No one had ever asked her that. "I don't know. I was asleep."

"That's good. What would you like for breakfast? You can have whatever you want, as long as it's breakfast food: oatmeal, cream of wheat, pancakes, French toast, or eggs. You decide and then Father and I will have the same."

Mary Kate had never had a choice before. She simply ate what was served.

"What's French toast?"

"You've never tasted French toast?"

Mary Kate shook her head.

"Wonderful. It will be like an adventure."

Mary Kate nodded.

"You get cleaned up and dressed and by the time you're finished, breakfast will be ready."

Mary Kate stared at her with blank eyes, turned and left.

"You called me Father."

Hilda looked up from her coffee. "Did I? I didn't realize I'd said it."

"It actually felt right. She will have to call us something. If we used the terms Mother and Father, she may pick it up automatically. We certainly don't want to be Hilda and Carl."

Hilda was standing at the counter, breaking eggs for the toast.

"Think back three months," she said. "It's incredible, the changes in our lives. Your promotion, a new car and a new daughter."

"And last year we bought the house," added Carl. "How does it feel for you, Hilda? All these changes."

She thought for a moment. "I can't bring myself to trust it. It's as if, one night we'll hear marching boots coming up the driveway and the door will be broken down. The Gestapo will come in, break all our furniture, throw us into the back of a black Mercedes and fifteen minutes later, we'll be in Auschwitz again."

Hilda dipped the pieces of bread in the egg mixture, and then dropped them onto the skillet.

"Perhaps there's no real escape from a concentration camp," she said quietly. "It's like the obese woman who loses two hundred pounds, yet every time she looks in a mirror, she sees a fat lady. No matter how far we run, Auschwitz is one nightmare away."

Carl slammed his hand on the table. "No! Don't say that! If that's true, the Nazis have won. We promised each other before we left Germany that we'd never speak of it again. America would be a new life for us. All our dreams have come true. Why can't we simply enjoy what we have?"

"We do enjoy. We will always get pleasure out of what we have accomplished. I just think that you can take all the painful memories and store them in a locked room in the dark corner of your mind. That doesn't mean they go away. You carry that room with you through the years and it becomes heavier and heavier. Eventually it sinks down into your subconscious and when you sleep, the door swings open and we once again see the dead-eyed children and the arrogant camp commander and all the death. You can't wish away your past." She refilled their cups.

"Perhaps you're right," Carl said sadly.

"I'm afraid I am. Now that we have Mary Kate, I think it may be important to remember, to realize that we have something in common with our new daughter. We have each been victims of massive human cruelty. If we wash it away, we can be victims again. I think those painful memories can make us more understanding, more compassionate parents." She paused, spatula in hand. "Perhaps the fact that we found each other was not a coincidence."

"What else can it be?"

Mary Kate appeared in the doorway. The conversation stopped.

The Hanson family sat down to a normal American breakfast.

Chapter Sixteen

1948-1952. Fort Collins, Colorado.

The first breakfast at the Hanson house was a great success, as were the next dozen or so meals. After a week, Hilda could no longer contain herself and she began to teach Mary Kate table manners.

Mary Kate felt, since she managed to successfully move the food from the plate to her mouth, no changes were necessary.

While Hilda was teaching Mary Kate how to eat properly, her daughter was giving Mother a tutorial on patience. No sooner did Hilda lose her temper, than Mary Kate would glare at her with the intensity of a body blow, making it clear; force, whether physical, mental or emotional would not be allowed. A détente was reached; Mary Kate would try to change and Hilda would stay patient and pleasant.

A week after the table lessons began, the three Hansons went on their first field trip, a tour of the Colorado State University Music and Physics Departments, and then to lunch in the faculty cafeteria. It all went smoothly. The rules of food management were followed and when Mary Kate was introduced to her parents' colleagues, she smiled and said, "It's very nice to meet you, Mr. Whatever." This created in Carl and Hilda a hitherto unknown sensation: the feeling of parental pride. They were taken aback by its intensity.

Hilda contacted the District School Board and set up a course of study that would correspond with the Board's standards. There were still three weeks before school was to open, so they took Mary Kate on a trip to Chicago, where they visited the museums and sights of the big city. Her favorites were the zoos, both Brookfield and Lincoln Park.

After Chicago, they drove to St. Louis and toured its wonderful zoo. The zoo had a small pack of wolves, including a big gray and white that happened to wander to the fence and stare at them. Mary Kate was thrilled.

"She's looking at me! Hi Sheila! It's Mary Kate! You look lovely. I have a picture of you in my bedroom." The wolf stared at her for a moment then trotted back to the pack. "She's going to tell the others. Isn't that exciting?"

Carl leaned close to Hilda. "Sheila's a boy."

Hilda grinned. "I'll never tell."

The Hansons arrived back at Fort Collins a week before the start of school. Mary Kate was elated when they pulled up into the driveway.

I'm home, she thought. *My very own home.* She ran to the front door to see her very own Sheila.

Carl disappeared into the bowels of the Physics Department and reappeared each night for dinner only to run back to school again.

Hilda took Mary Kate to Hoover Elementary School, four blocks from the house. They met with Miss Everett, the second-grade teacher. She agreed to supply test materials to the Hansons.

And so, on September sixth, 1948, the Hanson Elementary School opened for business. They began small. Mary Kate was barely thirty-eight inches tall.

Six hours a day, either Hilda or Carl would work with their daughter on reading, writing and arithmetic, geography, common knowledge, and the study of logic, philosophy and religion that they called abstract concepts. Her hunger to learn was insatiable. While she was still shy with everyone outside the family, she slowly began to relax with the Hansons.

On the first of February, in the middle of a snowstorm, Carl and Mary Kate were sitting at his desk playing a game. The rich aroma of Hilda's brownies hung in the air.

Carl had created a mathematical game he called Power Lunch. It was based on the concept that the larger numbers could eat the smaller numbers. They took turns drawing marbles with numbers on them out of a hat, till they each had ten. The numbers ran from one to twenty. They each rolled the dice and the one with the highest total, shouted "Lunch." and captured the opponent's two marbles. It was an exercise in addition and subtraction.

The first time Mary Kate won, she let out a scream and laughed: a head back, mouth open, laugh. Carl had never heard her laugh in the five months she'd been at the house.

He became so excited he grabbed her hand and pulled her through the sunroom and into the kitchen, shouting, "Last one in the kitchen has to eat an extra brownie!"

She cried, "No! No! Never!" laughing hysterically.

Carl and Mary Kate were both finishing their second brownie when she head Hilda playing piano in the music room. Gulping down the last of her milk, she dashed down the hall and into Hilda's room.

"Mother! I won! I beat Father in a math game and he's the smartest man in the world."

Hilda laughed and Mary Kate ran into her arms and they hugged like mothers and daughters do every day, but this hug was special. The very first hug is always special. Hilda's heart was aching with happiness and tears were flowing down her face.

Mary Kate pulled back. "Mother, you're crying. What did I do?"

"Nothing, my beautiful daughter, I'm crying from happiness. Older ladies often cry when they are happy. I'll take you to a wedding and if you close your eyes, you'll think you're at a funeral."

Unnoticed, Carl stood at the door, a smile on his face and also one small tear, which he quickly brushed away.

From that day forward, Mary Kate was a model child. She joined in the conversations, took an interest in Carl and Hilda, laughed at their jokes and by June 5, she was referring to them as Mom and Dad. However, no matter how many people she met, she never moved past the formal stage. Always polite and courteous. Always reserved and shy. Her grades were spectacular, to the point where the Hansons let her move ahead into third grade material for the fear she might become bored.

It was mid June. Carl and Hilda were sitting in the library with cups of after-dinner tea. Mary Kate was in her room reading Albert Payson Terhune's "Lad: a Dog." To Sheila.

Hilda put down her Agatha Christie and took a sip of tea. "Carl, I'm worried about Mary Kate."

"Of course. you are. She's doing wonderfully well. Who wouldn't worry?"

Hilda smiled. Carl had changed every bit as much as their daughter. He was lighter. More likely to see the humor embedded in their lives.

"I'm serious. Think five years from now. Mary Kate will be fourteen, but she'll look like a twelve-year-old. And, at the rate she's advancing, she'll be a freshman in college. A curiosity. She'll never be accepted, which means isolation."

"I know. I've been thinking about that lately. I think I have an answer. What's the weakest area of study in the American educational system?"

"Languages."

"Yes. They learn to read and write in French or German, but can't speak it."

Hilda laughed. She had the talent of instant enthusiasm.

"Of course! That's brilliant. We'll teach her German first, which should be fun, then we'll move on to French and then Latin."

"Right. We'll cut her regular studies down to thirty minutes each, and then spend the rest of the time on German. That should slow her progression and in a year she'll be speaking like a native."

"I like it, but what about Russian instead of Latin? I have a feeling Russian may be a good language to know in the future."

"All right, Russian it is."

Carl mused for a minute. He took out his yellow oilskin tobacco pouch, filled his pipe, lit it and took a few puffs to get it going. "What's our final goal for Mary Kate? When she walks out of this house, a mature adult, what will she be?"

"Well, she'll be an intellectual, compassionate, open, young lady capable of long range relationships with the ability to become a good wife and mother. I suppose we have to use the word we hate, normal."

"And she's made steady progress, amazing really. What hasn't changed?" asked Carl.

"Her social interaction. She's polite and well spoken beyond her years, but she also manages to make it clear that she's not available for conversation. She mostly uses one-word answers to questions, turns away and refuses to make eye contact. It all adds up to 'Please don't bother me.' She must have met a hundred people in the last year and the pattern remains ironclad."

Carl relit his pipe. "We have a number of young men in our department working on their PHDs. They're Associate Professors now, but I could create a position for my most promising fellow. We could call it Associate Department Head. Once a week we could invite him over for dinner and a conference. Mary Kate will get used to him and hopefully learn to relax with someone other than you and I."

For the second time since the conversation began Hilda smiled. "That should help, but I think we should plan on sending her to Hoover the last year or two. She needs to learn how to get along with her peers. Otherwise, her teen years could see a great deal of turmoil. For all of us."

And so, the Hansons set their plan into action. Mary Kate's German advanced rapidly. By the end of the first year she was translating English to German and vice versa. She also could carry on a simple conversation in German. Hilda and Carl decided to give her another year of their native tongue.

The third school year, 1950-51, they switched to French. Her social skills did not improve. Their friends saw her as painfully shy. She never warmed to any of the Associate Department Heads that came to dinner. Though she was never purposefully rude, she never understood that ignoring them was a form of rudeness. When she was ready for seventh grade, Mary Kate rebelled.

"Mother, I simply don't want to go to Hoover. I see no reason why I should. I'm perfectly happy here at home."

"All right, we live in a democracy. We'll take a vote. Your Father and I vote go. Now, you and your friends can vote. Count them up. We've got two. How may do you have?"

Mary Kate glared at Hilda. Her Mother said as gently as she could. "Now, do you understand why you should go to Hoover Elementary?"

Mary Kate's brows slowly unfurled. Her jaw relaxed. She looked out the kitchen window, sighed and said, "Yes."

MAXINE

Chapter Seventeen
1948-1954. New Orleans.

The world was changing rapidly, and my life was joining the throngs of people who went this way and that, in new directions, with new views and ideas. The war had ended, first in Europe in May, and then in Japan in August. Servicemen returned home, some to waiting arms, others to disappointment.

One evening in October, Madame and I were sitting outside in the courtyard and I expressed these feelings to her.

"I feel as if something is coming, something big, but I have no idea what."

"If you feel it, it is so, chère."

"I wish I had some clue as to what it is."

"You are watching for several things alike to make their appearances? What you say, la coincidence?"

"Yes, Madame. I have seen no signs."

She pulled her sweater closer around her body and stood. "Come, it grows cold out here. Let's go in my kitchen and I will brew us some tea. Then I will read your tea leaves for you."

"I didn't know you read tea leaves, Madame." I followed her through the French doors into her kitchen.

"There is much you do not know about me," she said, laughing.

Later, after we had drunk our cups of bracing hot beverage, she gave me instructions.

"You have drunk all your tea except a tiny bit?"

"Yes, Madame."

"Hold your cup in your left hand, thus," she said, and demonstrated the action. "Now swirl the contents clockwise, that is from left to right, three times. Vite! Quickly!"

I did as she told me, swirling the delicate china cup rapidly.

"Now turn your cup over onto the saucer, carefully. Là! Let it stay for a minute, so it drains well."

We sat and stared at the cup, the kitchen clock loudly counting the seconds in the background. I wondered if the cup had been handed down to her from her grandmother, as she told me many of her belongings had been.

When I turned the cup back up and Madame began to tell me what she saw, it was apparent tea reading was not my forte. I saw nothing but dark dregs of tea: Madame saw the future.

She frowned and turned the cup this way and that before speaking.

"There are changes coming. Many changes. The time has come for you to use your gift in earnest. You will help many people. You will..." she paused, then set the cup down. "That is all."

"What else were you going to say, Madame? I will what?"

"That is all. You will help many people, for many, many years." Suddenly she had turned serious, stern. She picked up both our cups and saucers and took them to the sink.

"It is late, and I am tired. You will leave now, please."

This was very unlike Madame. I said nothing, but went upstairs to my own apartment, puzzling over what changes were to come, and how I was to help people.

* * *

The next day at work—I was still the housekeeper at the LaCroix house—I looked at the cook and said, "Rosa, you must not go home tonight. Promise me, Rosa, that you will not."

She looked startled and frightened at my pronouncement.

"Why? What do you know?"

"I don't know what, but something bad is going to happen. Don't go home tonight. Do you have someplace else you can spend the night?"

"Yes, I can go to my sister's house. She'll let me stay there," she said as she crossed herself.

Everyone in the residence knew that I lived in Broussard Court, Madame's quad of apartments, so I'm sure they thought she was tutoring me in the mystical arts, which, of course, she was, but not in the way they thought. My gift of knowing was growing, but I neither knew nor cared about the Hoodoo Madame Badeaux practiced. Madame's reputation was such that I, too, was respected because of her closeness to me. Rosa spent the night with her sister, and the next morning she found that someone had broken into her apartment and trashed it. It was the crazy boyfriend of the woman who lived the floor above, and he had been so drunk he had gone to the wrong flat. If Rosa had been home, she would have been injured and possibly killed. In my mind, I could see this.

Rosa soon told the story of my prediction to everyone she knew, and I was the subject of many whispered conversations and more than a little apprehension, as if I were going to predict dire happenings for anyone who looked at me.

Not long after, Mrs. LaCroix told everyone they were closing the big house and moving to Mobile, so we would all be without jobs. While others fretted about finding new employment, I was not worried. My gift assured me everything was in divine order.

At the Beau Villa Hotel, the next place I worked after the LaCroix household, I was hired to be the supervisor of the service personnel: maids and bellmen and such. I enjoyed meeting the new people there, and the hotel, which wasn't large, was like supervising a private household, only with more bedrooms and baths.

A returning serviceman, Jimmy, ran the elevator. He sat on a stool by the controls and took people up and down all day. When he had a break, he took the crutches that replaced his missing leg and slowly made his way to the café next door. His depression spilled over like a dark cloud, shadowing everyone around him.

One day, as he was taking me up to the eighth floor, I said to him, "Jimmy, your life is about to change."

"You mean it can get worse than this?" he said bitterly. "Comin' back as half a man? My gal taking one look at me and high-tailin' it away, sayin' she couldn't handle being married to a cripple? What's worse? Is I gonna lose my job?"

"You're going to get a new leg. An artificial one. It will take you a while to get used to it, but in a few months you'll be walking without crutches."

I got off at the eighth floor wondering what caused me to say that—it just came to me. Jimmy stared at me, mouth open, closed the elevator door, then the folding gate, and pulled the lever that started the elevator back down. He didn't even wait for me as he usually did.

Jimmy was his usual, morose self until the following week when he returned to work after his days off. He was watching for me and called out from his place on the stool.

"Miss Maxine! Miss Maxine!"

I walked over to the elevator.

"I's gettin a leg, Miss Maxine, jess like you says. I went for my appointment at the VA, and they tole me about it. They measured n everythin', and they's makin' me a leg. I oughta get it in 'bout a month, and they says when I got enough practice I be able to throw away these crutches." His smile lit up his face. "How you know, Miss Maxine? How you know dat?"

I didn't know how to answer him, so I just smiled and walked away.

MARY KATE

Chapter Eighteen
September, 1952. Fort Collins, Colorado.

It was the day after Labor Day. Mary Kate and her mother were sitting in Hilda's Chevrolet station wagon outside Hoover Elementary School. Cars were stopping, dropping off children for the first day of class. Groups of students were walking along the sidewalk. Some were riding bikes. Mothers were walking with toddlers.

Twelve-year-old Mary Kate had been quiet all morning. Hilda could feel the tension building. "Are you OK, Sweetheart?"

"Yes." Her yes sounded more like a no. She began to shake.

Hilda had seen this before. "Remember the day we brought you home from the orphanage? You were terrified. You knew something terrible was about to happen. How did that turn out?"

Mary Kate nodded.

"If you like, I can come in with you. Mrs. Austin said we could, at least for the first day. It's up to you."

Without a word, Mary Kate picked up her books, stepped out of the car and walked quickly across the street, clutching her books to her chest like a drowning swimmer clamps onto a lifeguard. All around her, children were jostling each other and shouting to friends they hadn't seen for three months. The air was overflowing with chatter and laughter. No one seemed inclined to go inside.

Eyes straight ahead, heart thumping away, she marched forward with total focus. She couldn't look behind her for fear of running back to the car. She didn't dare glance sideways, afraid of meeting the eyes of a stranger who would immediately see the terror she was feeling. The tiny two-legged juggernaut steamed through the sea of students, an irresistible force. A telescope in a pile of binoculars.

She'd been here before with her mother and knew the way to her homeroom. Once she entered the lobby, she turned right and powered down the locker-lined hallway to the last door on the left. A sign next to it read *7th Grade*.

There were four students scattered about the room. Mrs. Austin was standing next to her desk in the front of the wall-sized blackboard.

"Mary Kate!" said the pleasantly plump, blond teacher. "I'm so glad you could make it. Your mother sent me your test grades. You'll be a fine addition to our class. We seat our people in alphabetical order at Hoover. I'll show you to your seat. You'll be right in the middle of the room."

She walked down the second aisle and stopped half way down. "Number thirteen." Mary Kate sat down in the one-piece chair and desk. "The number is stenciled on the sides of the desk. Just lift up the top and store your books inside. Any questions?"

Mary Kate remembered to smile. "No thank you, Mrs. Austin. I'm fine." The bell sounded.

In the next five minutes, twenty-five more children filed into the room. Mary Kate kept her head buried in a book. She could feel twenty-nine pairs of eyes probing the new girl. Most of the class had entered Hoover in Kindergarten. A new face was exciting. She was wearing a dark blue skirt and a white blouse. Her saddle shoes were also blue and white.

Mrs. Austin tapped her desk with the bottom of a stapler. Silence. "Welcome back to Hoover Elementary, everyone. It's good to see your smiling faces again. The young lady you're trying unsuccessfully not to stare at is our brand-new student, Mary Kate Hanson. Mary Kate has been home-schooled by her parents who are professors at Colorado State, and they made sure she took all the tests you've taken. Mary Kate, would you stand up and say hello to the class?"

Why don't I get down on my hands and knees and crawl out the door? Then they'd have nothing to stare at. She stood and felt herself trembling.

"Mary Kate, I saw the record of your test grades; nothing less than an A for the last four years. Your mother said you were studying languages. Could you tell the class about that?"

In a voice made small by stress, Mary Kate squeaked, "Yes, two years of German, two years of French and my parents and I are teaching each other Russian."

The previously grinning students were now simply staring. The smiles had disappeared when they realized the grade curve had just been shattered. If Mary Kate got an A on every test, there was no reason why the entire class couldn't do the same.

The attitude change was picked up by Mary Kate's sensitive antenna and her heart sank a few inches. She sat down. Mrs. Austin had meant well, but Mary Kate hated being singled out from the rest of the class. She'd spent the first part of her life as the Dresser Drawer Baby. A curiosity. When her story appeared in the Denver Post, the attention starved orphans, most of whom had never received so much as a Christmas card from the outside world, reacted with jealousy. "What makes you so special?" still echoed in her mind.

She spent the rest of the morning trying to go unnoticed. Mrs. Austin did a verbal review of what they'd learned last year. She'd ask a question, then look for a show of hands. If none appeared she'd glance at Mary Kate, who was busy counting her fingers.

Mrs. Austin suddenly realized she may have put Mary Kate in an awkward position and did not call on her the rest of the period. Mercifully, the bell rang for morning recess. The stampede was immediate.

"You have fifteen minutes!" Mrs. Austin shouted at the backs of twenty-nine students. "Mary Kate, I'd like to talk to you for a moment." Mrs. Austin walked down the aisle and sat in the desk next to Mary Kate's.

"I'm afraid I embarrassed you earlier. I should have understood you weren't used to speaking in front of a class. I apologize."

Mary Kate managed a smile. "I've lived a fairly isolated life. It's been just the three of us for as long as I can remember. That's why I'm here, so I can learn to interact with my peers."

Mrs. Austin stared at her new pupil, who was going to have a problem fading into the crowd. The girl spoke in complete sentences and projected a mature quality in everything she did. The very fact that she spoke of her "peers" instead of "kids like me," reflected the years spent with intelligent, well-educated adults.

"I'll tell you what, Mary Kate, I won't call on you in class. You raise your hand when you feel comfortable. OK?"

"Yes, that would be fine. Thank you."

"Good girl. Now, you can stay at your desk or go outside. It's up to you."

She stayed inside.

The day finally ended with no further contact with either her teacher or her fellow students. As for Mary Kate, she found the material they covered rather bland and was struck by the passivity of her classmates. She was soon bored and began to bring a book to school.

She was in her second week before she decided to go outside and read during recess. She found a picnic table in the shade of a large tree and settled in.

"Mary Kate?" She was startled. No one had spoken to her in the week she'd been here and she'd begun to relax into the routine.

A plump, dark-haired girl with horn rimmed glasses sat across the table from her. "Hi, I'm Dalia Malik, I see you everday, and you never talk. I thought you might be lonely."

Mary Kate thought a moment then said, "Not really. I don't think I know what lonely means. There's always a book to read. Or a thought to explore or a walk to take. I've seen you in class, of course."

There was a rather long pause.

"Is your father Carl Hanson, head of the Physics Department?"

"Yes, why do you ask?"

"Because my mother knows your parents. She teaches art at State and your father gave her the first paying job she ever had. She likes to tell the story. She says her assignment was painting a wall. Don't know why she thinks that's funny. Then she says she painted a wolf on the wall."

"Yes. That's my room she painted."

Dalia laughed. "That would make you the Dresser Drawer Baby, wouldn't it? My Mother told me the story. What was it like, living in a dresser drawer? Weren't you scared?"

Mary Kate's heart began to race. Sweat broke out on her forehead. She was back at the orphanage. "Dresser Drawer Baby. Dresser Drawer Baby." They chased her around the playground, laughing and taunting her. "Baby, Baby." She ran and ran.

Then she was back at Hoover. She tried to breathe and to her horror, found that she couldn't catch her breath. She was dying. She knew it. She dropped her book and ran. She had to get home, had to find Sheila and...and what? Her brain had descended into chaos. No thought would stay for more than a second, it would flee the scene of this dying. Thoughts of Mother and Father raced by and disappeared.

Then she was home, but the door was locked. She screamed and collapsed, falling down the steps and curling into a fetal position in the grass. She sobbed, completely drained and slept.

An hour later Hilda found her, sitting in the grass. Her face, red and sweaty. Her hair was a mess with grass clinging to it.

"Mary Kate, what happened? You fell asleep out here, didn't you? You lost your key?"

Sheepishly, she looked up at her mother and shook her head, feeling ashamed and stupid. What had happened? How could she have forgotten she had a key and had been using it for days? Without a word, Mary Kate stood, walked up the steps, used her key and left her mother standing, staring at the closed door.

Mary Kate never told Mother and Father about her first panic attack. A label she didn't know until much later. If there was ever a chance she would enjoy the give and take of public school, it was gone now.

* * *

Life at the Hanson house changed. The intimacy that had developed between the Hansons soon faded away. Without the intense day-to-day interplay that was an inevitable byproduct of home schooling, Mary Kate grew apart from Mother and Father. It wasn't the drama of falling off a cliff. It was gradual and subtle.

The free-flowing conversations at the dinner table, the camaraderie they enjoyed, fell away slowly. Longer stretches of silence. More misunderstandings. Shorter answers. A profusion of "fines." And silence.

As always, Mary Kate was polite and courteous, but she was moving into her teenage years with the requisite infusion of unruly hormones.

There was no shouting or fighting in the Hanson house. That would be "making a scene." Mortal sin territory. Yet Carl and Hilda mourned the loss of their beloved daughter. Gone was the shared laughter, the whispered confidences, the occasional hugs.

Whatever the problems she had at school, stayed there. When asked about friends, she was evasive. Her grades remained, as always, straight A's.

The house seemed to change the most. It seemed larger, emptier, less comfortable, colder, at times almost resentful. Like a huge complex mirror echoing the emotions of its people. And like its people, the frustrations were kept safely inside.

MAXINE

Chapter Nineteen
1954-1956, New Orleans.

A year or so after I told Jimmy about his new leg, I got an offer from another hotel. It meant more duties, more employees to supervise, and more money. I didn't really need more money, since I lived on very little, and wealth meant nothing to me, but I knew I was supposed to be in that new place.

I had worked there a few months when I found one of the maids huddled in the supply closet, crying.

"What it is, chère? What is wrong?" As I put my arms around her I knew the answer to my questions. "There, shh, it is all going to be all right," I said as I put my cheek atop her head. "Your child will have a good home. She will be healthy and loved. Shh."

I closed my eyes and rocked her in my arms, while my mind took me back to my childhood home in the bayou. I knew what this girl was feeling, not only because of my gift, but because I had lived it myself. A baby on the way and no husband in sight. The shame that would come to her family because of what she had done. The disappointment in the man she had thought loved her, and the heartbreak to learn he did not. The whispers and murmurs that swirled around her—and me. I lived it again through her thoughts, even though I knew her child would survive, as mine had not.

"There is a place for you," I said, as she stepped away from me and wiped her eyes. "Have you heard of the Florence Crittenden Home?"

She shook her head. "No m'am."

"It's a good, safe place for young women in your situation. You can go there and they will protect you. They will give you a place to live, get medical help and everything you need to have a healthy baby. When the time comes, they'll find a good home for her with loving parents."

"It'll be a girl, then?" she asked. She had already heard about me and my knowing.

"Yes. A girl."

She smiled at that, then her face turned serious again. "My father threw me out of the house when he found out. I stayed with a friend last night, but I have to find a place soon."

"Then take off work now. Go to the Florence Crittenden house. Your job will be waiting for you tomorrow when you come to work."

She started out of the closet, and then turned back.

"It's like people say? You have the sight? The second sight?"

"Some call it that, yes."

She smiled again. "Thank you."

* * *

Word got around among the employees that I could tell the future, and I was bombarded with questions until I firmly told them I could not call up the information at will.

"If the spirits tell me, they tell me," I said. "Do not ask me any more. If it is something you need to know, I will inform you." I learned something from this experience, to hold my knowledge close. I did not want the reputation my gift was apt to bring me. I did not want hordes of people coming for advice. Finally, they left me alone.

My gift continued to grow, and I often knew what was going to befall my co-workers and the guests who stayed at the hotel. I kept the information to myself, however, unless it involved the person being in danger. The second-floor maid was going to meet a new man tonight, and she would eventually marry him. It served no purpose to tell her. The guest in room 423 would find her lost ring when she returned home. She would be happy to know that, but I didn't need to tell her. And so it went. I was always full of secrets, happy and sad.

During all this time, the spirit of the young girl continued to visit me at bedtime. By then I was sure Madame Badeaux was correct, and this was the spirit of a live person who called on me. For one thing, she

95

grew and aged, just as a real person does. I figured if she were the spirit of a dead person, she would remain the same each time, looking as she had when she had died. But as the years went on, she grew taller and sometimes her hair would be in different styles, just as a real girl would change it.

I always smiled when I saw her, and after a while I began to speak to her, just a little. At first that made her disappear, going back to where she came from, I assumed. She usually visited me a couple of times a month, never regularly, and several months later when I said, "Good evening," to her, she answered.

"Good evening."

That must have shocked her, to say it aloud to me, because she looked startled and vanished. So, I went back to just smiling for a few times, then tried it again.

"Good evening."

"Good evening," she said, and this time she stayed, drifting around and studying my room.

One evening, after our usual brief exchange, she looked as if she was summoning her courage. Finally, she became brave enough to ask a question.

"Where is this?"

I thought for a minute. I had never given any study to the thought that the spirits that came to me didn't know where 'this' was. I looked around me.

"This is my room. It is in New Orleans, Louisiana."

"Oh."

All this went on over the time I worked at the LaCroix household, and in the two hotels. One evening I was very late getting home, and she appeared to me soon after. She stood there, watching me until I spoke. "You look sad tonight," I said.

She was quiet for a few moments, and then said, "Girls were teasing me at school today. It makes me feel sad when they do it."

"Why do they tease you?"

She shrugged her shoulders. Finally turning back, she answered. "Because I am different."

"Different? How?"

"Just different. Not like them." She continued her study of my books and knick-knacks. "I'm not like anyone I know. Like coming to visit you. No one else I know can do that. And sometimes I know things are going to happen before they do."

I was curious. "And how do you do it, come to visit me?"

"I don't know. I just lay there, and I want to be someplace else, and then I am floating above my body. I can see me, there on the bed."

"Yes."

"And all of a sudden, I am here."

"And what brought you here, to me?"

She shrugged her shoulders. "I just end up here. I don't understand how or why."

"It is where the spirits send you, I guess."

"The spirits?"

"Yes. The spirits."

She was quiet, watching me remove my jewelry and brush my hair.

"I've been able to do it for a long time now, since I was a little girl," she said quietly.

I smiled and said, "I am different, too. I'm very different than the people I know. Except for one, my landlady, Madame Badeaux. You and I, we have things in common. Sometimes I leave my body and travel, too. I have friends I visit in other places."

She smiled at me and I smiled back.

"Perhaps, when you are older, they will no longer tease you."

"Maybe."

"Your parents, are they different too? Do they speak of knowing things others do not, or traveling outside their bodies?"

"No. And they don't like for me to speak of it, either."

She looked down at her feet, then back up at me.

"I'm adopted," she said, and disappeared.

I changed into my nightgown and had climbed into bed and pulled the covers around me when I had another guest. I was turning about, getting into my usual sleeping position when a motion to the side drew my attention.

It had been many, many years since the fantôme of my great-grandfather had first made himself known to me, but there he was once again, dressed in his full regalia of skins and adorned with quills and beads.

"Grandfather!" I said, and sat straight up in bed. On his first appearance he had told me about my talent, my gift, as he had called it, and I immediately presumed he must be here to tell me something important.

"Granddaughter."

"It's very good to see you again," I told him. "I have not forgotten the other time you visited me, when I was a small girl."

He nodded. "I have watched over you all these years."

"Have you?" I asked excitedly. I had never given any thought to that premise, that my great-grandfather watched over me.

"You have done well. It is good that you help others with your gift."

"Madame Badeaux has been a mentor. She has helped me a lot."

"Yes, it is good we sent you to her."

"Sent? We? Who...how?"

"The spirits. We arranged your life so you would come here to her. We often send people to Madame for her counsel and encouragement."

My mouth dropped open. So many questions were vying to burst forth. The first ones exploded from me. "How did you arrange my life? How did you make me end up here?"

"Child, don't you know that all of life is arranged if you listen to the spirits? They will guide you in the way to go. You were born with the gift of knowing, and since you listen to the spirits, instead of ignoring them, you follow your path. Your mission is to use that gift to help others. Now is the time for you to have helpers in that mission."

"Helpers?"

"Yes. You will have one who will be with you always, and understand and assist in the work you are to do. There will be others, later, who will aid and support you, but they will not have the same kind of knowledge you and your helper have. Do not doubt it, they will be helpers too, even if they don't know that they are guided by the spirits too."

"When am I to meet my helper? Soon?"

"You have already met her."

I looked questioningly at him.

"It is your daughter, Shallah."

Chapter Twenty
September 1956. New Orleans.

The next few days I walked around in a daze, filled with anger. Grandfather would not tell me a lie—I knew he wouldn't. Nor had the spirits ever told me untruths before. Why would they now? Shallah was alive? Had my mother and Angelina taken her and given her to someone else to raise, as he told me? In my heart I knew this was true. Even though they did what they thought was best, both for the baby and for me, they had deprived me of something precious—my child. The way Grandfather had told me about it, I got the impression it *was* for the best—the way it was supposed to be, divine order. But now I had neither room nor time for anger about the past. The only thing that mattered was the present. And the future.

My heart ached and I wanted my daughter. Grandfather had said I would find her and we would be together, but how was this going to happen? He hadn't told me how, but said it was to be my next journey. I dreaded challenging my mother, but it had to be done.

"You know I have the gift," I said to her. "I know things."

"Yes," she said. "I know this to be true. Do you have something to tell me? A warning?" She crossed herself and sat up straighter in her chair. I had gone to the house she and her husband shared, and we were sitting in her living room.

"It is something I know. Something Grandfather told me."

"Yes?" She nervously played with the handkerchief in her hands. She probably thought I was going to warn her of some impending disaster.

"I know my baby was not born dead. I know she lived, and that you gave her away to someone."

She gasped and held her hand to her heart, then covered her face with the other one.

"I was always afraid you would find out. I thought you would know we were lying when we told you."

"What I want to know now is who you gave her to."

"You have to know, chère, that we did what was best. I knew we were going to have to move to a town, someplace where we could find jobs, in order to survive. I could barely feed the two of us. Your baby was better off with two loving parents to care for her."

"Shallah. Her name was Shallah. Say it." I was furious.

"Shallah. Yes. I understand. And I told Angelina to tell the people she gave her to that her name was Shallah."

"And who did Angelina give her to?"

"I don't know, chère. Truly I do not. Angelina said she knew of a couple who couldn't have children and wanted one badly. They were not from our parish, that I do know."

"Then where do they live?"

"I don't know, I don't know. It was no one in our community—no one we knew. But I don't think they lived too far away. Terrebonne Parish, perhaps, or maybe farther west, or even to the east."

"Angelina will know. She is the one who arranged it."

"Oh, chère, Angelina is gone. She died three...four years ago."

I stood and walked toward the door.

"I'll find her. I'll find my Shallah, see if I don't." I pushed open the screen door, stepped out onto the front porch and looked back at my mother. "She's your granddaughter, you know. You have missed these years with her, just as I have. Have you ever thought of her all this time?"

"*Mais oui,* I have thought of her often. I trust that the Lord has kept her safe and happy. I pray for her each time I go to mass, just as I pray for you."

I went to Madame and told her the story. I had the feeling she already knew the details without being told, either by me or anyone else in this world.

"What will you do, chère? How will you let the spirits guide you to her?"

"I don't know, Madame. I must think on it."

We were sitting in the courtyard. A breeze entered. It gently moved the fronds in the jungle of tropical plants, and then moved on. She lifted her face to the sky, closing her eyes. "There is a storm coming. Not as bad as some, but it will take several lives."

I had felt the signs but ignored them in the turmoil over the discovery my Shallah was still alive. "Will we be safe here in New Orleans?" I thought we would, but I no longer trusted my instincts.

"Oui. We will be safe here." She chuckled. "They give these storms names now. This one they call Flossy."

As I started to leave, Madame Badeaux stood and placed her hands on my shoulders, looking directly into my eyes.

"I have told you, have I not, there is no such thing as death? You only move from one side of the veil to the other. And one with excellent gifts, such as you, can move back and forth, from the side of the living to the side of the spirits, with ease."

"Yes, Madame, you have told me."

"And I also have told you, when you leave your body and go spirit walking, you must always stay connected to your physical form, to return to it, or else you will find yourself caught on the other side, unable to return except as a spirit, and your body will die."

"Yes. You have told me this, also."

She leaned forward and kissed me on the cheek. "You are destined to help others, from this side of the veil and the other. This is what I saw in your tealeaves.

"Go now, and do what you must."

I went to my apartment, to my bedroom, and started making preparations to go spirit walking, when the girl appeared by my bed. She was a beautiful woman now, most full-grown.

"A storm is coming!" she said. "I'm frightened. My parents won't leave our home, and I know we will die if we don't!"

"How do you know you'll die?" I asked.

"Because I know things. I know things that will happen, but I don't know how."

Chills ran through my body once again.

"Your name—you have never told me your name," I cried out.

"Shallah," she said. "My name is Shallah."

Chapter Twenty-one

With that pronouncement, she disappeared.

My daughter!

It had been my daughter visiting me all these years. Was she trying to find her birth mother? She'd once told me she was adopted. Perhaps the spirits sent her to me without her having any input into the matter. I had watched her grow into a lovely young woman. At least I had the benefit of seeing that much of her, and it was better than nothing.

I quickly prepared to find her. If she thought she would die in the hurricane she must have inherited some gifts also. I had to go to her.

I took the statue of the Virgin Mary from the top of my dresser and placed it on the floor. All around it I placed candles in sparkling crystal holders and lit them. With the light off, the flickering flames furnished a soft glow to my room. I knelt before the statue and said a prayer to the Mother Mary, asking Her to protect me in my travels and to protect Shallah, too. Then I said a prayer to God, ending as I always did, 'Thy will be done.'

I stretched out on the floor in front of the statue, my head pointing north. Lying on my stomach, my arms above my head pointing toward the collection of candles surrounding Mother Mary. Slowly, I relaxed each area of my body. Toes, feet, and ankles: check. Calf, knees, and thighs: check. So it went, until every muscle was completely at rest. I felt myself floating, floating—up from my body, until I was looking down at the figure on the floor. It was me, but not me. The real me was free of that body, free to go wherever I wished.

I thought of Shallah. Not the unformed vision of who my child might have been, the one I tried to imagine when I first learned my daughter was still alive, but the Shallah who I knew and loved. The Shallah who had been visiting me all these years. The Shallah who had only left my presence minutes before.

Then, I was traveling through cloudy skies. I sensed the power of the unleashed storm gathering around me. As soon as I began to worry about whether I could survive the battering, should it become stronger, I found myself in another candlelit bedroom.

There was Shallah, kneeling beside a bed, head bowed in prayer. I stood looking at her.

My daughter. My beautiful, daughter.

My heart was so filled with joy it overflowed into tears.

"Shallah?" I spoke her name for the first time.

She looked up.

"You came!" she said, and stood, a smile lighting her face.

"Yes, I came. Where are your parents?" It hurt me to call them that. I was her parent, not them. She had inherited this from me...this gift of knowing and traveling, not from them. I knew this was unfair. They'd raised her and I hadn't. Hopefully, they had loved her. But she was a part of me in body and in spirit. She began to cry.

"They're in the front room where they've have set up an altar, and they're praying to be saved from the storm. I told them it was too late. I told them we should have left when we could have, but they wouldn't listen to me. They kept saying it wasn't going to be a bad storm." She wrung her hands in anguish, tears rushing down her face. "They never listen to me, ever. I tell them about things that are going to happen, but they turn away. They won't believe me."

"You've done your best. You've warned them. They have to live their lives the best way they know how. That's their right. Whatever their fate is has already been recorded." She lunged toward me and I took her into my arms and stroked her hair. When she finally calmed down, I said, "Shallah, you do know you're adopted, right? You told me that once."

"Yes. I've known since I was a small child. I overheard my aunts talking about it. 'They got her from some Cajun family', they said. And it sounded shameful, like being Cajun was somehow bad."

"It's not. No one is shameful by birth. Only what you do can be shameful."

"They say what I do is shameful. Knowing what's going to happen. Sometimes when I told the children at school what was going to happen to them, they thought I caused it. They called me a witch."

I took her by the shoulders, surprised I was solid enough to touch her." Don't be ashamed of your gift. That is what it is, you know, a gift. It's who you are.

"Your great-grandmother was a traiteur, a midwife and healer. She knew, without being told, where she was needed, and she went to the side of the sick person and healed them. And your great-great-grandfather was an Indian shaman. He helped his tribe by telling them where to plant and where to hunt. He was a wise man who helped others."

"An Indian?" Shallah's eyes grew wide, and she sat down on the side of the bed.

"Yes, an Indian," I sat down beside her.

"An old Indian man has visited me ever since I was a little girl. Many years ago, he told me someday I would find my real mother, and we would never be separated again." She looked down at her hands in her lap. "I told my parents the first time it happened, and they scolded me for making up stories. I never told them again when he came." She looked at me shyly. "How do you know all this?"

"Because the old Indian man visits me, too. He's my great grandfather and the one who told me you were alive. Shallah, I'm your mother."

"You came to find me!" she said and burst into tears.

I gathered her into my arms. "Of course. As soon as I knew you were alive and found out the girl who has been visiting me is my daughter, I came."

"When I asked about being adopted, they told me my mother didn't want me—that she—you—gave me away." She sobbed.

"When you were born, my mother and the midwife told me you were born dead. We were poor, you see, and my mother was afraid we couldn't take care of a baby. She thought you would have a better life than one you would have with us."

"Am I Cajun? Like my aunts said?"

"Oui," I smiled. "You are half Cajun."

"And my father?"

"He was a very handsome man, a photographer who came to take pictures of the bayou and then went away."

"Oh!"

All the time we had been talking, the storm was raging outside, and the house creaked and groaned in the wind. We began to hear the sounds of flying debris hitting the sides of the building. Crashing sounds surrounded us. The brunt of the storm had arrived.

"You must go back," Shallah said. "You must go back to your body, or you will die!"

I pulled her closer to me. "There is no such thing as death, chère. You only move from your body into spirit form. And I am in spirit form now, am I not?"

"Yes."

"And when you visit me, you are in spirit form, are you not?"

"Yes."

"I'll never leave you, Shallah. We won't be separated again."

When I spoke those words, a mighty roar enveloped us and everything went black.

When I awoke, the stars were twinkling above me—millions and millions of diamonds in a beautiful black velvet sky. Shallah was beside me, holding my hand. I smiled at her, and she smiled back.

* * *

"Where am I?" asked Shallah.

I laughed. "Shallah my love, you are holding hands with your mother, lying on the living room rug in my apartment. Look around. You've been here many times."

Shallah grinned. "It looks different this time."

"But I have plans. For instance, I plan to stand up. How about you?"

We not only stood, but later I took her downstairs to meet Madame, who was sitting in the courtyard having a cup of tea. She rose when we entered.

"Madame, I have a surprise for you." I said as Shallah and I walked toward the table.

"And a very pleasant surprise it is. I am Madame Badeau and you are Shallah, the newly found daughter of Maxine Thibodeaux. You're not only very beautiful, but very welcome. Won't you sit and have a cup of tea? A cup for the newly found mother, Maxine?"

"Yes, thank you Madame. How much do you know of what happened?"

"A good deal more than all of it. Your favorite shaman was here this morning."

"Great-grandfather was here?"

"Yes. He was as giddy as a hundred- and seventy-year-old man gets. Everything was evolving exactly as planned. He also told me what was to happen next. He'll lay it all out for you, soon."

Shallah and I spent the rest of the day in a deep discussion of the past. There were so many holes to fill, so many memories to share. We were exhausted by ten o'clock and went to bed.

"You can sleep in the bedroom that used to be my mother's. Are you going to be OK?"

"I'll sleep like a log. That's what my..." She caught herself and froze.

"It's OK, Shallah, really. You've spent your whole life with two people who loved you. And you loved them. They'll always be a part of your memories. So, go and sleep like a log, just as your...?"

"Father used to say," said Shallah. "When I was young, every time I saw a log, I'd wonder if it was sleeping."

One o'clock that night, I was pulled from a dream by the sound of crying. I slipped out of bed and tiptoed to Shallah's room, eased the door open and walked over to my daughter's bed.

"She's sleeping," said a familiar voice.

I whirled around. Grandfather, feathers and all, was sitting in a chair across the room. His eyes seemed to be lit from behind, and he was smiling.

"She'll have a difficult time, but she's a very adaptable girl and she'll soon be far away and very busy. She'll have no time for grief."

I gasped. "You're taking her away from me?"

The old Indian raised his hand. "No, no. We've had enough of that. You two will be working together. I promise you. Now, think of this. You and Shallah are part of a very complex undertaking that began before Shallah was born, eighteen years ago. So far, everything is moving ahead as planned. Right on schedule."

"I don't understand, Grandfather."

"You will in a few minutes. Let me tell you a story.

"Tomorrow, at a ranch in Arizona, a young lady, Anita Amades, will be changing linen and cleaning a guest room. As she's leaving, she will be met by her lover, a wrangler named Rick.

"'I've got a surprise for you,' he'll say to her. 'I'm no longer working here.' Anita will be upset. 'You're leaving?' she'll ask. 'So are you,' he'll tell her. 'We're headed for Jackson Hole, Wyoming, where I'll sign on as head wrangler at Spangler's horse ranch. We'll get married as soon as we get settled in our house on ranch property. It's all set up. I've been working on this deal for a couple of weeks.'

"'I was hoping for a more traditional proposal, but I'm too happy to quibble,' she'll tell him, and he will reply, 'You'd better go tell the boss you're quitting.'"

"That's a nice love story," I told Grandfather, "but what does it have to do with me?"

"Listen. You'll understand.

"The next day, a tourist by the name of Wally Wallace will, on a sudden whim, enter Madam's shop. Wally's a very pleasant, friendly fellow who manages the ranch in Arizona. The owner will have called him to get some information on a horse and in passing will have mentioned Anita's quitting after working there for five years. Anita practically ran the ranch house and guest quarters and will be hard to replace. When Wally comes in, Madam will turn him over to you."

"Of course, I'll take it from there. I assume I am to fill Anita's position?"

"Yes. That is correct.

"Next month, Jim, the elderly cook, will pass away and you, with all your training, will have taken Anita's place in every way and will convince the owner and Wally to bring in Shallah to take Jim's place. Shallah is already a very good cook, and much to her surprise, will suddenly know hundreds of recipes. You two will then be in place to help execute the final elements. You'll be using everything you've learned from Madam, your work at the LaCroix family home, your time at the two hotels, everything."

"But that means I'll have to leave Shallah for a month."

"Yes. I'm sorry, but she needs time to grieve. After that, she'll be all yours."

Shallah began sobbing again. I sat on her bed and brushed her hair from her eyes. She awoke and smiled at me. I kissed her forehead and turned back to Grandfather. He was gone.

BILL

Chapter Twenty-two

May,1957. Rensselear, Indiana.

Two days after graduation, Bob Myers and I were sitting in the Saint Joseph's College rec hall, nursing Cokes. The small college and seminary sat in corn fields just outside Rensselear, Indiana.

I was either going to New York and try to break into the theater or go into the seminary. Bob would be joining his father's accounting firm, then marry just before Christmas.

"You don't look very happy, Bill. What's going on?"

"I look as happy as you do."

"Well, then, what's the plan? Priest or actor?"

"I don't know. I'm not even sure I believe in God any more. And I'm less sure there's a big demand for another actor. Besides, I'm tired. I need a break. Sixteen years of school, you know what I mean?

"Now, you, you've got it made. Your father's company. Even if you screw up, what's he gonna do? Fire you? And if you don't marry Judy, I might. A great girl, and she loves the ground you trip over."

"But that's the trouble. I feel as though I've never lived."

"Accountants aren't supposed to live. They're expected to tally."

"I've never had an adventure. I've never been anywhere. I feel like one of those paint-by-number people."

"You're not that exciting."

"Come on, Bill. I can start any time I want to at Dad's. Let's do something adventurish. Just once."

"OK, Bobby-boy. I've got it. Your favorite author is Mark Twain, right?"

"Yes."

"Guess what town is one state over and two hundred miles southwest of Rensselear."

"Aha! Hannibal, Missouri!"

"You must have gone to college. Hannibal, Missouri, the birthplace of Mark Twain. We hitchhike down there, visit all the sights, the Mark Twain cave, his home, the famous fence, and when we've had our fill of Mark, we float down the Mississippi River on a raft or...something. Sound like a winner?"

"Do you really think we could?"

"Only if we want to. First thing we do is find ourselves a pair a pair of emerald slippers."

* * *

May, 1957. Hannibal, Missouri

Bob and I were standing on the bank of the Mississippi, staring down at the sunken jon-boat three feet out.

Myers turned to me. "It's not exactly the Queen Mary."

"But it is a sunken ship. Salvage law says we can raise it. We won it and everything it contains."

"What are we going to do with a fourteen-foot jon-boat filled with mud?"

Two days later, we launched the U.S.S. Silverfish with a bottle of Coke broken over its bow. It gently slid down the bank. Luckily, under all that mud in the boat were two oars. It was meant to be.

As the ship pulled away from the shore, thousands of cheering fans filled the air with confetti. Children ran along the bank waving balloons with "Bob Myers and Bill Landon, Our Heroes," printed on them mainly in sequins. The band played....

Well, maybe not.

"Did you check the lifeboats?" asked Captain Bob.

"You're rowing it, sir."

Two days later, we hit a tropical storm. The boat filled with water, sunk, and we barely made it to land, which, fortunately, was inhabited.

Six hours later, I stood with Bob at the bus station. He was going to Indianapolis and the arms of his fiancée.

"Next time I'm in need of abject misery, I'll call you. Hopefully, I'll have lost your number," he said.

"Come on! It's called an adventure. You said that's what you wanted. They don't come with a guarantee."

"You sure you won't go back with me? Last chance."

"I think I'll hitchhike down to New Orleans, and then maybe L.A. I'll call you when I get back. You'll be glad to see me by then."

* * *

June, 1957. Jackson Mississippi.

It was ten o'clock on a miserable night to be hitching a ride, and I'd passed up miserable two hours ago. Because I was wearing Levis, shirt and jacket and it was pouring rain, I was as close to invisible as you can get. For my next ride I could very well be impaled on the hood ornament of a speeding car.

A dark, four-door sedan slowed and pulled off the road. The driver jumped out, ran to the drainage ditch and relieved himself.

Grabbing my waterlogged duffle bag, I jogged toward him. He turned and saw me.

"Hey! Could you give me a lift? Please? I'm trying to get to L.A. the hard way. Outside of being dumb, I'm harmless."

He laughed. A good sign.

"Sure. Throw your duffle bag in the back."

"I don't want to soak your passenger seat. I'll sit in the back. I'm a human puddle."

Another black sedan swooped in behind us, splashing to a stop not ten feet from my new best friend's car. Four men with guns in their hands, all pointed at us, jumped out. The driver, a chunky man in a yellow poncho, walked forward.

"Raise 'em."

We did.

It wasn't his commanding voice that did the trick; it was the largest nickel-plated forty-five I've ever seen. Then again, every gun pointed at your face is the largest gun you've ever seen.

Poncho spoke. "Mel? Take these heah boys back yonder ahind the cah an' sit 'em down. Keep your gun on 'em."

Bald, paunchy, wearing a dirty white sleeveless tee shirt under filthy bib overalls, Mel walked us back.

"Sit yo' self down, boys."

You could tell Mel was a follower, because his gun was just an ordinary thirty-eight special.

We sat in the mud. "What's this all about?" I asked as Mel hopped onto the trunk of their car and sat staring into the rain.

Probably a zen thing, I thought as I waited for an answer. I looked at my friend. Skinny, buzz cut, prominent cheekbones and teeth. He was gazing placidly at his feet.

Hell no! I thought. Placid was for later. All my life I've hated bullies. Maybe I can't move faster than a bullet, but at least I can play with Mel's brain.

I stood up.

"Hey, boy! Whatcha doin'?"

"I've got a cramp. Just stretching my leg," I said nonchalantly.

I took a pencil out of my jacket and a notebook from my back pocket, wiped off the mud, and squatted down in front of the license plate.

"Could you move your feet for a second, please? I can't read the numbers through your boots."

"Shit!" he said.

I wrote down the numbers and then stood. Mel hopped off the trunk. We were now standing nose to nose.

"Oh, Mel," I said. "Glad you're still here. Would you give me your full name, please?"

Mel lifted his thirty-eight. "How 'bout a bullet 'tween your eyes?"

"Name first."

"Jimmy! I think we got trouble heah!"

114

Poncho came running.

I could see my duffle bag fly through the air and land on the edge of the ditch. Then the front seat followed. They were tearing my new friend's car apart.

Mel and Poncho conferred for a moment. Poncho walked up to me and pointed his hand howitzer at my forehead.

"Y'all causin' trouble, boy?"

For the first time, I saw his face: perfectly round and red, with wire-rim glasses covering small eyes.

"No trouble. We're both American citizens, minding our own business, when four guys pull guns without explanation and dismantle my friend's car. Any sane man would easily decide who's causing the trouble. You're not robbing us, or the first thing you would have done was ask for our wallets. And you're not cops, or you would have wanted to see our IDs. So, who the hell are you?"

Poncho shifted from one foot to another. "I'm thinking" is written across his forehead in invisible neon.

"OK. Forty minutes ago, a drugstore a half-mile from heah was robbed. Two young men got fifteen thousand dollars worth of prescription drugs, put 'em in a leather valise and left in a dark four-door sedan. Now, I'm askin' y'all, what would you think if'n you saw you two?"

"And I'm going to ask you again," I said, "Who the hell are you?"

"We're sheriff's deputies." He paused, gritted his teeth. "Have y'all got any identification?"

"Yes, sir. Thank you for asking."

I handed him my wallet. It was still raining and too dark to read my license. He looked confused for a moment, then stuck his gun under his arm and pulled out a small flashlight, which he turned on and put into his mouth, retrieved his automatic, and studied my license.

After a minute or two, he looked up at me and said, "mneneth?" Realizing he still had the flashlight in his mouth, he grabbed it and put it in his pocket. "

"What's your damn name, boy?"

"Bill Landon."

"Age?"

"Twenty-two."

"Where you from, boy?"

"I've been in college in Rensselar, Indiana. I just graduated."

"I knew from the funny way you talked you didn't belong heah."

"Don't worry, I'm leaving as quickly as I can."

"Ah hate a wise ass."

I smiled. "I suppose that means no Christmas card this year."

He threw my wallet in my face, turned and stomped off.

A half-hour later, my new best friend, Larry Ledbetter, and I pulled into the freight yard parking lot.

"You sure you know what you're doin', Bill?"

"I'm never sure, but standing out there on the highway trying to get a ride in a rain storm is like being buried alive, and I'm not going to do it anymore. Besides, there are no deputies on freight trains. Hopping a freight is positively surgical compared to that."

"You sure do talk funny."

"Thank you, Larry, I appreciate that. Just think, you'll remember this night for the rest of your life. Cool, right? It's called an adventure, and may you have many more. Thanks for the ride."

I got out of the car, took my soggy duffle out of the back seat, waved to Larry, and walked past the control shack, where an old man was standing in the window, watching.

Minutes later the rain had moved on and I was standing in the middle of the Jackson freight yard. It was eleven-thirty and long dark behemoths slid quietly to and fro, occasionally connecting to another with a mighty metal on metal crash. Wedded, they moved on as one.

There's something about a freight yard that's sweetly mysterious. I was checking the chalked manifests for a freight heading west. Lowest number, east coast. Higher number, west coast. LA is one hundred one and my final destination. I'd found a few LAs, but no open boxcars. That's the way to travel.

In the distance, sirens, like electronic wolves, were coming from two or three directions. I tensed. Were they looking for me? They were getting closer. Damn! I wasn't going through one more playtime with the deputy Bozos. I was just too tired. There'd been no sleep for two days.

A cop car drove into the entrance, followed by another. Then another. The boys got together for a little logistics, and then fanned out into the yards.

Freight yards are actually lit at night. Towers around the perimeters give off a cautious light. At best, it's semidarkness. Perpetual dusk.

The cops were an easy sixty yards from me. I walked over to a car, grabbed the ladder and pulled myself up. The cop wannabes had emptied my duffle bag onto the ground in the pouring rain. It now weighed at least fifty pounds. I struggled. My arms were letting me know this wasn't a good thing to do.

When I got to the top of the ladder and threw my duffle up onto the car, I thought my arm was going with it. I hung there, gasping for breath, fighting to regulate my breathing. I could hear the cops getting closer.

Climbing up two more rungs while still holding onto the top one, I gathered all my strength and catapulted myself up and onto the roof, grabbing the metal walk to keep from falling back. Made it.

The steel walk runs the length of the car, about eighteen inches wide. It's crosshatched with serrated metal so you won't slip and fall off the train when it's raining. Great idea unless you want to sit or lay on it.

I took out a pair of Levis and spread them lengthwise on the walk, then put a couple of shirts over that. I'd no sooner lain on the walk than I heard *thunk, thunk, thunk, thunk:* the sound of a train taking up slack as it starts to move. Was it my train? I won't know till I feel my car lurch. It finally does.

I heard a cop shout, "Hey! There's someone on top of this heah train!"

I scrunched down as flat as possible in case they started shooting. Then I heard the final *thunk, thunk, thunk, thunk,* and we were moving. Up ahead, the thunks began again, faster than before. More shouting, more thunking, and then the shouting faded away. We were leaving.

Blessed train.

A few minutes later, I sat and watched the lights of Jackson, Mississippi go to black and I let out a sigh of relief. I was exhausted. You pay a price for an overdose of adrenalin and I fought to keep my eyes open. My system was demanding sleep.

Walking to the center of the car where it's slightly more stable, I tied my duffle bag to the grid with the strings, then I laid down and slept.

I woke. Something was wrong. I was no longer lying on the walk. I was sprawled on my face, my left arm hanging over the side of the boxcar. With every bounce I moved another inch toward the edge. I was terrified. Couldn't move, afraid I'd make things worse.

We hit another bump and my left foot was now hanging over. Frantically, I swung my right arm toward the walk. I could feel my body topple over the side.

Falling. Falling down into the black of a Mississippi night. Feeling only sadness.

I opened my eyes. Stars. Millions of the most beautiful stars I'd ever seen. I was lying on my back on top of a freight train, racing toward L.A.

Chapter Twenty-three
June, 1957. Texas.

As the train headed west from San Antonio, I sat in the boxcar watching the scrubland cook. It was late spring, but the sun was doing its summer rehearsals. It was hot. The heat invaded deep into the center of my body. I was smothering in it. The train started curving south.

Ah, it's warmer down south, isn't it? Oh goody!

I got up, stumbled into the darkness of the boxcar, curled into a ball on a piece of corrugated cardboard and tried to sleep. It's never easy sleeping in a moving freight train. The car constantly sways side to side while bouncing up and down so you're spending half the time in the air.

I woke because the train was slowing. I knew because the sound had modified. The clicks weren't coming as fast as before. I looked out the door.

We're in cabbage world!

Tiny cabbages by the thousands in irrigated splendor. Not a house, tractor or human being to be seen. The train came to a stop.

Well, at last a great opportunity to see lots of cabbages. Imagine the stories I'll tell my kids, if I ever have any.

Because of moisture from the irrigation, it felt hotter, more oppressive, than the dry scrubland. I was awash in sweat. I spent the next half-hour watching cabbages. The nice thing about cabbages is they're quiet. The desiccating glare of the sun forced me to shut my eyes. I saw brilliant pink for a moment, opened my eyes, and then continued to watch the show. Something was different. It didn't make sense, although I couldn't kick the feeling. Ah, there it was, a tiny dark spot straight out near the horizon, just a dot.

Perhaps it's irrigation equipment, I thought.

I settled in and watched it. Not because it was in any way remarkable, more because it wasn't a cabbage.

I took out my red bandana, dried my face and arms. It cooled me for a few moments. Then I relocated my dot, and it seemed larger now. If that were true, the chance the dot was a water pump went way down. I moved to the front of the boxcar, taking with me the illusion dark is cooler than light, in spite of the fact the steel sides of the car were too hot to touch. I counted to sixty. I wanted to both cool my brain, in case I was having hallucinations from the heat, and also give the dot time to define itself. It sounds silly now, but made perfect sense to a brain baked half way to done.

I casually walked to the door, looked off to the right as though I'd lost all interest in dots. I glanced straight out to where the dot had been. It was not only larger, but also closer. It was moving toward the train. I could see some vague definition now, shaped like a human, dark colors: brown and green. Yes! It was a man and he was running straight toward me. I felt adrenalin race through my veins.

Who is he? What does he want?

I ran to my duffle bag and pulled out my hunting knife. Back at the door I watched as he came closer and closer. Suddenly I felt foolish. I took the knife back to my bag and left it.

I could see him clearly. He was an older man, around forty, and he was black, wearing shabby clothes, work shoes, coming hard. Then it was *thunk, thunk, thunk.* I braced myself. *Thunk, thunk, thunk.* The train was pulling out. He heard it too. Both man and freight train picked up speed. He reached the tracks, but the door was now twenty feet beyond him. He sprinted along the side of the car. I lost sight of him. I stuck my head out the door. There he was, two feet from me. Trouble was, he was running full out, too fast to turn and jump on. I leaned out and stretched my left arm toward him, holding to the door jam with my right.

"Grab my wrist," I shouted. He locked onto my arm as I did his. "Now, jump as high as you can. I'll pull you aboard." He jumped. Using the doorframe as a fulcrum, I pushed with my right arm and pulled with my left. He swung up in a great arc and flopped down onto the floor of the car.

He laid on his stomach, his head toward the caboose, gasping and coughing, then crawled into the darkness, and sat with his legs splayed out, eyes closed. I watched. Luckily, he didn't realize how dangerous a move we just made. I should have had my head examined for trying it. Both of our hands were covered with sweat. If either of our hands had slipped, he would have been sliced meat. Oh well. We made it.

So, we sat facing each other, but a car apart. We didn't try to talk, and we wouldn't for a while.

Perhaps twenty percent of the people you meet on freights are wanted by the police. Usually, it's simple desertion or robbery. But it might just as well be murder. So, there's a natural caution, a holding back when someone new comes on board. Even if the train is quietly sitting, there's no conversation for a while. When you do speak, there's no exchange of names. Besides, a moving train is too loud for conversation. There's watching. You're stuck in a boxcar with someone who, by his very presence, is abnormal. Otherwise, he'd be on a bus or driving his car. He'd have a job, a wife, kids, a house; therefore, he's abnormal. You've got a spectrum from quirky to psychotic. Best be careful, watch.

He did and I did. I dozed.

When I looked up, he was sitting in the doorway, his feet hanging over the side, staring at the passing scrubland. Not exactly the Rose Bowl parade, but it's what we had.

I went over to my duffle, checked to make sure my knife was safe and pulled out one of my self-contained meals, a box of Twinkies. I took two, went to the door and offered him one. He looked up, smiled, took one and nodded, "thank you."

I returned the smile, nodded 'you're welcome,' went back to my spot and ate dinner. When the train stopped again, we'd talk.

It was late afternoon. The sun was about to duck behind the horizon. Cooler air was already making life easier. The sound changed, the same chord but with a few notes missing. The train was slowing. It wasn't braking but coasting. Miles later, we finally came to a stop. As the silence rushed in, the lack of noise was a shock.

Life on the rails is so different from Main Street. Your entire environment is contained in a noisy uncomfortable box the size of your living room. Everyone who enters your room will be a stranger, one that you will never get to know and will never see again. You're constantly looking for clues, because your well being, your very life, may depend on how you react to what's about to happen. So, you watch, listen and feel the vibrations of the beast you're riding.

Later, when your adventuring is done, you reenter Main Street. When you do, it takes time to adjust to the fact it's not necessary to be constantly aware, forever watchful and sure- footed; if you trip or lose your balance on the ever-moving floor of the car, you could join the dead. Later, you could live casually, even carelessly. All the roads are marked. All the processes are agreed upon. The steps are numbered. You don't even have to look at the people who pass through your days. Why should you? There'd be no penalty if you don't. There might be if you did. "Why is that man looking at us?" And you grow to like the ease of life. But you're also conscious of a certain loss of intensity that made every moment so meaningful. Important. Every day an adventure.

We sat together at the door. We were both dehydrated, and I cursed myself for not pulling a cabbage. We could have gotten some moisture from chewing the leaves. I waited for the question. It came.

"You got any water?" he asked.

"No, sorry. This morning the train stopped in front of an irrigation ditch. I drank as much as I could, just me and a dozen cattle. They didn't seem to mind."

He smiled. "They're good that way."

"Yeah. Where are you headed?"

"I'm goin' home, son."

"Sounds like you'll be happy to get there. Where's home?"

"You ever hear of Drydon, Texas?"

"Nope."

"Well, it's just south of nowhere at all."

"Oh yes, I've been through it. Do you have family there?"

"Sure do. Yes sir, I got me a wife, Emma, and two boys, seven and ten, and a little piece of land no bigger than the palm of your hand, but it's enough so's I can grow what we need." He beamed.

"Sounds perfect."

"You ever hear anyone say vegetables make the world go 'round?"

I laughed. "Well..."

"It's money that does it and I ain't got none of it."

"Me either."

"But you also don't got two kids goin' to school in September, when they'll need books and pencils and decent clothes so kids don't shame 'em, and doctors who says they's healthy and got all their shots, and a dentist to check their teeth and—"

"I get the idea. Wish I could help."

"So...off I goes, lookin' for work."

"What kind of work do you do?"

"Mechanic. Worked for Suggs Ford for up to two year ago. Had for twelve years. Then old Mr. Suggs up and died, and no one wanted to buy it cause it weren't makin no money, and I'm out of a job. Had some savin's, but that didn't last but a year. Then they took my truck away, and now we're livin' off what we can grow. Had to find work somewhere, so I starts hitchin', but nobody picks me up. Two days and I hadn't got but thirty miles. Then a farmer headin' north stops for me. I saw the train tracks and I hopped off. I'd catch me a train to somewhere. Lots of trains, but they don't stop. After three days one does, headin' east and that's how I found McHenry Vegetables, cabbage, beans, and broccoli, two thousand acres of 'em. A hundred twenty-five dollars a month, room and board. That was in March. Figured I'd stay to the end of August, be home in time to get the boys off to school." He paused.

"But it's not August yet. What happened?"

"Well, I figured I'd find out how much money I got so far. They tally it all up afore you leave, give you a lump sum. So, I goes to the office and asks to see Mr. Ledbetter, the bookkeeper. When I told him what I wanted, he got my file and started workin on his addin' machine.

After a bit he looked up and said, 'You've earned a total of two hundred and eighty-nine dollars, minus expenses.'

"What expenses? I asked him.

"'The largest one is insurance, followed by what you owe the company store. The work clothes, boots, nine cokes a day at twenty-five cents apiece, two comic books, thirteen bags of potato chips plus numerous penalties for working past your assigned times. It's all here,' he said.

"Ok. Now how much do I got comin' as of today?"

"Twelve dollars and fifty-seven cents."

"I jumped up and ran out, back to my dormitory, put on the extra pants and shirt I bought and headed to the cabbage field. When I get there, what do I see but a big ol' freight train just a-waitin for me. Then it starts movin'. I run as fast as I can and when I thought I couldn't take another step, I see you at the door, lookin to help me on, a mighty nice sight. I forgot the pain in my legs and I jest naturally flew." He laughed.

"Good to have your company. How about another Twinkie?"

"Long as the kitchen's still open, don't mind if I do."

It was morning. Our train picked up speed. We were sitting in the door enjoying the normal temperatures while they lasted. "How will you know when to get off?" I shouted.

"When the train stops," he yelled. We both laughed at my stupid question.

The sun was high in the sky when we finally came to a stop. He looked at me and said, "Well this is where I get off, son." But he doesn't. "I don't know what I'm gonna say when I get home. Emma, she don't want me to go. She begged me to wait, but there was no work. I promised her I'd bring home enough money for the boy's school things. I told the kids that I'd bring 'em each a present, and they was all cryin'. I walked out of the house and down the road. Hardest thing I ever done. I had to make my body move 'cause it didn't want to go. I reached the road and the boys come runnin' to me.

"Take us with you, papa. Please take us. We be good, you'll see."

124

"Then I'm cryin' and I shoo them home. 'You got to stay and take care of your Mama. You got to be the man of the house. I be back afore you know it.'"

Silence. Tears were running down his face. I didn't know how to stop his pain. Putting my hand on his shoulder, I held it there. He slipped off the train and turned to me, took a roll of comic books from under his shirt. "For the boys," he said. He turned and began walking, stopped, looked back. "My name is Jim."

I nodded. "My name is Bill," I said.

He nodded and walked on. I sat there watching him get smaller and smaller until he was just a dot on the horizon.

Chapter Twenty-four
Tucson, Arizona. 1957.

The train moved steadily through New Mexico and into Arizona. I kept thinking about Jim, wondering how his homecoming went. Also, about his lack of bitterness. He'd been cheated; why wasn't he railing against McHenry Vegetables? Where was the rightful indignation? No hatred. Amazing.

It was a sunny day in the Sonora Desert. Spring in Arizona means wild flowers blooming in assorted colors—white, yellow, red, and purple—fed by the fresh rains of winter. Soon they'd all be gone.

But, on that day, I sat in the door of my boxcar, watching the flower show, with a sense of pure contentment, as we flowed deeper into the desert, heading west.

The train stuttered as it slipped along the rails. *Clickity-clack, clickity-clack.* I pretended what I was seeing was an unending sheet of painted scenery, unrolling before me, and I was a one-man audience.

The rhythm slowed and a highway appeared, running easily alongside the train. A barbed wire fence added to the clues; we were coming to a town. I stood in the door, looking for a water tower. Usually, it would have the town's name proudly splashed across its side. A crossroad with stoplights flew by.

We lost our *clickity-clacks* to *tick-tick-ticks.* I stepped away from the door and sat in the semi-dark. It's illegal to ride the rails. Finally, we stopped in a large freight yard with tracks crissing and crossing in some great complex pattern. I tried to nap.

"Hello!"

I looked up. A head peered at me from the doorway.

"Sorry to disturb you," it said.

He was young, perhaps low thirties, with a pleasant face, marred by a broken nose pointing left. He was wearing a blue gray uniform. *New to coppery, but at least he's not a deputy sheriff.*

I grabbed my duffle bag and threw it to him, walked to the door, sat, rolled onto my stomach and slipped to the ground. I smiled.

"I'm on my way to L.A. I wasn't going to visit...ah, where am I?"

"The fair city of Tucson."

"Doesn't seem fair to me."

"I.D. please." I handed him my wallet. He looked through it, handed it back.

"What's waiting for you in L.A.?"

"The Pacific Ocean. I've never seen it, and since I'm just adventuring, it's as good a place as any. It'll probably be similar to the Atlantic. Beachfront. Lots of water." I continued smiling. It was my best look.

"You sound like a college student."

"Just finished. This trip is my graduation gift from myself."

"We have a quota system here and I'm one stop short. Sorry. Tell you what; I'll try to get you a two-man cell. It's Friday, you don't want to be in the drunk-tank over the weekend. Watch your head."

* * *

CLANG! The steel door slammed shut. I was in a drunk-tank. Think of a square birdcage sitting in a box. Only this cage was thirty feet to a side, with eight feet of walking space around its perimeter. A row of bunk beds was on two sides, leaving an arena with a toilet sitting in the middle, for entertainment. Hanging on each of the outside walls were coiled fire hoses, in case of riots.

It was Friday afternoon. The courts were closed, so I'd be here till at least Monday. Drunk-tanks are fine during the week, but on Saturday night, it can be dangerous. I envisioned forty or fifty falling down drunks, every one of them mad as hell. Only in the movies are there funny drunks.

127

CLANG! "Bamberger." A guard stood at the door. He had a steel rod and was beating on the bars to get attention. "Let's go, Bamberger, you're out of here!"

Halfway down on the right a middle aged, heavyset man walked quickly toward the door. When they leave, they never look back. Three seconds later, he's gone. Free to sin again. Suddenly, I was very tired. I lay on the soft, gray-striped mattress. I floated gently into a deep sleep.

CLANG! CLANG! CLANG! "Supper time," shouted our culinary drill sergeant. "If you don't want to eat don't come to the door. If you take a tray don't spill any. The maid's been suspended for conduct unbecoming a human, and you're taking her place. You'll have fifteen minutes to eat, at which time you'll slide your tray out through the slot. Don't bother to give your compliments to the chef. He's fully aware of what he's doing to your digestive system. Bon appetite."

I felt like applauding. That was the first laugh I'd had since my arrest. A tin cup of cold water and hot pinto beans in a sauce you wouldn't want near an open flame, sobered me up considerably.

And so it went. People entered. People left on bail. The beans and hot sauce were served three times a day. The guard's routine never varied, and I laughed each time. I dozed and stared, had an occasional thought, and then dozed again.

Then it was late Saturday afternoon. Three University of Arizona grads in town for some sort of a game got an early start on the party. They were ushered in to the tune of three testosterone tantrums, and then they settled down.

They had no idea they were the opening act for the Saturday night follies, the Fools Parade, as predictable as war. I composed, in my mind, a letter from the International Association of Monkeys accusing the human race of slander, with a nasty P.S. to Charles Darwin.

By eleven, the main attraction was in full swing. It would peak around two in the morning, after the bars closed.

I was sitting in my bunk next to a man in his fifties. He was tall, with a great head of wavy, steel gray hair. He had all the wrinkles of an

128

outdoorsman, a cowboy, perhaps. The crowd was building nicely, about forty. The noise was half way to intolerable.

My neighbor seemed peaked. I tapped him on the shoulder.

"My name's Bill."

"I'm Floyd."

"Are you okay?" I asked.

"No...DUI...My second arrest. I may lose my license." He rubbed his face.

"How'd it happen?" I asked.

"I live outside of Phoenix, where I buy, sell and trade horses. A client's looking for an Appaloosa for his daughter, so I spread the word. Yesterday, I got a call from Danny Dowling. He owns a horse ranch just north of here. He's got a gray gelding with a good black splash on his hindquarters. He's only two hours from me so I drove down this morning, picked up all the info, pictures, price and I was about to head home when he said his wife just told him she was pregnant with their first child, and would I have a drink with him. That was at one thirty. Well, I guess I left the ranch about three drinks too late."

"Don't worry, Floyd, you'll get through this. By the way, what's the name of Danny's ranch?"

"It used to be called Spirit Ranch, but Danny calls it the Catalina Horse Ranch."

"Cool name, where is it?"

"On Sabino Canyon Road, at the foot of the Santa Catalina Mountains."

"Why didn't he call it the Santa Catalina Horse Ranch?"

"I don't know. Maybe he doesn't believe in Santa."

There was a scuffle outside the cage. Three guards were trying to force a Hispanic into the arena. They pushed and pulled. He ignored them. Two more officers joined the game. The drunk disappeared into a large mound of guards. This insane pile slowly moved into the cage. Then the guards made a mad dash for the door.

CLANG. The drunk, bull-rushed the steel door and beat on it with his fists. From what I saw, he had a sixty percent chance of breaking the door down. He was no taller than I, five-ten, but he was built like an old iron safe. He whirled around and glared at his fellow inmates.

He roared, "Who took my straight razor?" It's as though we all agreed to stop talking in that instant. Silence.

Now, the possibility of making it through a strip search with an undiscovered straight razor implies an extra orifice unknown to medical science.

"Who's got it? I had it when I came in here."

Oddly enough, no one spoke up. He began to pace up and down the arena like a huge sulking insect. "I want it and I want it now," he yelled even louder than before.

I wanted to tell him the guards probably took it when he was strip searched, so I raised my hand to get his attention. He ran over to me. I smiled. Before I could open my mouth, he grabbed my coveralls just above my navel and I was no longer sitting on my bunk.

Mr. Pit Bull toted me to the center of the arena as easily as a human would carry a lunch box. He dropped me on my back. My head hit the concrete floor and I tasted blood. I'd bitten my tongue. He grabbed my coveralls again and in one swift movement, lifted me above his head and just stood there, holding me with one arm.

"Give me my razor."

I knew then, I had to kill him instantly. Anything less and I'd be in big trouble. Oh, I could mention my war wound, or beg for mercy or appeal to his humanity. Somehow that all seemed like a waste of time, so instead, I did the very worst thing possible. I giggled. I couldn't stop. I was hanging in the air at the mercy of a box of angry muscles and all I could do is giggle. A salute to the power of nervous energy. He scowled. I imagined his tiny yellow teeth chewing on my throat. I was terrified. I heard myself laugh. Then I realized I was spraying blood all over his pissed-off face.

He couldn't believe my stupidity. I felt myself being lowered and suddenly I was flying through the air, a piece of human litter, casually tossed away. My head hit the concrete again. Darkness.

I don't remember a thing from that moment until Monday morning, when a blinding headache snapped me awake. It felt like a litter of rats was inside my skull, gnawing their way out. I closed my eyes and practiced an exercise I'd taught myself as a child. It involved complete relaxation and both acknowledging and accepting the pain as a necessary message from my nervous system.

The pain eased. I was lying on my cot with my hands folded over my chest. Floyd was gone.

CLANG... CLANG...CLANG "Breakfast!"

My favorite comedian went through his routine in a voice loud enough to curdle glass. I didn't laugh. When I returned my tray, I asked the guard if I'd been lying on my cot all weekend. He looked at me oddly.

"No, you've been up and about. Didn't miss a meal. Why?"

I shrugged. "Just curious."

By ten-thirty, I was standing in front of the judge, a scrawny, sunburned man with thin white hair, wearing a permanent frown. I was wearing my very best smile. My story: college...gift...Los Angeles. I left out the quota part. It sounded too much like an excuse.

He didn't seem to notice me.

"Thirty days at the county farm."

I nodded my head and continued smiling.

His face softened. "However, providing you're out of Tucson in one hour, I'll suspend your sentence as a graduation gift."

I think he winked.

I collected my clothing, duffle bag and shoes. I pulled out the inner soles. I kept twenty-five dollars wrapped in cellophane in each shoe for emergencies. It was still there. I was out of the jail in ten minutes.

MAXINE

Chapter Twenty-five
The Ranch. Arizona. 1957

So! Here I am. Born and raised in the bayou, water all around. And where do the spirits send me? To the desert. The only water around here is in a big tank, and it is precious, not to be wasted. The scant amount of water here does not bring food, like the water back home brought the fish and shrimp and mussels, but it does maintain life. Here the main food comes from the cattle that are raised not on this ranch, but nearby.

The spirits must have a sense of humor to do this to Shallah and me. Yes, my daughter and I are together for the first time since she rested in my womb. I came first, and a month later, when the cook died, she joined me, just as we'd planned. We are to work together to help those who are sent to us. I can't say that I know exactly how this is going to happen. Back in New Orleans, there would be people who would be in my life, either momentarily or daily, and what I was supposed to say to them would just pop into my head. Is it still going to work that way? I expect so.

I do know this is where we are supposed to be. I have that knowing. This horse ranch in the desert is where our works will be done. But..., but what? There is more to this ranch than is apparent. It is a ranch of spirits. Spirits who don't know they are spirits. Can that be?

Mysteries upon mysteries. Whenever I get used to something, like knowing things, and spirits popping in on me, and out-of-body travel, then comes along something else I have to get used to. I wish Grandfather would come back and explain more to me.

He has only come to me three times, so far. Once it was to tell me I had the gift of knowing. The second time was to tell me Shallah was still

132

alive and I was to find her. And the third time was to prepare me for the future. This future. But I have the feeling I will be seeing him more often.

I did find her, just as the hurricane roared inland, taking homes and people with it. Hurricanes have always meant two things to me, birth and death. Maybe that is why we are now in a desert. There will be no more hurricanes: no more birth and death for us.

I think my true calling is starting, here in this barren region. Just as Madame Badeaux had Broussard Court, and the spirits sent me and others to her there, I suspect this ranch will become my home, and the spirits will send people to me to help or be healed.

But I will not work alone, as Madame did. I have Shallah, for one thing, and Grandmother is here, and all these other spirits who do not know they are spirits, and I think someone else is coming. Will he be another spirit? I can't tell. But it is a man. And he will join in this healing. He is coming, and I will know him when I see him, and I will welcome him to this calling.

BILL
Chapter Twenty-six

I was sitting in the back of a cab parked along Sabino Canyon Road, fifteen miles northeast of Tucson. The sun was shining gently in a light blue sky. The temperature had dropped down into the mid-eighties. The Santa Catalina foothills stood ahead of us. To the left was a shallow valley with a large mound in the middle. On top of the mound sat a series of buildings making up the Catalina Horse Ranch. To the left of the driveway was a long, low main house, modern, horizontal timbers and lots of glass. A nod to Frank Lloyd Wright. On the other side of the road, just below the mound, sat the stables and corrals.

When Floyd told me of his time here, I'd remembered all of my boyhood dreams of working on a ranch, the books I'd read on horses and tack and the life of a cowboy. After I left jail, the next step in my journey seemed obvious; I'd get a job at the ranch, fulfill my boyhood dream, then move on to L.A.

Now that I was actually there, I felt stupid.

When I confess to never actually riding a horse, they're going to think I'm retarded.

I tapped Juan, the cabbie, on the shoulder. "I think I'd better go back to town."

He turned around and grinned. "Hey, you're here. You might as well ask them for a job. What are they going to do, shoot you?"

I sighed. "I was hoping it wouldn't come to that."

He stared at me. "OK, listen. No! No! No!" He grinned. "Feel any pain, yet?"

I laughed, "OK, let's go."

We drove down the long dusty road, past the stables, up to the ranch house. I paid Juan. "If I give you three extra bucks, will you wait five minutes? I'll either come to get my duffle bag or leave with it."

"Sure, I need a siesta."

"Thanks, Juan, you've been a big help!"

I looked up and saw a lady standing in front of the taxi, wearing a tan blouse and a peasant skirt. She was small, perhaps five-two, shiny black hair, olive complexion, thirty-five. Smiling. I assumed she knew Juan. I got out of the cab and walked toward her.

She said, "Don't worry, you'll get the job."

I was about to say, "What job?" when she took my arm.

"Come on, I'll take you to the office. The owner's name is Danny. He'll be sure glad to see you."

So, she thinks I'm someone else, which means I'm going to be an unpleasant surprise.

"I think you've made a mistake. I'm not the person Danny's looking for."

"Of course, you are."

We walked along the back of the house. To my right was an in-ground swimming pool. Ahead, attached to the house, were three housing units running down past the pool. The sign above the door read, *Office.*

The lady pulled me in. "Danny, here's someone you should talk to." She squeezed my arm and walked out.

I saw the owner standing behind a large desk.

"Hello, my name's Danny Dowling. What can I do for you?"

"My name's Bill Landon." We shook hands.

He was a tall man, broad, with red hair and freckles on pale skin. In spite of his size, he looked like Huckleberry Finn, all grown up.

"I'm looking for work."

"Sit, sit," he said, and we both do. "What have you done, so far, Bill?"

What in God's name can I tell him? I'm caught and the truth shall make me gone.

"Well...to start at the beginning," I stalled. "Nothing when it comes to horses and ranches."

I stood.

"That's perfect." he said.

135

I sat.

"I can get all the wranglers I need to work the horses, however our yard man quit this morning. I want someone who's willing to do all the other jobs it takes to run a ranch. It's hard work."

"Well, I've worked hard since I was twelve. All through high school and college...construction, digging ditches, working on a bailing crew on farms..."

"OK, I've got the picture. We pay a hundred twenty-five a month plus room and board. I don't know how good a cook your mom was, but mine's better. That lady who brought you in is Maxine. She unofficially runs this ranch. Or I let her think so, I think. Well, is it a deal?"

I nodded. "It's a deal."

"Good. Now you sit here, I'll get your foreman, Wally, and he'll lay out your duties. He'll be glad to see you, because he was going to fill in until we got a new man."

As soon as he left, I walked back to the cab, grabbed my duffle, thanked Juan and ran back to the office. I barely sat down when I heard footsteps.

Danny's coming back. I'm ready for this.

"Bill, this is Wally, our foreman. Believe me, you're in good hands. I'll see you two later."

"OK," I said, "But first tell me why this used to be called Spirit Ranch."

He laughed. "People believed the dome was an ancient burial mound. Bunch of nonsense."

I smiled, grabbed my duffle, and followed Wally back toward the road.

Wally was another big man, but very different. He looked like a run-away accountant. Horn rimmed glasses, big nose, big bones, wide hips. An awkward man.

We stood in front of a ten-foot corrugated water tower. There was a bunkhouse eight feet from it, the first of three along the driveway to the back of the property. They all looked alike, white, eight by twelve, small window front and back.

"The first bunk house is yours." He walked over and opened the door. "Come on in, but be careful where you step. There's a bunkhouse tarantula in here. You don't want to kill it."

"Why not? How can I sleep knowing it's in here?"

He laughed. "Look, you've got a choice. If you kill it, you'll soon be overrun by cockroaches, silver fish, ants, mice, pack rats. Every critter on the ranch will want to winter at your house. Tarantulas don't care about you. You don't look like lunch. So, he doesn't sting you and you don't kill him. Just remember three rules: always turn your light on before you get out of bed, knock your boots against the wall before you slide your foot in, and keep a piece of bread by the door. It attracts bugs and mice; he eats them and stays in the bunk house."

Wally stepped outside, walked over to the tank and kicked it.

"This is your baby. Just about every night, it will overflow. The splash will wake you. You'll get up and turn off the valve. In the morning, when you wake up, say on your way to the john, you'll turn it on. And because we're all using water, everyone's helping keep the tank happy.

"Where's the washroom?"

"Ah-ha, you plan on going to the bathroom while you're here?"

I didn't know if he was trying to be funny or what, so I play it straight.

"Yes."

"Good plan. The john is right there on your left."

I turned left. Fifteen feet away was another bunkhouse with two doors. Because it was behind the tank, I hadn't noticed it, but it was easily twice the size of my cabin.

"The door on the left," Wally said, "is the bathroom. Try to keep it clean. The other door belongs to Maxine. Behind Max's room is Shallah's. She's the cook and Max helps her when we have guests."

And so it went for the rest of the afternoon. The swimming pool, the stable, the horses, the tack room. A lesson on how to properly saddle a horse. How to run the gray Ford tractor. Where to go when Max needed supplies, how to pay for them. Danny had three sable and white collies. They had to be curried every other day.

At four o'clock Wally said, "Your eyes are glazing over. You'd better take a nap. You'll hear the bell ring at five-thirty which means half-hour to dinner in the main house."

A nap sounded perfect, but I smelled awful and felt worse. It had been an exhausting four days. I walked over to the bathroom and went inside. Toilet, shower, washer, dryer, sink with mirror, also, a generous stack of towels on a small table. I threw my clothes into the washer. Then I took a long hot shower. I stood in that wonderful, scalding water for fifteen minutes, and it slowly washed away the dirt and grime of the freight car, the wanna-be cops, the strip search, the drunk tank, the Hispanic dynamo and his straight razor, the blinding headache, the fear of rejection, and any doubts I ever had that this was a truly beautiful world. I stepped out of the shower relaxed, sleepy, and at peace. My clothes were washed. I put them in the dryer, wrapped my towel around my middle and sprinted to my bunkhouse door. I dove in, went to my duffle bag, pulled out some nicely wrinkled clothes, laid down on the bed and without a thought of my tarantula, I slept.

Ding, ding, ding. The dinner bell sounded. I went over to the main house and walked into a foyer. The kitchen was straight ahead. To the right I could see the vast dining room, commanded by a huge plank table with a large bowl of fruit sitting in the middle. Obviously, I was early. I walked the length of the room and stepped down into what appeared to be a lounge or rec room. No one else was here. The room was all windows on three walls. Window seats with red leather cushions ran continuously around the perimeter. A black grand piano stood in the right corner, keyboard facing the back window. I walked over to the piano. I expected it to be out of tune. It wasn't. As I sat at the piano, I could see a large natural stone fireplace on the inside wall, sofas on each side. Three guitars leaned against the wall next to it. The remainder of the wall was a built-in bookcase, filled with books. All my preconceived notions of the "ranch world" were wrong, or perhaps this was a unique ranch. Wally came in with two other men. The old song ran through my mind, "*I can tell by your clothes that you are a cowboy.*" They must have all shopped at the same store. Blue work shirts, Levi's with big gaudy buckles, and Western boots. I made a note to buy a pair of boots and a silver and turquoise buckle. I wanted to fit in. Oh, and a Western hat.

Maxine appeared at the doorway.

"Dinner's ready, guys."

Dinner was a blur. When I was a child of six, I had accidentally cut my left eye in half with a paring knife, leaving a white scar down the middle of the cornea. Luckily, I lost that unfortunate eye in a fight (one of many) when I was seventeen. With a plastic eye, I can pass for normal, but the shyness lingers. It always intensifies when I have a group of people around me. I have to be on guard.

"Turn your head, not your eyes. Keep your eyes looking where your face is pointing," said the doctor.

I can, but it creates a tension in me, which is enough to insure I'll immediately forget all the names and most of the faces. I do remember Miss Emily. She was an elderly lady in a wheelchair who sat across from me. She had braided black hair with gray streaks, the two braids coiled over her ears, large brown eyes, and the sweetest smile I'd ever seen.

I excused myself from the table. As I walked away, I could actually feel the tension flow from me like water down the drain. By the time I sat down behind the piano, I was relaxed. Out of habit, I usually sat where I'll be least noticed and with my back to a wall. I could see the sun slipping behind the hills. Wally and the two wranglers came in. They sat in front of the fireplace. One of them made a fire. In the evening, it gets quite cool in the desert. It goes from summer to late fall in fifteen minutes.

Wally picked up a guitar and strummed it. The three talked of horses, the rodeo coming to town in the summer, who's hiring, and Shallah, the cook. I hadn't met her yet, but apparently she was a great beauty. I was enjoying the conversation, half dozing. They sang cowboy songs with more energy than voice, and we were having a rollicking time. They stopped singing and discussed the next song. They were speaking softly. I couldn't quite pick it up. What I did hear was the piano playing. The keys depressed one by one in no apparent order or rhythm. I stifled a laugh.

Back home in Illinois my elderly friend, Frank Spryer, had spent his early days out west, in Wyoming, around the turn of the century. He told me that the ranch hands always initiate the newest tenderfoot by pulling a prank on him. When he started working at a ranch in Cody, they tied him hand and foot then threw him on a freight train heading west. He ended up in Pocatello, Idaho. It took him three days to make his way back to the ranch, where he was promptly fired.

So, the magical playing piano is a prank by Wally and the boys. We'll see. The piano continued to play. It was obviously a player piano. I opened the top and looked inside: sounding board, strings, hammers. Nothing else. Now I was impressed. This was getting good. I pushed the piano two or three inches but no wires ran up the leg from a hole in the floor. I went back to the keyboard and ran my hands along it to see if I could sense anything unusual. Nothing. The piano continued to play and I could feel the keys move under my hand.

The boys had thrown themselves into another song. They were twenty feet away and hadn't noticed anything unusual. I suddenly realized they might not even be aware I'm in the room. I walked over to Wally.

"Wally, could I talk to you for a second?"

"Sure, what's up?"

"The piano is playing by itself. Come on, see for yourself."

I grabbed his arm and pulled him toward the piano. I could barely hear it tinkling. Then it stopped. We reached the quiet, silent, non-playing piano. We stared at each other.

"It really was playing, Wally."

He put his hand on my shoulder. A look of kindly pity enveloped his face.

"You've had a rough day. Why don't you turn in?"

I leaped at the idea.

"Yeah, that's it. Nerves, fatigue, sure. I'll just sit here a second. Then I'll hit the sack. Thanks, Wally."

He went back to his singing. I sat behind the piano, just to prove to myself that it was indeed my nerves and not some demon Steinway, out to do away with my sanity. My neck and shoulder muscles began to loosen. Good. Relaxed. Just an episode to file away with all of the other things I don't understand. The piano began to play again. I jumped up, hurried out of the rec room and walked quickly through the dining hall. Maxine was coming from the kitchen, toward me.

"Well, good night, Maxine, I'm going to turn in."

She stepped up to me, put her hand on my chest to stop me.

"The piano was playing, wasn't it?"

There was a long pause while I tried to absorb what was happening.

"How do you know?"

"The spirits are welcoming you to the ranch. They want you to know that as long as you're here, they'll keep you safe. They know who you are."

"I'm here purely by accident. I'd never heard of the Catalina Horse Ranch before this weekend."

She smiled, shook her head, turned and walked out the door

Have you ever had something happen in your life, so beyond explanation, that you have no choice but to dismiss it? There's no way to grasp it. No platform of knowledge from which you can make sense of it? I was a trained Catholic boy, with sixteen years of religious education behind me. I may have lost my faith, but I couldn't go where this was leading me. I'm Catholic. We don't believe in the spirit world, we believe in God. So, I simply chased it from my mind and went to bed.

Chapter Twenty-seven

I woke at sunrise, put the piano recital out of my mind, showered, shaved, turned on the water in the tank, and walked down to the stable. I fed the horses three bales of hay. Danny kept between twenty and thirty horses. They began to come into the small corral for breakfast. I cleaned out and refilled the water trough. I took Danny's personal horse, Braddock, out into the yard. Then I mucked out his stall, replaced the straw, fed and watered him, walked him for fifteen minutes and put him back into his stall. Two burros came up to the corral. They walked to the fence, laid down on their sides and scooted under. Time for breakfast. Burros are very smart.

I walked up the hill to the kitchen and checked with Maxine to see what she needed from town. Shallah, the cook, was there. She was young, maybe eighteen, dark brown hair, big brown eyes, and a small nose. She had a complexion copied off a fine ivory carving and a wonderfully ironic smile. She was spectacular.

She did not encourage familiarity. You sensed it. A reserve. To her credit, she managed to be friendly at the same time. A magical juggling act.

I ate breakfast. You could have anything you like, steak, eggs, pancakes, oatmeal, French toast or all of the above. It was pancakes and sausages for me. Yet, there were no fatties here. Every one worked it off and then some. That day, because we had no guests (potential buyers) coming, I would be digging ditches along and down the side of the dome, to drain standing water during rainstorms, if we ever had one. And so my day went. Uneventful, yet fun. At least for me.

One night, after I'd been there a week, I woke up at two-thirty to shut off the water tank. As I turned to go back to my bed, I saw flickering lights in Maxine's window. Fire! I ran to the window. The cabin was filled with lit candles, too many to count. Maxine was lying on the floor face down, her arms out in front of her. She was wearing a beautiful white night gown and was either sleeping or in a trance. A statue of the Blessed Virgin Mary was standing on a table in front of her. Did she fall asleep while praying? If so, what were the chances she would burn the bunkhouse down? Should I pound on the door and wake her? Should I wake Danny, Wally, anyone? She didn't seem to be in immediate danger. I went back to my bunkhouse, bundled up, took my straight chair, put it outside, and sat watching Maxine's window. I was looking for any change in the flickering pattern. By three, I saw Maxine's silhouette move past the window. The lights slowly dimmed and went out. I went back to bed and slept till sunrise.

I woke and did my chores. This day we'd be having buyers: a family who had chosen three horses from our brochure. Although Danny didn't need the money, he wanted the ranch to be his own personal success. His family created a fortune making ice cream in Seattle: Dowling's Family Ice Cream. When they died, he sold the company for a bigger fortune. The money bought him this ranch, plus a hefty bank account.

I was out at the pool, vacuuming the bottom, when Max came by with an armful of linen. She looked as though she'd had a full night's sleep.

"Hi, Bill. How do you like ranch work?" She laughed. Everyone there hated to clean the pool.

"As far as I'm concerned, it's fun. Good people, soft bed and the best food I've ever had. What could be better?"

"Good. Stay happy."

"By the way, you scared the hell out of me last night."

I told her the flickering light story.

"Yes, I went to England last night to visit a friend."

"What?"

"Mr. Doyle. He lives in a suburb outside of London, but he thinks of himself as a Londoner. He's a writer."

"Really? What sort of a writer?"

"He's got a whole shelf filled with his books. Detective stories, I think. They're too thick for me to read."

"And you say, his name is Doyle? Do you know his first name?"

"I think his name is Arthur, but he's Mr. Doyle to me. I've only seen his full name on books."

"And do those books say, Arthur Conan Doyle?"

"That's right. You've heard of him?"

"Yes, I've read all his works, about Sherlock Holmes and Dr. Watson."

"Oh, for Heaven sakes, I've heard of them! I'll ask him about that next time I see him."

Why was it, every time I talked to little Maxine, I walked away with a mystery?

"Would you say Mr. Doyle is healthy?"

"He seems to be."

"That's interesting, since he died in 1930."

She laughed, an "oh you!" sort of laugh. "I know that, silly."

She turned and walked toward the units.

"Maxine, you've got to explain how you can fly to London without a plane and talk to someone who's no longer on this planet all while you're in your bunk house!"

She continued walking and entered the last unit without so much as a backward glance.

After I finished the pool, I found Wally in the tack room repairing a torn bridle. The odor of fine leather, like warm mahogany filled the air.

"Hi, Wally, you got a second?"

"Barely. What's the problem?"

"It's Maxine."

"Did you get into a fight with her?"

"No, no, nothing like that. I like Maxine. Damn. This is difficult for me. I don't get into other peoples' lives. I enjoy people, but it's more as an observer."

"Yeah. I know."

"How long has she been here?"

"Hmmm. Let's see. How long have you been here?"

"About a week."

"That's right. Well, she came, I'd say, three months before you. Said she'd never worked on a ranch. Then she dug right in and sort of took over. In a good way. Jimmy, our old cook died, and she brought in Shallah. You know how that turned out. Now that Max, Shallah and you're here, we're in pretty good shape. Why are you asking about her? Something's happened, right?"

"Where's Max from?"

"She's a Creole, from New Orleans. I think she's also half Cherokee. Not unusual down there."

I nodded. "Have you ever noticed anything, well, strange happening?"

"You mean in the last four months? Outside of you, no." He laughed. "I can see you're chewing on something. When you're ready to spit it out, we'll talk."

Chewing on something was right, but I hadn't a clue what it was. Danny was in his office. He was pulling files for the horses he was going to present.

"Hi, Danny, do you think I might take the truck for an hour? There's something I've got to do in town."

"Does it have to be done today?"

"No, could be done tomorrow."

"That would work better. If the family hates the horses they've picked from the brochure, you might help catch and saddle alternatives."

The next day dawned perfectly, clear, blue sky, warm, gentle sun, as though it was gathering strength for the summer. Sneaky old sun. I moved through my chores quickly. Maxine needed supplies from Safeway. Good. I didn't have to ask Danny for the truck. I told her I might be back a little late. It was two o'clock. Checking the list, I saw no frozen food. I could shop first and not risk anything defrosting.

An hour later, I pulled into the parking lot of St. Anthony's Catholic Church, looking for a logical explanation for the strange happenings at the ranch. I'd been taught by Jesuits in college, and I needed the calm, orderly thought process of a priest. The church building was the usual faux adobe you see all through the Southwest. So much more peaceful and reassuring than the pretentious gothic or the businesslike modern churches. I found the rectory, rang the bell, and waited. I could feel my heart beating. I had planned on entering the seminary until I'd lost my faith. This was the first church I'd been to in over a year.

An elderly, white haired priest opened the door. He smiled. "Yes, my son?"

Tears welled up in my eyes. "Father, could you give me a few minutes of your time? I'm afraid I need your advice."

"Of course, I'm not due in the confessional for an hour. Let's go into my office."

We made our way through the rectory, a rectory like so many I'd been in, with piles of books, thick carpets, crucifixes large and small, the beautifully done picture of Jesus with His hand raised in greeting, and an open heart radiating rays of light. All enclosed in an exquisite silence that would muffle any scream of anguish, soothe any battered soul. We entered his office. Spare, as I knew it would be, used only for counseling.

"My name is Father Eippers. Now, what do we have here?"

I told him what happened at the ranch, and that I haven't been taught to deal with matters of ghosts, spirits, things of that sort. He sat in thought, searching for the one explanation that covered all the elements. He looked at me and stated with complete certainty. "It's quite obvious, of course, you were drunk."

A jolt of electricity ran through my body. I stared at him, speechless.

"The only other explanation is, naturally, that it's the work of the devil."

My mind flipped back to the Middle Ages, when the devil got credit for all the fun. I stood up, shook his hand and thanked him for his help.

Driving back to the ranch, I had to ask myself if this is where I should be. I felt drawn to L.A. for many reasons. This was not the ranch of my boyhood dreams. Perhaps it never existed in the first place. Good people. I liked them, but I was not equipped to deal with the spirit world. Should I leave now or give the ranch a little more time? I decided to stay one more week, then if another happening occurs, I'm out of here.

MAXINE
Chapter Twenty-eight

So, the spirits in this place have a sense of humor, do they? Well, they're lucky they didn't scare this new man to death. Too many doings like pianos playing by themselves and he's liable to leave, then how are they going to help him? And how is he going to help me? They'd better think about that!

He's here to learn. I know that, although it's one of those things I don't know how I know. Somewhere along the way he's lost his faith, and he needs to find it again. The spirits have sent him here to do that. But he's not the only one. There's someone else coming, someone who needs us both, needs us all, to find and acknowledge her talent, her gift, her true self. I don't know yet who that will be, only that it is a female. Maybe Bill will find himself in helping her, whoever she is.

But it is obvious Bill knows nothing about spirits, nothing at all. And between the mysteriously playing piano and my visiting London to call upon a friend who has been dead for twenty years, he is liable to bolt and run before he learns of his gift, his ability to help others finding their way through life.

The day I first met him, I was walking to the main house and off in the distance I saw the dust being stirred up by a car coming along the road leading to the ranch. That time, my knowing came a couple of minutes before I laid eyes on the person. I knew it was someone coming to find a job here, and I knew the spirits sent the person. I didn't know until he got here that it was a young man, and that he had no experience, none at all, with ranch work, much less spirits. He doesn't have a clue about what is really going on here. He'll learn to accept the mysteries of life. He'll wonder about them, mull them over, but eventually he'll accept them.

If what he sees, or what I say, doesn't frighten him away, that is.

I didn't know anything about our piano playing spirit until the music happened to me on my first night here. It is the spirit of someone who used to play the piano here in the past: the past century, perhaps, or the roaring '20s. Or maybe the spirit of someone who will play here in the future. There is no such thing as time in the spirit world. The piano played when Shallah arrived too. She laughed when it happened.

So here I am, organizing the household of a ranch full of cowboys. Cowboys with no cows, just horses. A household full of spirits who don't know their true mission isn't the horses, it's helping those who need this place, the Spirit Ranch. Shallah is here, too, cooking. And another helper, who doesn't know he's a helper, has arrived. Each of us needed, each of us arriving just as planned, divine order.

The other one, the woman who needs helping, will come when the time is right. This I do know.

How do I know, you ask?

I just know things.

BILL
Chapter Twenty-nine

Life moved on at a steady, understandable pace for a few weeks. It was late June. I was walking from the stable to the house, twenty feet above the valley floor. Topping the rise, I saw a dark shape ahead of me in the road. It looked like a black chicken. Moving closer, I saw it wasn't a chicken at all, but a raven. Having only seen drawings of ravens in books on ornithology, I hadn't realized they were so large and serious. I stopped. He calmly watched me as I watched him. His feathers looked as though they'd been oiled; shining purple and blue, he was one handsome bird. I wanted to study him before he flew away.

I could only compare him to the crows of my native Midwest. He was almost twice the bulk, with a wider chest, thicker neck and a large dangerous looking beak. Quite impressive. I then realized we'd been staring at each other for over a minute. I took a step forward. He shifted his feet. Crouched. He seemed ready to fly and did, straight to my right shoulder, where he landed, then swiveled around, so we were both facing the same direction. My whole body stiffened and a little piece of panic formed in my stomach. His beak was now inches from my remaining eye.

Laughter. Slowly, carefully, I turned left. There was Maxine, having just loads of fun.

"Relax. He likes you. You look like you've been starched."

Giggling, she turned and walked away. Stiffly, like a badly made robot, I reached my left hand over to my right shoulder. The raven stepped onto it, and I brought my hand out away from my face. I noticed that I'd been holding my breath, and inhaled. The bird made a soft *kreee* sound. He was obviously tame. Someone's pet who'd lost his way. Perhaps I looked like his owner. He'd soon realize his mistake and fly off, but my brain immediately projected into the future. It was exciting, thinking of a living thing in my life. I didn't know how that would work, or if it would. I pushed those thoughts from my mind. Time for a shower and dinner. Right on cue, *ding, ding, ding.* Half hour.

I threw him gently into the air. He flew to the roof of my bunkhouse. How did he know where I was going? Hey! I was looking straight toward it. Best not get too spooky. He was just a lost bird. I showered and shaved, stepped out of the bathroom. He was still on the roof, making those little *kreee* sounds, as if he were talking to himself. I walked toward the dining room. He flew ahead, landed on the orange tile roof of the main house and watched me.

After dinner, I went to the bunkhouse to pick up a book I wanted to finish. The bird flew ahead of me and perched on the roof, and then followed me back to the main house. By this time, I was feeling comfortable with him. I decided to call him "Nevermore," from the Poe poem.

The next day, Wally asked if I'd like to ride the wire. Every Friday, someone rode along the barbed wire fence of the big corral to check for breaks. It was three strands, a quarter mile per side. The small corral had a board fence, because you can't break a horse in barbed wire.

"Sounds like fun," I said.

I saddled up Red, a tall chestnut.

Nevermore stood on the stable's peak, watching. No one knew he was at the ranch except Maxine. This would be a good test for him. We'd be out in the open desert, far from the house. Would he fly away? I headed out and, for the first half, he flitted from post to post. Then, he decided it was easier to ride. He spent the rest of the time perched on my left shoulder. Today there were no breaches. I went back to the ranch with a firm feeling I had a pet raven named Nevermore. It was interesting and strangely calming.

From that day on, time flew at the Catalina Horse Ranch, no pun intended. Nevermore was discovered and became the ranch mascot. After all, he was friendly, clever and always curious. He loved playing tag with the collies. They, of course, chased him when he came near. He ran with an odd side to side gait, till they were within biting distance, then up he flew, circled the yard and started the game again. If he saw a collie napping in the sun, he'd sneak up behind, grab its tail, give it a good yank and the chase was on. You could almost hear them mutter, "That damn bird."

I tried to keep people food out of his diet, but it was a losing battle. He developed a system for panhandling. When he saw someone sitting at the green picnic table by the pool, munching on, say, potato chips, he stood directly in front of them and watched their every chew. His stare was so intent, so focused, that eventually his gaze took on an aspect of adoration. Oddly flattering. The diner felt, as he or she executed another successful transfer of chip from bag to mouth, Nevermore would break into spontaneous applause if he only had hands. For such devotion, he deserved at least one potato chip, perhaps two. Or three.

Miss Emily spent much of her time in her room, knitting or reading. She had crippling arthritis. Every morning Maxine came in and worked with her to keep her joints from freezing up. Then she had Maxine wheel her out to the pool, where she read or visited with the staff. Every month I drove her into Tucson's main hospital for a check-up and any change needed in her medication. She had been a long-time friend of Danny's parents. She's family.

It only took a few days for Nevermore to discover Miss Emily. From then on, she was a part of his daily routine. As soon as Max wheeled Miss Emily out, Nevermore would fly to her, perch on the arm of her chair, and spend time communing with my sweet lady. She'd murmur something to her little black friend, and he'd answer with *kreee*, his version of a purr. What secrets must have passed between those two?

To stop Nevermore drinking from the pool, I left a bowl of water outside my bunkhouse. He'd fly in with an insect in his beak, hop to the bowl and dip it in the water before eating it. Why? I have no idea.

Days sped on at the ranch. There was always a Nevermore story told at dinner. In a strange way, our mutual interest in him, created a bond between us and we came together as a staff.

Plans were being made for a big Fourth of July party. It was an annual affair with the horse community and was the most important party of the year.

Wally, Danny, the wrangler George, and I were building an open-air pavilion between the main house and the pool, to bring shade to the guests. We already had a cement floor poured and after chores, we raced to finish by Sunday. Unfortunately, Nevermore was sure he could help. *There must be something a smart bird can do,* he seemed to think. He was right, of course. He could drive us crazy, constantly underfoot. We kept shooing him away, but he was positive it was a new game. Danny referred to him as "that damn bird."

Saturday afternoon, we finished the pavilion. It was twenty by twenty-four feet, with a cement path connecting with the walk that ran along the house and the three units. Now Miss Emily could have shade in which to sit and read and didn't have to depend on Maxine to wheel her across the yard, a bumpy, uncomfortable way to travel

A truck pulled into the yard with three Porta-potties, which we placed behind the pool. Folding chairs arrived along with two extra picnic tables. Maxine and Shallah were preparing salads and casseroles for tomorrow. By seven thirty, we were done. We straggled into the house to a cold dinner, and we were all in bed by nine.

One o'clock Sunday arrived, with the party people right behind, singles, couples, families. Danny was in his element: shaking hands, hugging, laughing at the unfunny jokes, schmoozing like a born politician. The people spread through the compound. Some swam. Others lounged under the pavilion. Sun-lovers played horseshoes or were down at the stable, riding carefully chosen pre-saddled horses. We only had five rigs, so we held the rides to ten minutes and kept them in the small corral. We called it the 'small corral', though it was larger than a basketball court. Wally, George and I were there to keep order. Most of the riders were kids, but a few men came down to ride a particular horse. They brought their brochures with them. We let them into the big corral with the hope that they would turn into buyers. The temperature was a hundred and thirteen, so the riders didn't stay out in the open desert for long.

It was two o'clock. Time to bring the food out. Wally and George shut down the horse show, while I ran up the hill to help carry the food out to the three picnic tables we'd set up between the pavilion and the house. The ranch was filled with laughter and squeals from the pool, good conversation and an atmosphere of holiday fun. At the end of the day, there'd be fireworks for a grand finale.

The food theme was "Tex-Mex Meets America." Each dish was labeled mild, medium or hot, with the name and main ingredients. Before long, Wally came up to help, which freed me to check on Nevermore. I looked into the sea of Stetson hats and fancy belt buckles under the pavilion. Finally, I saw him hop above the crowd, then disappear.

He was the surprise of the party! Circulating through the group like a Washington hostess, he hopped from shoulder to shoulder. Everyone wanted to see and touch the tame raven. He, apparently, enjoyed being seen and touched. Amazing! He was as good as Danny at working the crowd. It suddenly dawned on me. He'd been part of a petting zoo. Had to be. It's not normal for a bird to be that comfortable in a tangle of humans. I walked off to get more chairs.

Someone screamed over by the food tables. I ran through the crowd and saw Nevermore standing in a bowl of Potato Salad, pecking at some cheese enchiladas. Shallah was desperately trying to shoo him away.

"No, no, no," she shouted.

Nevermore ignored her. He was busy having lunch. I reached the table, swatted at him with an open hand, but he simply hopped to the next table. He'd played this game before. Both Shallah and I lunged for him. He hopped onto a platter, scooped up a piece of ham and flew off with it down toward the stable.

"Landon!"

I turned and looked into the red, enraged face of Danny Dowling, his eyes bulging, his face contorted.

154

"Either that damn bird goes or you go!" He glared at me with something similar to hate.

I was too stunned to speak. I stared at him for a moment. Then, I walked slowly down the hill. The sky was a brilliant blue. I barely noticed the people walking past me were talking and laughing as they headed for the buffet. I didn't want to leave the ranch. I felt at peace here. I was happy, but how could I throw my friend away?

If I left, it would mean I'd go back to riding the rails, with a raven. Impossible. How would I hitchhike with a large black bird on my shoulder? I could take a bus. Can you see me buying two tickets to LA? The ticket agent would ask, "Where's the other passenger?" I'd reply, "He's up on the roof."

I reached the stable. It was deserted. Everyone had gone for the food. Then I saw him. He was standing on a fence post, preening. It was an after -meal ritual. I decided not to ask him what he did with the ham.

I'd made my decision. I'd tell him to leave, and if he refused, we'd go together. I walked up to him, my heart feeling like a lead fist in my chest. He stopped his feather fussing and looked at me. His shiny black eyes gave no hint of remorse. I glared at him, working up a sizable portion of anger.

"Go away! Go on, go away, I don't want you anymore." I shouted.

He cocked his head.

"Go on! Get out of here!"

He turned his head and looked at me. Then, he flew away. Just like that, he left. Just went. I watched him get smaller and smaller as he flew toward the Santa Catalina Mountains, till he was just a dot. And then he was gone.

I wanted to scream, "Come back! I didn't mean it." But of course, it was too late. For the first time in many years, I cried. I couldn't seem to stop. My legs gave out and I slid down the post and just sat there. For a long time.

The next day Danny called me into his office. I sat in the red leather chair, feeling numb. I watched him. He picked up a pencil. Tapped it on the desk for a moment. He leaned forward.

"About yesterday," he paused. "Look, I lost my temper. I just want to say I'm sorry about that."

"You were just reacting to the moment."

"Yeah, it turned out fine. Few people even noticed it and those that did, thought we'd actually staged it for laughs...we had no trouble cleaning it up. He landed in the potato salad first, so all we had to do was follow the mayonnaise foot prints." He paused again.

"Ravens don't drool, do they?" He grins. "By the way we actually sold that big chestnut gelding to a man from Douglas. He's the one you let into the big corral. He mentioned you. Said we had a good staff." He tapped his pencil on the desk for a moment. "The bird's gone?"

"Yeah."

"Well, we're going to miss him."

I nodded. "Especially Miss Emily," I said. "They were very close."

He tapped a few more times. "And you."

"Yeah."

MAXINE
Chapter Thirty

We had another spirit visiting on the ranch for a few weeks, although even I didn't recognize him until he made himself known.

A raven had attached itself to Bill, going most everywhere Bill went and generally amusing everyone with its antics or irritating everyone by getting in the way. The only other person so honored was Miss Emily. Nevermore, Bill's name for the bird, enjoyed sitting on the arm of her wheelchair and seemingly holding long conversations with her. She would talk and he would turn his head as if listening.

Nevermore was entertaining until he hopped into the middle of the 4th of July meal, destroying much of the food. At that, Danny gave Bill the choice of getting rid of the bird or leaving the ranch himself. I think it was a hard decision for Bill to make.

The day before that big scene, I was walking back to my cabin when with a swoop of his large black wings, Nevermore landed by my door.

"Hello, bird." I opened my door and the raven hopped in ahead of me. "Well, make yourself at home," I said.

Immediately the bird disappeared into a cloud of mist and instead there stood my great-grandfather, clothed in his usual native garb. I hadn't noticed until then how many of the feathers that ornamented his clothing were the black-purple of the raven.

"Grandfather!" I said, surprised, as I closed the door.

"Granddaughter. Did you not know it was I, in another form, that had been visiting with you these many days?"

"No, Grandfather, I did not. I didn't know you assumed other than human form."

"I am from the Bird Clan of my tribe, as was my mother. As such, I can assume the form of a bird now that I am a spirit. We of the Bird Clan are messengers, and we are responsible for teaching the importance of the positive and negative events in life. Have you not realized I bring you notice of important changes coming to you?"

"No, Grandfather, I had never thought about it in that way."

"My father was of the Red Clan, and it is from him I gained my other gifts of knowing about what some people call death. I have many attributes from my father's clan, as do you. You have many talents from both your father and mother's sides."

"Yes, my mother told me about my grandmother and how she healed people. Grandmother came to me while I was carrying Shallah in my womb, and helped me through her birth."

"I have been visiting with your grandmother, talking about the mission you have before you, and about how best to complete it. My bird-self will be leaving soon, but I wanted to speak to you before I left, to be sure you knew the meaning behind the appearance of the raven."

"What *is* the meaning?"

"Bill was becoming increasingly doubtful of his place here. He has always been a loner, but to complete this mission he must feel he's part of this group of people. He was melancholy and needed cheering up. So, I came in the form of a friend, a bird friend, and now he's happier, more at home here on Spirit Ranch."

"Spirit Ranch?"

"Yes. That is the true name of this place."

"It fits."

"Tomorrow, I will play the Trickster again. It will be so infuriating the second time, the owner will give Bill one final chance to get rid of me or being fired, leaving Spirit Ranch for good. It's time for Bill to decide if he's part of this mission or not."

"But Bill doesn't know anything about any mission, like we do."

"Not consciously, he doesn't. But the spirits are tickling his subconscious mind now, hinting there is more to life, more for him."

"I thought he was brought here to learn about himself."

"Yes, that is true. And as he learns, he can help others."

"If he chooses to stay."

"Yes, Granddaughter. If he chooses to stay."

"And you don't know, Grandfather, which he will choose?"

"No. It is in his hands."

* * *

The next day I related all this to Shallah as I was helping in the kitchen. We had tons of food to prepare and set out for the guests who were coming, and we had been working for days getting ready for the big party.

"I haven't seen Grandfather since we came to the ranch," she said. "I wish he would visit me."

"He said the Bird Clan were messengers, and they bring messages of positive and negative events."

Shallah stopped slicing tomatoes and stood thinking. "Hm. I guess that's right. Every time he came to me, it was to bring word of something good or something bad."

I slipped a cookie from a tray. "Did he tell you anything about cooking?"

She laughed. "Actually, yes he did. I wanted to cook since I was a young child. I would try to help my mother, but she would shoo me from the kitchen, saying she could work better without me underfoot.

"Later, when my father was more successful, he hired a cook, and sometimes she would let me help. She taught me many things, many recipes."

"She did an excellent job. You're a superb cook."

"Thank you. When I was about seven Grandfather told me I would be a cook someday, that it was my gift, my talent. He said people would value me for my cooking ability and for my sweet spirit. Of course, I didn't know he was my grandfather then, not until you told me."

"He was right on both points," I said, smiling at her.

"Maxine, does it bother you when I refer to them as Mother and Father? As my parents? I know we agreed we wouldn't mention it, that you are really my mother, but does it bother you when I use those words?"

"No, Shallah. I understand. You lived for many years calling them that. Naturally you would continue to say mother and father." I said

159

this, but in my heart it hurt. It hurt that I had lost years with her. It hurt I had not been there to see her talent grow. It hurt that it would complicate matters and lead to explanations for her to call me Mother. But at least I was with her every day, and little by little the hurt was going away.

* * *

The celebration was a huge success until the raven, using his Trickster talents, once again walked through the food and snatched away what he wanted to eat. That was when Danny gave the ultimatum. "This time, you make damn sure he stays away. If he comes back here again, you're out of here for good."

For the second time, Bill chose to stay, sending the bird away, although he was so troubled that he and almost went with the bird. I know it was a hard decision to make. But what I also know is it was a test—a test of Bill's commitment to our mission, even though he knew nothing about it.

But what I also know is that Danny regretted his outburst of temper that banished Nevermore. Afterward, he wished he had not said it. But it had to be. The spirits decreed it.

Danny didn't know it, but I did.

BILL
Chapter Thirty-one

A week later, Danny asked me if I'd go into town, pick up some dog food and then take Miss Emily for her check up. I had been painting the bunkhouses pine needle green and this would be a welcomed break from the hundred-ten-degree temperatures that left me exhausted at the end of each day. I jumped at the chance.

"Good," he said. "Take Wally's station wagon. It's more comfortable for Miss Emily."

And for me too.

Danny walked back toward the house. Max came out of the kitchen and passed him as she headed my way. I could see by her face she was troubled.

"You're going to town today. Taking Miss Emily."

"I know. How did you know?"

"Don't go."

"Why not?"

"Today's Tuesday. Wait till Thursday."

"But Max, Danny says—"

"Please!" she said, with an intensity that scared me.

She stared at me for a moment then turned and walked back to the house. If anyone but Max asked me not to go and gave no reason, I'd ignore them. But I'd seen enough to know Max wasn't simply anyone.

I went to lunch. Danny was there, talking to Wally about the two horses the ranch was trucking to Flagstaff. Danny turned to me, "This couple bought right out of the brochure. Apparently, they're too busy to come down here." He rolled his eyes.

"Danny, I've got a blazing headache. Could I go to town Thursday?"

"It's the heat. Stay out of the sun today. We're out of dog food, but you can go tomorrow, you'll feel better then."

That night, right after sundown, Danny knocked at my door. He had one of the collies on a leash. Wally was standing behind him with a carbine under each arm.

Danny said, "Listen."

I heard what sounded like a dog whining.

"The coyotes are trying to lure the collies into an ambush. One of them is pretending to be injured while the others are hiding behind the bank of the arroyo. They'll kill the dogs if they can." He handed me the leash. "You hold Lad." He also gave me a spot light. "We're going to surprise them. When I say, 'now,' shine the light on the far bank. The coyotes' eyes will reflect the light, and then we'll shoot. Got it?"

"Got it."

The three of us made our way around Max's bunkhouse to the edge of the arroyo.

"Don't worry about noise. They know exactly what's happening. That's why we need Lad. He'll get them tasting blood and they'll lose any fear of us."

We lay down on our stomachs and peered over the bank at the whimpering coyote, lying on his side. Lad started growling and the coyote began struggling to stand. He was yipping pitifully, pretending one leg was broken. Danny was on my left, Wally on my right.

"OK" Danny said. "Now!"

I turned on the spot. It lit the entire far bank. Ten sets of tiny spotlights glowed and both men fired instantly. The coyotes were gone. It all happened in half a second. The arroyo was empty.

I kept the light on as we climbed down one bank and up the other. We found one dead coyote. Danny picked it up by its front paws and dragged it out into the desert. Wally tapped me on the shoulder. He said something, I could see his mouth forming words. I grabbed his arm.

"I can't hear! I'm deaf."

Wally laughed. "You'll hear fine by morning," he shouted.

I laughed. At least I think I did.

The next day, hearing restored, Miss Emily and I left the ranch a little after noon. We passed Maxine, standing by the stable with her arms crossed. Watching. Miss Emily's appointment was for one. We picked up the dog food, two fifty-pound bags of kibble, then crossed town to the new hospital on the outskirts of Tucson. We discussed how a pack of wild dogs could plan an ambush. How do they communicate such a complex plan, without the ability to speak? How do they pick the stalking dog? Decide the time. The logistics. Could there be some sort of pack telepathy? We consciously avoided any mention of Sunday's party, and Nevermore. I drove a bit slower than usual, remembering Maxine's plea.

We made it to the hospital with time to spare. Forty minutes later, a nurse wheeled Miss Emily back into the waiting room. The car was parked off the main entrance and we carefully put her into the front seat. The putting in and taking out of Miss Emily always made me nervous, sure I'm hurting her and she's too much of a lady to mention it.

Feeling relieved to have escaped whatever mishap Maxine envisioned for us, I relaxed and chatted with Miss Emily about her knitting, which I thought was unique and possibly with commercial value. We hadn't gone more than a mile when a green Hudson ran a stop sign at the same moment we entered the intersection, hitting our left front fender with a heart stopping sound of metal on metal, forcing us off the road into a ditch. We were jerked around and in mild shock when we finally came to a stop. I automatically checked my precious body parts. Everything seemed OK.

"Are you all right Miss Emily?"

She winced. "My wrist hurts. I hope it isn't broken. And I've got a pain in my side. I must have hit the door. Is the other driver injured?"

"I can't see him."

The Hudson was sitting ten yards down the road. I didn't see the driver, perhaps he'd gone for help. Then we heard sirens coming from three directions.

Twenty minutes later we were back at the hospital. Miss Emily had a broken wrist and a cracked rib. The police came in and told us the driver of the Hudson was dead. They questioned us for fifteen minutes. We weren't much help. It all happened so fast I never saw the driver. Now, I'm glad his face is not part of my memory. He was eighty years old. The doctor came in and informed the police he apparently had a heart attack or a stroke. He thought the man died well before reaching the intersection.

Wally came to take us home. Miss Emily had the nurse sign her cast. She had her chest taped up and had us promise not to make her laugh. I suppose it was a funny thing to say, and bless her for trying to keep our spirits up, but the ride home was a thing of silence.

We all felt the oppressive weight of a man's death. Who was he? Did he have children? Grandchildren? Was there a Miss Emily sitting alone in an empty house wondering what's taking her husband so long? Questions. Questions.

I'll ask Max. She knew this little trip was going to end badly. But how could she possibly have known? There are entirely too many things I don't understand.

Maxine was waiting for us when we drove up to the house. Wally and I united Miss Emily with her wheelchair. Wally brushed off my apology for wrecking his car and Maxine gave me a big hug then pulled back.

"Are you OK?"

"Me? Sure."

We locked eyes. "I want answers Max."

She smiled sadly, turned and walked away. She looked back.

"Please," I said as firmly as I could.

She nodded. "OK."

"Thank you."

"Let's go down to the stable," she said. "It's more private there."

We walked side by side, then stood at the fence, gazing at the sullen, dusty brown hills.

"I'm ready," I said.

She sighed. "You've been ready for a while. I'll explain what I can and no more. It won't answer all your questions, but you'll simply have to accept it."

"All right. It's got to be more information than I have now, which is none."

She took a deep breath and continued staring straight ahead.

"If you had gone to town when Danny asked you, Tuesday, you would have left the hospital just as you did today. The green Hudson would have hit you broadside. Wally's car would have rolled over twice. Both Miss Emily and you would have been killed. You went twenty-four hours later and he hit the front of the car. Miss Emily was injured and you didn't have a scratch. If you had waited forty-eight hours, as I told you, you would have seen him go through the intersection and his car would have later crashed into a tree."

"I don't understand."

"All right, let's say that every human is connected to all the other humans on the planet. It is like a terribly complex ballet. We're all in the dance together."

"OK. OK. We're all connected. But, how does my not going into town affect a man's death? I'm a non-dancer, a neutral element. I sit out the dance. And how do you know these things? Is this why I'm here, to save Miss Emily's life? And what are these spirits that welcomed me to the dance? Ex-humans? And how did you get involved in all this? And—"

"I've explained what I can."

Ding. Ding. Ding. She gently touched my face. "You'd better get ready for dinner. You'll be very hungry."

That night I ran through Maxine's explanation in my mind. I threw away her claim that we're all connected to each other. It's a variation of every man is your brother. It's nice but it doesn't make sense to me in this context. And it's nothing I can either prove or disprove. However, I do have direct evidence of her connection with the spirit world. The piano was not only playing, but it was reacting to what was happening in the room. It was perfectly controlled. Shutting down when I brought

165

Wally over, then starting again, when Wally went back to his singing. Maxine was in the kitchen, forty feet away, she couldn't have heard the piano. Yet, she knew when I left the rec room. Then she came out of the kitchen to meet me, and deliver the spirits' welcome.

I can dismiss her trip to London as some sort of self-hypnosis, but how do I dismiss her knowledge of the accident before it happened? A good guess? I go into town three or four times a week but Max has never cautioned me to drive safely. And what about Nevermore? Did he appear to insure I stay at the ranch? When I decided to leave with him, did he fly away to remove my reason for leaving?

If there's a spirit world, and that's the only explanation that covers the facts, there's life after death and the next logical step is; there's a God. What sort of a God? I don't know. I have a feeling I'll never know. Still, knowing a God exists is more than enough for me. Is this why I was brought to the ranch? Why do questions always outnumber answers? I may have found God, but my faith, my belief in organized religion, is still dead.

I go back to my John D. McDonald novel, where the good guys are big, strong and handsome and the bad guys might as well have *Sleazy Criminal* tattooed on their foreheads.

Chapter Thirty-two

The next day began as they all did, with chores, a trip into town for supplies, pool cleaning and collie brushing. It was just after lunch when Danny called me into the office. I sat down and waited for him to speak. He moved paper around for a minute, and then looked up.

"So, how are you feeling?"

"A little achy, but a whole lot better than Miss Emily. I feel guilty of course."

"Why do you feel guilty?"

"Miss Emily was my responsibility. Under my care."

"You know, of course, how illogical that sounds."

"Sure, it's a pure emotional response. Probably magnified by the old man's death. Not much I can do with it, but give it time."

He stared at me.

"I asked you to go into town Tuesday. You said you had a headache and could you go Thursday. The natural thing would be to say Wednesday. Did Max have one of her premonitions?"

He wasn't showing anger, just curiosity. This meant he wanted simple reinforcement. I decided to tell him.

"Yes, she said she had a bad feeling about Tuesday and Wednesday. But strongest on Tuesday."

He shook his head. "That Maxine is something." He fell silent a moment. "By the way, on the last Sunday in July we'll have a guest coming to stay till September. It's a girl. Her name is Mary Kate Hanson. Eighteen. She'll be dropped off by her father. She just graduated from Fort Collins High in Colorado. Her adopting parents were best friends with Mom and Dad."

"Like Miss Emily."

"Yes, it is an interesting story. They were German Jews in the 1930s who changed their name to Hanson months before Germany made it illegal. The Nazis wanted to ensure no Jew could hide behind an Aryan name. The timing probably saved the Hanson's lives.

"Mr. Hanson was a physics professor. She taught music. In late forty-three, they were accidentally discovered by a friend from their past, who informed the Gestapo. They were arrested and sent to a concentration camp. Luckily, they were both in good health and were put to work rounding up other Jews to be eliminated. It's something they never talk about. It must have been horrific. The American Army, at the end of the war, liberated them.

My father was a science fiend. Worshiped Albert Einstein and had read a number of Doctor Hanson's articles. After the war, Dad, with the help from a friend in congress, sponsored Carl and Hilda, and then Dad found a position for Carl at Colorado State. The first three weeks they were in America, the Hansons stayed with my parents, and they've been friends of the family ever since. They were at my wedding, in Seattle.

Today, they both teach at Colorado State. That's one half of the story"

"Ah," I said. "The other half is the daughter."

"And that's the story you'll be involved in."

"Me? I'm the yardman. How could I be of any help?"

"I'll tell you after you hear Mary Kate's story. It's almost as heart breaking as the Hanson's.

"She was born in 1940 in Denver, to a pair of criminal alcoholics. She spent the first year and a half in a dresser drawer. They only took her out to feed her and clean her. Even that wasn't done on a regular basis. They gave her no attention, much less affection. If she cried, they shut the drawer.

"Her parents were arrested for felony theft. Later, the police found her in their hotel room in an advanced stage of starvation." He picked up a yellowed piece of newspaper. "According to the officer who found her, 'She's a great baby. She didn't even cry when we picked her up. As a matter of fact, I've never heard her make a sound.' They rushed her to a hospital and when she was healthy, she was sent to Social Services.

She couldn't walk or talk, and was the size of a five-month-old. After she was evaluated, they shipped her off to a state orphanage, where she stayed for seven years.

"In 1948, Mr. and Mrs. Hanson read about The Dresser Drawer Baby, in a follow-up article in the *Denver Post.* They had no children and didn't want any, but something in her story touched their hearts. The thrust of it was: here was a little girl, withdrawn, silent, given to fits of crying, and totally unadoptable, through no fault of her own. People were looking for Shirley Temple on "The Good Ship Lollipop." This girl had all the charm of a stone. For whatever reason, they adopted her and spent the next ten years working with her, trying to fill in all the holes she'd been handed by life. They've done a great job. Unless you have a sharp eye, she'll appear perfectly normal. But she has little natural personality. She's almost too perfect. Cautious, mannered, as though she's reading a script.

"She'll be going to Colorado State in September, and even though the Hansons will be at the same school, it's huge. They'll only see her in the morning and evening. As you know, college isn't like high school. She may only have three classes one day, two the next. Lots of time in between, so they worry."

"Doesn't she have girl friends going to Colorado State?"

"She doesn't have any friends at all. Kids sense she's not like them and shy away from her. Most of them know her story. Different isn't good in high school. Same is good. The Hansons feel she still needs to be socialized. Be with new people. People who aren't as judgmental and rigid as teenagers, who'll accept her for whatever good qualities they find in her. Personally, I think she's a sweetheart. By the way, she's brilliant."

"I can see where this is going. You do realize I'm not trained in psychiatry?"

"Exactly. Mary Kate's had access to those people all her life. She doesn't need that. She just needs a friend. Someone her age."

"Me."

"Yes." He smiled. Which disappeared instantly. "Not a lover. Do we understand each other?"

"Understood."

"She's in no way ready for romance."

"When do I meet the parents?"

"You don't. Dr. Hanson will bring Mary Kate down. I'm sure he'll want to talk to you."

"Look, Danny, you and I haven't spent much time together. After all, you're my boss. You really don't know me very well. Are you sure about this?"

"Max and I went over this at length. We're both convinced it will work." He paused. "Actually, it was Maxine's idea." Tapping his pencil on his desk he asked, "You're not gay, are you?"

"No. Not that I know of."

"Too bad. That would have taken away some of the worry."

"Sorry, I can't help you there."

"As for your job. Do your regular chores. We won't give you anything extra. That will give you plenty of time to socialize. If you need the truck to go to the movies or a picnic or just sightseeing, ask. You'll get it. Have we got a deal?"

I let it sink in for a moment. "It's a deal. But what if we hate each other?"

Danny grinned. "Impossible, you're both good people. What's not to like?"

Chapter Thirty-three

It was the last Sunday in July, arrival day for the Hansons. Everyone there knew the story of Mary Kate and the dresser drawer. Danny told the staff at dinner the Tuesday before. Asked us all to be especially kind and welcoming. I told Miss Emily about my new part time job. We decided to work on it together.

The Hansons were due for dinner. Danny said we'd wait till they arrive, so we might eat a little late. Right on time, the dinner bell rang and a blue-gray Mercedes nosed its way up the hill. Danny and Jan were there to greet them. He opened the passenger door and out stepped the most beautiful girl I'd ever seen. She was wearing blue jeans and a blue and white-checkered shirt. With dark brown hair and finely carved features, she was perfectly proportioned, slender, and not an inch over five feet tall. Think of a miniature Maureen O'Hara. She smiled and shook hands with Danny and Jan, but as they turned to say hello to Dr. Hanson, her smile stopped instantly and she stood expressionless as if she'd simply shut down. Waiting. That perfect face in repose.

The entire staff had gathered to welcome them. I was standing next to Miss Emily, holding her chair in case someone accidentally nudged it.

When she saw Mary Kate, she grabbed my hand and said "Oh, Bill, she's lovely."

I whispered, "Perfection."

"I haven't seen her in years." she said.

Mr. Hanson walked around the car with Danny and Jan. He was perhaps five six, bald, with a ring of snow-white hair, wearing an expensive gray suit, white shirt and paisley tie. He looked all of sixty-five and harbored no illusions of becoming a cowboy.

The four walked toward us. Danny introduced everyone to the Hansons, who smiled and nodded to each of us in perfect unison. The only break came when they arrived at Miss Emily. Mary Kate bent over, hugged her and they exchanged *good to see you.* Dr. Hanson took her hand and patted it.

Dinner was mostly a dialogue between Danny, Jan, and the Hansons mostly on family, business, school, horses, and the food. It wasn't uncomfortable for us, because we could enjoy Shallah's wonderful food.

It occurred to me I'd only seen Jan a few times since I'd been here, and I'd never seen her look lovelier. We'd never spoken. I was told she was Italian. She had black hair, an olive complexion, and a pleasant laugh. There were rumors she was having a difficult pregnancy. She spent all her time in the suite. It was said she hated it here. I hoped not. For her sake.

After dinner, we were all in the rec room. Miss Emily and I were sitting together, enjoying the warm feeling flowing through the room. Jan had retired to the Dowling suite. Both Dr. Hanson and Mary Kate had a small group of people surrounding them. Good. They should feel thoroughly welcomed by now.

Miss Emily and I were discussing taking a trip tomorrow with Mary Kate. She thought we might give her a little more time to settle in. I agreed. While Mary Kate and her father were busy with others I asked, "How is Jan doing with her pregnancy?"

She replied, "Yesterday, the doctor came in and ordered her to bed, and her mother in Seattle wants her to come home and have the baby there. I'm afraid it's going to cause trouble between Jan and Danny."

"Let's hope not."

Dr. Hanson was now sitting before the fire, reading a magazine on Quarter horses. I didn't know what Danny had told him about our arrangement, so when I went over and reintroduced myself, I'd decided to let him lead the conversation. He did.

"How long have you been on the ranch, Bill?" he asked, making it a point to look me square in the eye.

"Two months, but it seems a lot longer. So many things have happened here."

"Yes, it's an active life, I'm sure. Do you like ranching?"

"Yes. There's more to it than you'd think. I can't see myself leaving anytime in the near future. Mostly because of the people. It's like one big family. Did I hear Danny say you teach physics at Colorado State?"

"Yes. I'm in my thirteenth year there. Why do you ask?"

"Oh, I have a few questions I'd enjoy exploring with you, when you have the time."

"Well, I'll be leaving Tuesday afternoon."

"That soon?"

"A tight schedule."

"Why don't I let you decide when you have an open ten minutes. I'm sure you'd like to spend as much time as you can with your daughter. You'll see me wandering around the ranch, looking lost. Just give a whistle and I'll be there."

He shook my hand. "I look forward to it."

"Good to meet you, sir."

I went back to Miss Emily.

"How was your talk with Dr. Hanson?"

"Fine. But I can tell he'd rather talk about something other than himself. That's a little unusual."

As we chatted, I noticed Mary Kate continued her pattern. While she was conversing, her smile was there, but immediately after, a door slammed shut. I also noticed something missing in her reactions. She didn't react with that instinctive flirty feminine way young girls learn from childhood. It's mostly in the eyes. They learn to manipulate Daddy. Control him and get their way. They learn it quite early. Mary Kate didn't use her eyes that way. She stared straight into the man's eyes without the sideway glances. It was a steady gaze. No batting eyelashes here. Was she too old to learn at eight, when she was adopted? I bet the kids at school picked up on that. She didn't look around the room or pick up a magazine. She stared straight ahead, sitting with her hands glued to her lap. Waiting, but for what? Could there be a distrust of what's to come? Fear? Is fear the core emotion? *Damn it I've got to stop this armchair analysis.*

I turn to Miss Emily. "I'm going to turn in. Do you want to go back to your room?"

"No thanks, sweet boy. I'll hitch a ride back a little later."

* * *

The next day was a runner. Everyone on the ranch, including the burros, needed something picked up or dropped off in town. It was good to be busy. I barely had time to shower and shave before dinner.

After finishing the last crumb from a piece of Shallah's pineapple upside down cake, I wandered down to the rec room, pretending casual. Mary Kate was sitting in a corner with her hands in her lap, in repose. I could feel my heart beating against my rib cage.

Why am I nervous? Even if she bites, I won't be that close to her.

I forced a tentative 'hello.' She flipped on the switch and there came that smile. A good smile.

"Hello. You're Bill, aren't you?"

"Yes. How did you remember?"

"You're the only boy at the ranch my age."

"I don't know about that. How old are you?"

"Eighteen, just."

"Ah. I was eighteen once. Didn't like it. But to be fair, I tried it for a year. At the end, I decided it was too tight. So, looking for a little more room, I moved up to nineteen."

"Really? Bold move. How did that work out?"

"Here I am at twenty-two. If this doesn't fit, I may take up drinking for a living."

"I understand there's very little money in it. I don't think I'd care for someone on a liquid diet."

I used a Groucho Marx voice, "And I don't think I'd like to be cared for."

She laughed, a light lilting laugh. "Give that man a cigar."

"Look, I don't know if anyone told you, but if you'd like to take a walk in the desert, don't go alone. At least, not the first time. The desert

174

can be a little tricky if you're not familiar with it. Anyone here will be happy to go with you. It would only take a few minutes to give you the do's and don'ts."

"Thank you for the warning. Is there anyone you'd suggest?"

I looked at her with the cutest grin I own. She laughed a very nice laugh indeed. I turned and walked away.

So, she had a well-defined sense of silliness. What a surprise. We both react to stress with humor. Of course, Silliness is non-threatening, innocent, surfacy, almost childlike. For people like us, it breaks down inhibitions. It could be the key to opening up Mary Kate. Helping her to relax. Making a real friendship possible. What was especially encouraging was we bypassed the formal, ultra polite stage. Psychologists say humor creates distance between people. Yes. But it's a safe distance. That's why people with a strong sense of humor are so popular. Especially in a group, when we have a tendency to feel self-conscious.

I walked to my bunkhouse feeling fifty pounds lighter. I'd felt an immediate connection with Mary Kate. She felt it too, I'm sure. It was as though we'd known each other forever. Were the spirits at work here? No way to tell. Can they influence your thoughts, your emotions? Could they be affecting Mary Kate? Before I drove myself crazy, I went to bed.

Chapter Thirty-four

I woke with a strong sense of excitement. A feeling of potential was in the air. I ran through my chores reliving the previous evening and my conversation with Dr. Hanson. His unusual sense of reserve at the possibility the subject might turn to him or his daughter. He could have been waiting till we were alone. That must have been it. I went through my encounter with Mary Kate. It couldn't have gone better. The second I started the silliness, she relaxed. The silliness won't last of course. We only went into it to release nervous tension. The longer we're with each other, the less the tension. Eventually, we'll learn to trust each other. And Mary Kate will find she has a true friend. Unless I screw up.

Dr. Hanson and Mary Kate were sitting under the pavilion, talking. He saw me and waved.

"Hello" I called. "How do you like our new pavilion?" I said as I walked to them.

"It's wonderful, did you build it?" asked Mary Kate.

"I helped. Considering my talent with a hammer, I'm surprised there wasn't a loss of life." I can't bring up our arrangement with Mary Kate here. Has Dr. Hanson changed his mind?

"Sit down, Bill. Take a break. You wanted to ask me a question?" He took out a pipe and filled it from a soft, yellow, oilskin pouch, tamped it. Lit it with a wood match and puffed to get it going. "OK, I'm ready," he said.

I decided to tell him of Maxine's theory. I took a moment to collect my thoughts.

"I'll describe a theory and you tell me if my friend is blowing pipe smoke, or if her theory is at least possible. I ask you because I'm in no way qualified to judge."

He settled into his chair and continued to work his pipe.

I told him about the accident and Max's warning. "She said if I'd gone on Tuesday we would have been killed, and if I'd waited until Thursday, we'd have passed the intersection before the old man's car reached it."

"You know, Bill, hearing her idea is fascinating, but in order to give you any sort of judgment, I'd need to know the steps taken to arrive at her conclusion. I tell you what. Give me a number. The first one that jumps into your head."

I think. "Six thousand two hundred ten."

"A very fine number, but without context it's just a number. Impossible to say it's correct or incorrect. What your friend is giving us is the final conclusion. What do you say, Mary Kate?"

"I agree it's a fascinating concept, but it creates thousands of questions. Six thousand two hundred and ten, to be exact."

"True," I said, "But if she's right, we'd have to reevaluate our image of the subconscious from a sort of super storage bin to an organ as powerful as a God. Well, thanks for the time. I'll see you two later."

I walked over to the office and knocked on Danny's door.

"Come on in."

"Hi, Danny. I thought we'd get together on the arrangement with Dr. Hanson. Have you spoken to him?"

"Only to the extent he thinks you're a fine, respectable young man, and if he thought you represented the caliber of males Mary would meet in college, he wouldn't be so worried."

"That's very flattering. I was a bit concerned. I guess I thought we'd sit down and have a good old man to man talk."

"No need. How about Mary Kate? What were your impressions?"

"At first, I could feel the stress inside her, which she masked by being super polite and correct. It's a common tendency. However, she was almost robotic. I assume time will erode some of that. I watched her during dinner. She didn't relax for a second. Perfectly perfect. A queen has never been so well guarded. I didn't talk to her Sunday night. I watched. I wanted to give her time to acclimate herself to her new environment. Last night when I reintroduced myself, she reacted with the same formality as expected, but for some reason I said something silly."

"You were probably nervous."

"I mean pure silly, and she responded with something just as silly. And we both relaxed. It felt as though the protective walls simply dissolved. I think that will be a key. I really do. Humor."

Danny stared at me as if I were a stranger. "Do you have a degree in Psychology?"

"No, my major was Philosophy with a minor in Psychology. Thought I might become a priest, with counseling as my specialty, so I've done a lot of extra reading."

"Huh," said Danny. "I can't believe it."

"What can't you believe? That I could be a priest?"

"No. That you're here with those qualifications at the exact time they're needed."

"A coincidence. They happen all the time."

"Yeah, what else could it be?"

"Oh, by the way," I sat in the red leather chair, "Miss Emily and I thought we'd take Mary Kate on a sightseeing tour tomorrow. We'll pick up a map from the Chamber of Commerce."

Danny pulled open a drawer. "Don't bother. We have plenty. I suppose you'll take Wally's station wagon."

"Almost have to. Assuming Mary Kate wants to go."

Dr. Hanson left after lunch. I was at the pool and watched Mary Kate and her dad shake hands, then wave at each other as he pulled the car out and headed down the hill. Max came out of the house, said something to Mary Kate, and they went inside. No tears. No negative body language. No emotion I could see from fifty feet away. Was it a feat of control or were they not close? Interesting.

Next morning, I was up at sunrise. I quickly did my chores and listened carefully for the breakfast bell.

Ding, ding, ding. I walked up the hill, showered and shaved, washed my hair and used a bucket of deodorant. You'd think I was taking my best girl to the prom. I went to the house and checked with Maxine in case she needed something from town. She didn't. Good.

"By the way, Max, I noticed Dr. Hanson left yesterday," I said. "How did Mary Kate take his leaving? Was she OK with it?"

"If I were to guess, I'd say she was a little scared. She didn't say it, but I don't think she's been away from home before."

"Oh, poor kid. We'll watch over her."

Max looked at me with a sly grin. "I've got an idea. Why don't you and Miss Emily take her sightseeing after lunch?"

"So, my pretty little spy, you've been talking to Danny."

"It'll take her mind off things." Her smile widened. "Have fun."

"We will, thank you."

She walked out the door, and I turned and went into the kitchen. Shallah was chopping onions at the butcher-block table. The odor from a simmering pot of her ever-special chili surrounded me.

"What do you think, Shallah?" I asked. "Miss Emily and I are going to ask Mary Kate if she'd like to go sightseeing after lunch. Good idea?"

She put her index finger to her temple and robotically intoned. "Always counter a negative with a positive."

I laughed at our insightful cook. "You're a surprising lady, Shallah. There's a lot more to you than you think."

She crossed her eyes, tilted her head. "Or perhaps there's a lot more to me because I think."

"That's it, of course."

"What would you like for breakfast?"

"I haven't asked Mary Kate about our day trip, yet. I'll wait till she gets here and ply her with food." Then I said in my best Boris Karloff voice. "Women always feel more receptive over a bowl of burnt gruel."

She grabbed a dishcloth and threw it at me. I ducked into the dining room and sat at the big table.

I waited. I was nervous. More on edge than when I sat in the cab on Sabino Canyon Road, debating whether or not to ask for a job, three months ago. I'm not the nervous type. I wouldn't be wandering around the country alone, if I were. But I'd only had a thirty-second conversation with Mary Kate. She's had time to think about it. Was the euphoria I felt the same for Mary Kate? Or did she breathe a sigh of relief when I left? Did I misread the conversation because I needed a positive reaction?

Stop analyzing everything. Stay in the present. This is where life happens.

Someone came in. I could hear a cheerful female voice talking with Shallah. I jumped up and rushed into the kitchen.

"Shallah, I'll have whatever Mary Kate's having. She's promised to be my taster this morning." I popped back into the dining room, sat, and waited.

Shallah stuck her head in. "Mary Kate's ordered pancakes with butter, strawberry jam and coffee. Sorry, Bill, but your valet died last night from exhaustion. You'll have to come and get it yourself."

She disappeared and I leapt up and leaned into the kitchen. "Let's see, that's pancakes, syrup and coffee, but remember, the doctor warned me against heavy lifting. My war wound and all."

Shallah grinned. "What if I just throw them at you one by one?"

I paused a beat. "What if I apologize? Mary Kate, I'm sorry you were forced to see the ugly side of ranching."

"Your tray is on the counter," said Shallah with mock sternness.

"Fine." Pause. "And if I get a hernia, you'll hear from my attorney."

"Better him than you."

The girls laughed. I did too.

"You're too quick for me, cooking lady."

I took my breakfast back to the table. Mary Kate came in with her tray.

"Do you mind if I sit here?"

"Do you have identification?"

"My, you're wound up this morning."

I took a sip of coffee.

"I know. I'm nervous."

"Really?" She set her silverware on the table. "One of your horses has a head cold?"

180

I poured some maple syrup on my pancakes.

"No, I want to ask you something but I don't know how."

"What is it you want to ask?"

"If you'd like to go sightseeing with Miss Emily and me. I assure you, Miss Emily is of the highest character."

Silence. Mary Kate spread butter, then strawberry jam on her pancakes.

I smiled. "What if I lie and say it was her idea?"

Silence. She cuts a piece out of the stack and forks it into her mouth.

"Perhaps, it was a bad idea." I said sadly.

Mary laughed. "I just wanted to see if you'd squirm under pressure."

"And if I did, would you pull my wings off one by one?"

"But it wasn't necessary. You didn't squirm at all."

"I will later, when I'm alone in my bunk house. Public squirming isn't a good idea." I took a sip of coffee. "Bit of a mean streak there. Did you notice?"

"You just looked sad."

"That's how I felt."

"Of course, I'll go. Now, cheer up or I'll sic Shallah on you."

That broke the spell. I laughed. "That's not fair. She majored in quiptology. Her mouth is a deadly weapon."

Chapter Thirty-five

It was two o'clock on a blue-skied afternoon. August hot. The three of us were in the station wagon. It was the first ride in Wally's car since the accident. I watched Miss Emily's reaction carefully. She seemed fine. That's my lady. While we lunched on Shallah's chili, Mary Kate had gone over our Chamber of Commerce list of 'sights.' She picked the Old Tucson Studios and the Mission San Xavier Del Bac. We were heading for the studio.

"I can't believe you two are taking time out of your day to cart me around."

"Well, that's what we saints do," I replied.

"Yes," said Miss Emily. "My world class knitting, and of course my world class reading, lies unknitted and unread. We're just a couple of...what would you call us, Bill?"

"I've heard the word saints bandied about," Mary Kate chimed in. "Quite recently, too. But it was said by the President of the Silliness League, Mr. Bozo, the clown.... Seriously, thank you both. I guess I'm not used to such kindness."

"We simply wanted to be sure you weren't alone after your father left," said Miss Emily. "Have you ever been away from home before?"

"Once, last spring, a pajama party at a friend's house. I did feel a little uneasy. All they talked about was their boyfriends."

"On the right," I said, "is the famous Safeway Store of Tucson, the only store in the world that actually sells real live pomegranates. As in that song "The Twelve Days of Christmas.""

"Now Bill, there are no pomegranates in that song," says Mary Kate.

I adopted an exaggerated French accent. "I laugh in your face. You've never heard of a Pomegranate in a Pear Tree?"

A desolate silence. "All right," I finally said. "I know obnoxious when I hear it."

"Thank God," said Mary Kate.

"Miss Emily, why don't you tell Mary Kate the story of the coyotes and the collies?"

I needed to pull back on the silliness. It was becoming strained, which defeated its purpose. Good. I could relax.

"I think we're here. There's the sign," I said. We saw a parking lot. I turned in. Ahead we saw a hundred or so cars, and beyond, a group of low buildings baking in the August sun. "Well, here we are," I announced, for absolutely no reason. "I think I'm going to stay in the car," Miss Emily said. "I've been here before. When you consider the heat, the crowd, and the uncomfortable ride across the desert, it doesn't make sense."

Mary Kate was clearly upset. "I wish you had told us, Miss Emily. I could have easily picked somewhere else."

Miss Emily smiled as if Mary Kate had just said her vanilla pudding was tasty. "I came along today so I could spend time with my very special friend and our delightful new guest."

"How about the Mission?" I asked. "I can hardly wait to see it again. There are accessible sidewalks and a beautiful church. You two will love it."

"Are you sure you want to sit here in the heat?" Mary Kate said.

"We'll keep the motor running and leave the air conditioner on," I said. "We don't want to come back to a beautiful lady, roasted to perfection. After all, what would we do with a wheel chair?"

Miss Emily laughed and Mary Kate swatted me on the arm.

"That's terrible."

I grinned. "Hey, lighten up. I was about to say something sincere. Can't have that."

"Go," said Miss Emily. "You're stealing my knitting time."

I was used to the heat, but after spending an hour in refrigerated air, our bodies went into mild shock. We stepped out of the car into an oven, set on broil. It felt like we were in the late stages of smothering. After a moment or two, I could breathe again. Welcome to summer in Tucson.

The Old Tucson Studio is an outdoor set created for the 1940 film, *Arizona*, starring Jean Arthur and William Holden. It's been used ever since for films and TV westerns. It's the typical main street out of the 1870s west, with crusty wooden stores, two saloons, a bank ready to be robbed, a sheriff's office, a small church and, true to Hollywood's idea of reality, no houses for the people to live in.

Main Street was crowded with Western hats and pointy-toed boots, fancy silver-and-turquoise belt buckles, Hawaiian shirts, short shorts, cameras and noise. A lot of kids with cap guns were *bang-bang*ing their way to happiness. Toddlers cried and people laughed, doing their best not to run into their neighbor. All of it seemed to add to the heat.

"What do you think?" I half shouted to Mary Kate.

"I don't know. I can't see the town for the people."

A little lady with a big red handbag pushed her way between Mary Kate and me, and, like a snowplow, cleared a path for us. Some people exude kindness. Mary Kate laughed. But I sensed a strain in her laughter.

"Let's walk through once and then go back to the car," she said. "I don't want to leave Miss Emily too long."

"Yes, I feel the same way. Ain't guilt grand? It's my favorite sport."

There was supposed to be a show: a bank robbery with bad guys and a good sheriff shooting it out in the street. More noise.

We finally reached the end of the street, and then turned back. I didn't mention it to Mary Kate, but I was still worried about Miss Emily. If the motor shut off, so would the air conditioner. We plunged back into the crowd.

We could hear a bunch of boys, shouting and shooting cap guns behind us. A boy who was apparently being chased tried to get past us, ran into my left shoulder and pushed me into Mary Kate. She started to fall so I grabbed her shoulder. She gasped and glared at me with a half-pound of hatred. She pulled her hand back as if she were going to slap me. I stepped back and raised my hands in surrender.

"Hey, take it easy. That kid knocked me into you. It was an accident. I couldn't let you fall."

She slowly relaxed. "I know that."

"I hope you do."

She nodded.

"Let's get back. I won't feel easy till I see Miss Emily's OK."

"Same here. Come on, I'll race you." I was attempting to lighten the moment. It would be impossible to race through this mob.

"If you want to race in 112-degree weather, go ahead." She spit out the words. "You can tell me who won when I get there. Assuming you're still conscious."

Not a word was spoken as we walked purposefully back toward the car. Ten feet before we reached it, Mary bolted forward. Slapped the hood. Turned. Threw her hands into the air. "I won! I won!"

"No, you cheated."

"Yes, wasn't it wonderful?"

"No, it was sneaky."

She started prancing like the new heavyweight champion, throwing jabs at the air.

"Sneaky and sly and cunning and crafty, and let's not forget underhanded," She threw an upper cut. She stopped and looked at me with a smug smile. "How's that for a sweet young thing?" she asked.

"You forgot deceitful."

"No, I didn't. It's just that one should never brag to excess." She said, suddenly prim.

I couldn't help smiling. I doubted she'd had many pure spontaneous moments in her life. I thought it was a good thing. A very good thing.

Miss Emily was listening to Beethoven's sixth and happily knitting when we got into that cool car.

"My, you two weren't gone long. I hope you didn't hurry on my account."

"No" I said. "We hurried on account of a 112 degrees and pure jealousy. Here you were, relaxing in comfort, listening to beautiful music, while we're out slaving through a noisy, pushy, sweaty mob. Wasn't fair."

Chapter Thirty-six

The trip to the Mission took less than fifteen minutes on Old Mission Road. We topped a rise and there it was, a mile away, sitting on the desert like a white dove. It stood in the stark valley in complete harmony, like an alabaster carving, its design a perfect balance of form and function. It not only spoke of God, it also welcomed man. Not a hallelujah hymn of praise, but a simple prayer to a listening God from humble man.

Mary Kate and I easily moved Miss Emily into her wheel chair and up the sidewalk onto the Mission grounds. The grass was thick and green enough to make an Irishman dream of home. A simple fountain burbled happily. The pure white church with its orange tile roof rose against the deep blue sky, solid, strong adobe made from the same dust we're heir to. A bell tower guarded the right side. A half-finished tower sat on the left.

"It's beautiful," Mary Kate said.

"I thought it might touch you," said Miss Emily. "What do you think, Bill?"

"I think we've just left the suburbs of Hell and are starting to come into Heaven."

The interior was equally impressive by its simplicity. The crisp white walls. The beautifully colored stained-glass windows, multiplied by the sun, painted translucent shields like mystical rainbows on the walls. Somewhere an organ played sonorous and sweet. There were twenty or so visitors, each alone in their prayers, sitting or kneeling in the pews. A sense of communal peace filled the church. There was a statue of the Blessed Virgin Mary on a side altar. I went over to say hello. I'd been able to reluctantly walk away from religion, but I couldn't seem to say goodbye to Her. It was an emotional attachment. The dogma was reason and logic. There was no emotional content. I asked Her to help

186

me find my way back to my religious family. My intellect told me I was talking to a plaster statue. My heart replied, *but that's Mother Mary.*

It was a quiet ride back to the ranch, each of us doing a little interior work. The fight between reason and emotion always drained me. I threw both the rascals out and concentrated on the simple act of driving a car. Miss Emily and Mary Kate were quietly chatting about the people at the ranch.

"Maxine is indeed a lovely person," said Miss Emily. "She comes in every morning, you know, helping me stretch and bend and giving me massages. If she didn't, the doctors think my joints would freeze up. Actually, I can walk a few steps, but if I overdo it, I'm in bed for two days. Maxine is always cheerful and positive and fun to be with. We spend a lot of time laughing, and I like her a lot.

"But I tell you, there's something mysterious about her. I've met very few people in my lifetime who don't like to talk about themselves. Maxine is one of them. I don't know one thing about her. She won't even lie about herself. She's completely guarded. Whatever thoughts are running around in her head never make it to her tongue."

At dinner, the three of us were exhausted from the heat and the emotional roads we've each traveled. We sat and quietly practiced the art of enjoying our food. Danny was at the head of the table. Always the salesman who needs the presentation to go well, he broke the silence.

"Well, how did your sightseeing go, Mary Kate?"

"We had a fine time."

I recognized this Mary Kate. The polite, well-controlled one.

"We stopped at Old Tucson, which looked like every movie western town I've seen. And then we saw the Mission San Xavier Del Bac. I wanted to see it because I enjoy architecture. I think every house should have some."

I stifled a laugh. Mary Kate noticed and winked.

"We toured the entire Mission. It was so beautiful, I was awe-struck. I walked to the car in complete peace."

Danny smiled. "I could use some of that myself."

Miss Emily looked up from her steak. "It has that effect on many people. I go there thinking, 'poor me,' and walk away whole again. I wonder if they rent rooms."

Danny slapped the table in mock anger. "Here! Let's have no talk of you leaving the ranch. What would we do with a wheelchair?"

We all laughed. "You'll never live it down, Bill, at least, not while I'm around."

After dinner I was sitting at the piano, noodling, when Mary Kate came into the rec room.

"I didn't know you couldn't play," she said, pretending surprise.

"Actually, I started life as a child prodigy. I wrote my first concerto while in the womb. Had to borrow the piano from my twin brother. Took me years of lessons to reach the point where I can't play at all."

"I see. And what happened to your twin?"

"He never came out. To this day, Mother is confused as to where that music is coming from. She'll be playing bridge with her lady friends when she'll break out in an elegant Bach fugue, and it's sort of like someone at the table's passing gas. She'll smile sweetly and shake her head as if to say, 'Don't look at me.'"

"I've come to apologize."

"I accept your apology."

She leaned on the piano while I continued my life long search for middle C.

"I'm serious."

"OK. What are you apologizing for?"

She looked down at the piano. "For this afternoon. Please."

Her face was as solemn as a grandfather clock. My heart staggered for a moment.

"I'll tell you what. Why don't we both apologize?" I said as gently as I felt. "I'll go first."

Then, because I was feeling entirely too vulnerable and suffered from a lack of courage, I said, "Because I'm the oldest and therefore the tallest. And I'm the only one here who can grow a mustache. You're not Sicilian, are you?"

She finally laughed.

"And, I once met Charlton Heston. He didn't notice. I'm sorry for touching you. May you never be touched again in your life. There! That's over. You're next."

"You're the silliest man."

"Only on the surface. One apology, please."

"I apologize for misunderstanding you. And therefore glaring...and cheating."

"I thought the cheating was fun. You should cheat more often."

"Thank you. I'll practice in my room tonight."

"Just think. If all problems were solved so easily, why, we could eliminate war. Imagine all those munition manufacturers standing on street corners with signs, 'will kill for food.'"

"You're bizarre."

"Now, if we want to discuss the touching and glaring we can, without guilt."

"Do you want to?"

"My M.O. is to analyze the life out of everything that catches my attention. Lifeless things can't hurt you. Sure, there's an odor, but it soon fades. I analyzed my way right out of the faith I lived by. It's sort of like burning down your own house, while you're still in it.

"And now we come to you, my dear. Why was your first reaction to being touched, anger? I've seen that before, but it's always been followed by laughter. You reacted with anger and you stayed angry."

"I know. I was almost at the car before I could get rid of it completely."

"Is it because I'm a guy person?"

"I don't think so. I think it goes back to my first day in high school. I'm short, only four foot eleven. In grade school, I could sort of hold my own. Once you were in your homeroom, you pretty well stayed there except for recess and lunch. Even then everything was on the same level and there were four doors you could use to go outside, and hall monitors, to keep the peace.

"In high school we had three floors with our lockers on the first floor. Each subject had its own classroom. You had ten minutes to get to your locker and then to the next class. The halls were like a constant stampede, with students pushing and shoving. They had hall monitors, but they couldn't see me buried in the middle of all the big kids. I panicked. I thought they were going to knock me down and just keep going."

"Sounds like a nightmare."

"I couldn't breathe. My heart felt like it was about to burst. I knew I was dying. I was so tense, I slowed everyone down. They pushed harder. I felt I was being buried alive. This seemed to go on for hours until finally everyone disappeared.

"The bell rang, and I knew I was going to be late, and I hadn't yet found my classroom. I forced myself to read the printed schedule. When I finally did find it, I walked in. The teacher was speaking to the class. She stopped and stared at me. Then the whole class stared at me. When the teacher asked me my name, I was too traumatized to speak. Or move."

"You poor kid."

"I held up my schedule. The students started to laugh. I wanted to run out the door but I couldn't make my feet do it. I just stood there like the Statue of Liberty, holding up my paper. Now, the whole class was laughing. The teacher saw what was happening and realized I needed help so she took me out of the classroom and calmed me down. Mrs. Henry was very nice."

"Good for her."

"When we walked into the crowd at the Old Tucson Studio, I was back at the first day of high school. Then, when that little lady with the big red purse barged between us. I could feel the panic in the pit of my stomach."

"I sensed you were upset but I didn't know why."

"All I wanted to do was go back to the car. I'm sorry I glared at you when you touched me, but by then I was in no shape to be rational. Besides, in my family, touching is done under very controlled circumstances and only on special occasions. And now we come to the ritual touching. We love each other, but we're not close."

"That's more common than you'd ever guess."

"When Dad and I were leaving for Tucson, my mother took me by the shoulders and touched her cheek to mine. She didn't realize I was scared and needed more. I'd never been away from home, except for that pajama party, and that was half a block away. I don't know what I was afraid of. I just knew I needed her to hug me, just as I've seen other mothers hug their children. Instead, she said, 'Take care of yourself.'"

"How do your parents address each other?"

"Mister and Mrs. Sometimes Father and Mother."

"So, there's not a lot of outward emotion flying around the house. When your father left the ranch the other day, how did that go?"

"Much the same as Mother."

I hit a few simple chords.

"Yet, you do have strong emotions. I could feel your stress when you arrived. Once you knew that we weren't going to shove you into a boiling cauldron and serve you for dinner, you slowly dismantled the walls."

"You're saying stress is formed by fear."

"As is anger."

"Yes, I see." She thought for a moment. "Even if you merely fear you're not going to get your own way. But my fears didn't take the form of thoughts, just stomach cramps and tight neck and shoulder muscles. On the drive down here, I spent half the time massaging my neck."

"If your fears were on the conscious level, you could have confronted them. Intellect and logic could have been used. Brought them out into the open. Daylight does wonders to quiet fears that grow in the dark corners."

"Why don't we sit by the fireplace," said Mary Kate. "This feels like a long conversation."

As she and I walked together, a thought popped up.

"I think you and I had the same reaction at Old Tucson. Didn't we both become more worried about Miss Emily, the deeper we went into the crowd? I felt the same anxiety you did. Soon, all I could think of was, got to get back to Miss Emily."

"You're right. Why didn't I see that?"

"What triggered it for me wasn't just Miss Emily, it was the people. They were too close, too noisy, too aggressive. I felt hemmed in; claustrophobic, with no sense I could have any control over them; fear, like you on your first day in high school."

"Yes, I think that explains it perfectly."

She smiled that beautiful smile of hers and my day was complete.

That night, I woke at four. Something was nagging at me, and I knew what it was. I was playing psychiatrist. Damn! I couldn't seem to resist analyzing, following the trail of therefores. I'd promised I wouldn't do that. However, I might be falling in love with her. Which meant protective instincts, nurturing impulses, the whole bunch of side emotions that come with that sort of love. All fertile soil for a compulsive analyzer. I couldn't let that happen. Couldn't! Wouldn't! A fine counselor I'd make.

Besides, she was too vulnerable; too young, incapable of dealing with the complications. She needed time to grow, learn, and become...Mary Kate. To find her stolen birthright: what every newborn enters this world with...trust. Because it's completely helpless, it must be able to trust the arms that hold it, the breast that feeds it, the smile that tells it, "You are lovable."

I was finally dragged down into sleep by an infinite line of therefores.

Chapter Thirty-seven

Mary Kate was waiting for her pancakes when I came in. I picked French toast and sausages. I waved.

"Hi, Kiddo," I said. "Did you sleep well last night?"

She polished a spoon with her napkin.

"It took a while. So many things running through my little brain."

I grinned. "Little? I'd trade yours for mine any day of the week. Except Thursday. That's my bowling night."

"Are you going to be busy today?" she asked.

"Having checked with my secretary, it appears I have a clean slate after lunch."

"Good. I hate dirty slates. You sort of offered to take me walking some day, and I woke up this morning, looked out the window at the clear, blue sky and said, 'Girl, this is some day.'"

I did a W. C. Fields. "Ah, a trip through the desert's flora and fauna. Until I turned thirty-nine, I thought fauna referred to Bambi and her gang of ruffians."

"It does."

We stared at each other in smug silence. We were unusually obnoxious that day.

"You know, some people do pushups in the morning," I said.

"Well, that's what we're doing. Mental gymnastics. Ensuring our synapses are well oiled and functional. Ready to fire. Did you think we were just being silly?"

"I was hoping."

After lunch, Mary Kate and I walked into the desert, our canteens filled. She was wearing blue leather boots, tucked in jeans, blue work shirt and a white western hat with a Salerno Butter Cookie tucked in the band. I looked at it and raised my eyebrows.

"In case we get lost," she said. "I thought there'd be more sand. Have they been trucking it out to the coast for their beaches?"

"Most deserts aren't mainly sand. The Sahara is one of the few that is. What we're walking on is caliche. It's a mixture of dust and salt, baked in the sun. This used to be a huge lake, an ocean really. Think the Great Salt Lake in Utah and the Salton Sea in California. Now it's called the Great Basin."

"So, what's so dangerous out here that I need an escort?"

High cirrus clouds floated above us, and a slight breeze moved in.

"Well?" she asked, with a tinge of impatience.

"Oh, I'm sorry. My head was caught in the clouds. Ah, OK, see that nice furry bush next to the barrel cactus? It's called a jumping cholla. The fur is actually thousands of barbs that come off so easily, they seem to jump out and imbed themselves in your skin. They're like quills of a porcupine. Very painful and extremely difficult to remove.

"Always be careful not to disturb rocks or debris as you walk. Scorpions, Tarantulas, Gila Monsters and other critters hide during the day's heat. They're out at night, so walking after dark's a no-no."

Mary Kate screamed and shielded her face with her hands.

"What was that? It was coming straight for me."

"I know. They do that all the time. They veer off at the last possible second. They're called Tarantula Hawks. They're a form of Jewel Wasp. They have excellent eyesight, so why they terrorize us, I don't know. Maybe just for the fun of it."

"I'm sure that's it. I heard him laugh as he flew by. What about rattlesnakes?"

"They're the true gentlemen of the desert. They'll warn you to stay away. When you hear the rattle, freeze. They have bad eyesight. If you don't move, you'll be invisible to them. Locate the snake and slowly back away."

"What about coyotes?"

"You'll never see them. They steer clear of people. Apparently, they think we give off an extremely irritating odor."

"That's it? That's all I have to worry about?"

"Well...," I thought. "Ah...don't eat the cactus. Why? Do you feel I over sold the danger?"

She frowned. "I think it was a sneaky way to get me alone with you."

"Me? You're calling me sneaky? Isn't this the same person who pretended she wasn't racing at Old Tucson and then lunged for the car at the last second?"

"That wasn't me. That was my semi-evil twin sister, Murray."

"Murray?"

We stared at each other in mock outrage.

"Murray was the one who stayed in the dresser drawer, while I was out gambling our inheritance away."

* * *

A half-hour later, I sat with Miss Emily in her room, which is larger than it looked from the outside. Piles of books were everywhere. Knitted wall hangings in rich warm colors, like soft, cozy, stained glass windows, were on every vertical surface.

"I think we're making a little progress." I said, sipping a cup of chamomile tea Miss Emily always had on hand. "Though, never having done this before, whatever I'm doing now with Mary Kate, how do I judge?"

"You're being a counselor, just as you trained yourself to be. As to how to judge the progress, take your own advice. Trust your feelings." She smiled that sweet smile and sipped a little tea. "I did sense a positive shift in her attitude. There seemed to be a more relaxed, natural texture I hadn't sensed before. Why not give yourself a bit of credit for that? Not all, of course. I do think she's picking up the tone of our ranch life and adapting to it. What happened on your walk today?"

"First off, everything was normal. She asked the right questions, made appropriate comments, all in that disengaged way. I could sense a modicum of anxiety. But not as high as when she arrived on Sunday."

Miss Emily daintily tapped her lips with a napkin.

"This is the first time you two have been alone together, it's natural she'd drop back into her stress management."

"At the end of our walk, we slipped automatically into our silly mode. She accused me of being sneaky, luring her out into the desert to be alone with her. I said she cheated on our race to the car in Old Tucson. She claimed that wasn't her, but her twin sister, Murray."

Miss Emily raised her hand. "That's all very cute, but—"

"Then she said Murray was the one who stayed in the dresser drawer while she was out gambling her inheritance away."

"Oh my. Neither of us has ever brought up that part of her past and she's never mentioned it. What was said after that?"

"Nothing. We had reached the pool. She turned, walked toward her room. I said, 'I'll see you at dinner'."

Miss Emily thought for a minute. "You know, Bill, she got off to a horrendous start in life. Our thinking has been concentrated on that unfortunate beginning as the source of her anxiety. There may be other elements we don't know about that have added to her stress."

"You mean, over and above the coldness of her parents? Interesting. That sort of environment usually pushes the child outward, looking for the warmth and affection lacking at home. Yet, she doesn't seem to have had a support system at school, teachers, close friends, father or mother figures. After school she went straight home and rode her bike, alone. For a teenager, she's pretty isolated."

"I think you're overly focusing on her parent's coldness. I know them. I feel their distancing themselves was a direct result of the protective walls Mary Kate hid behind for years. I don't think Mary Kate sees that clearly. She's the one who has to make the effort to show them that those walls are no longer there."

Finishing my tea, I said. "Your instincts are right on target." I rested my hand on hers. "Miss Emily, I couldn't do this without you. Are you sure you don't have a degree in psychology hidden somewhere in this room?"

"I'm sure. I've just lived longer than necessary."

Chapter Thirty-eight

Each night after dinner, Mary Kate and I spent the evening together in the rec room, reading poetry, short stories, discussing everything that came to mind. There was a lot of laughter going.

It was the third week in August. On the TV news, they announced the annual meteor shower. These travelers from outer space come from billions of miles away only to burn up when they hit our atmosphere. It was a spectacular show, but for me, a little sad. The phrase "I've been kicked out of better places than this," came to mind.

The next afternoon, I spent a few minutes on the phone with the weather bureau.

At one forty-five a.m., I stepped out of my bunkhouse, turned off the water tank, and headed over to Mary Kate's room. The ranch had shut down for the day. Silent. Dark.

I knocked on Mary Kate's door. Waited for a while and knocked again. Then again. I heard the door chain being connected. She opened it three inches.

"Who is it?" came a sleepy voice.

"It's Bill. Time to go adventuring."

Pause, as she deciphered each word, straining for meaning. Especially 'adventuring.' "Will I like it?"

"Unless you're comatose, you should find it very exciting."

"I'll be right out."

"I'll be under the pavilion. Wear a jacket and gloves."

I sat and gazed at the incredible display of stars, some shooting, some not.

We walked down the road, past the stables, and up to Sabino Canyon Road.

Ahead of us, we could see the black silhouette of a hill, blocking out the stars.

"What's in the backpack?"

"A spotlight, a blanket and a few other things we might need."

We trudged to the base of the hill.

"What time does the show start? I hope you have the tickets."

"This is a freebie. Starts in a half hour. Just enough time to make it to the top. You ready?"

"This better be good, Billy Boy."

"Here we go." I flicked on the spotlight. It lit the desert for ten or fifteen feet in front of us. The desert was not at its best under the harsh light. It looked as if we were filming an extremely cheap movie, 'The Witch and Her Cactus Lover.'

Coyotes yipped in the background. Pairs of eyes glistened in the dark, and then they were gone. There was an occasional rustle as the critter hurried away, wanting no part of us. The hill became steeper and we had to lean forward, so as not to fall on our backs. We climbed and climbed. I could feel the burn in my thigh and calf muscles. My back was letting me know it didn't sign up for this.

"Would you want to rest for a moment?" asked Mary Kate.

"I thought you'd never ask. Male ego, you know."

We stood as straight as we could, gasping for breath.

After we stabilized, Mary Kate piped up. "Let's go. We're almost at the top. I'll race you!"

"Oh no you don't, you're a known cheater."

We struggled on for another few minutes and then topped the rise. I checked my watch.

"It should begin in six minutes."

"What should begin?"

"If I tell you, a picture will automatically form in your mind which later will color your perception."

We found a small clear patch and spread out the blanket.

"Sit down facing east, away from the ranch."

We both did.

"Now, just relax and watch the sky."

"Oh! Look, a shooting star!"

A meteor scratched an arc in the dark sky.

"There should be more of them."

"There's another one."

"All on cue." I said. "Just as we trained them. We use the same ones every year."

Mary Kate swatted me on the arm.

A dark crimson line appeared across the eastern horizon. Mary Kate pointed to it. "What's that?"

"That, my dear, is the opening line of the show."

Slowly, the blood-colored string grew in thickness. Soon it took on a form, until it became an impossibly huge dome, taking up half the eastern horizon, then rose above the earth, a giant glowing ruby red ball, with meteors flashing across its overpowering face. You could almost hear the bass tones of a great organ, ominous, threatening. In my mind's eye, I could see two eyes snap open, then an impossibly huge mouth filled with shark's teeth forming an earth-eating grin.

"My God, Bill, what is it?"

"The moon."

"No, it's not. I've seen the moon all my life, its never looked like this."

"How does it make you feel?"

"It scares the heck out of me. It's so unreal looking."

"If you saw it every month, it wouldn't frighten you. It would fit into the template you have of the different phases of the moon. Our mind is chocked full of templates. That's how we recognize our world. Not just the visual template, but all sorts: sound and touch and ideas, concepts. Haven't you noticed that the average person has trouble accepting new ideas? They're scary. Threatening."

"So, Professor Science, what makes a giant red moon?"

"Heat ascending into the night sky creates a giant magnifying glass. As the heat rises it takes billions of dust particles with it which filter out all but the red spectrum"

"I don't care, it still frightens me."

"Do you want to go back?"

"If I leave the moon looking like a bloated demon, that's what it will be in my mind. Could we wait until it's civilized again?"

Chapter Thirty-nine

Two nights later, after we'd had a full night's sleep, we sat in the rec room watching the fire.

"When's your father coming down, Mary Kate?"

"Four more days."

"You're going to be glad to see him."

"Oh, yes. Though I'll be sad to leave the ranch. This has been like living on another planet. I'm so glad I came. The friends I have here are very special, and you're the first real friend I've had."

"What about your high school friends?"

"I didn't have any. I don't think I was ready to have a real friend. What you see today is not what I was in high school. I spent most of my time being frightened. The rest of the time..." She paused, gazing into the flames. "Look, I'd like to write to you. If that's all right."

"Of course, it's all right, silly person! But, I probably won't be here much longer. First, I'm going to L.A. and then head to New York."

"What are you going to do there?"

"Become an actor."

"I thought you were going to become a priest."

"Not much call for priests who don't believe in religion."

Playing with her bandana, she seemed to be mulling things over. "I don't believe in God," she said.

Suddenly, dots in my mind were being connected.

"Does that bother you?"

"No. My parents don't believe, either."

"Is that why you don't believe?"

"Not really. I've simply seen no evidence of his existence. Where was God when my birth parents left me in a dresser drawer? Or, when my parents were thrown into a concentration camp? And why, in the most Christian country in the world, do we have the highest murder rate? The highest crime rate? Why isn't a religious country morally superior? Why, when the vast majority of the world believes in a supreme being, does Earth have eight wars, on average, in any given year?"

"Did you express those views at school?"

"Yes! I'm not ashamed of them." Mary Kate stared straight ahead, her jaw clenched so tightly, I feared for her teeth. Her face was scrunched in anger. This is a side of Mary Kate we hadn't seen at the ranch. It spoke of angry confrontations and of teenagers' favorite pastime, labeling, those kids never saw the Mary Kate we know and we never experienced the bristly unpleasant side.

"Mary Kate," I said quietly. "Do you think you could do me a favor?"

"What?"

"Could you relax a bit? That way, you won't explode all over the carpet."

"I'm sorry, Bill. I wasn't angry at you."

"I know that, silly person."

We sat in silence.

"Look Mary Kate, I want you to enjoy a satisfying life. A happy life. That will be difficult to achieve if you declare the rest of the world idiots. I promise you, they will resent it. And they outnumber you by around three billion."

"I'm not afraid to stand up for my beliefs."

"Let's just say religion is a private, personal option in life. OK? It's like your sexual orientation. It's nobody's business but yours. Why not give yourself a gift of four years of non-conflict sport. Four years of the peace you enjoy here at the ranch."

"That's easy enough to say, but I can't be something I'm not."

"You won't become a different person by not saying a few words. When you go to college, find interesting people and exchange worlds. We all live in our own world. Explore another. Make that final move from the dresser drawer. You've had enough aloneness."

"I know."

"There's infinite delight and mystery out there, just waiting to be explored: sounds your ears have never heard; tastes with funny names, so rich and full your tongue will send you thank you notes; exciting, thrilling thoughts you can pluck right out of the air; stimulating people who can make your life richer by their very presence."

"And how do I find these paragons?"

"You'll meet them, and they'll like you. You're bright and beautiful, with a good heart. Simply shut down the Mary K. Hanson Advertising Agency for four years. If someone asks you about religion or politics, smile and say 'I'll tell you later.' Watch and listen. You'll find people who can discuss those subjects without being judgmental. But, be careful. Stay away from fools.

"Waiter? A good life for Mary Kate, please. Hold the conflict."

Chapter Forty

The next morning, Mary Kate came down to the stable and watched while I watered and fed the horses. It was another hot August day, but with a difference, a bit of wind. Dust devils formed, swept across the valley, then collapsed.

All the horses were in the small corral except Apache, a tri-color Indian pony Danny had bought last week. A short, stocky and very smart horse. He'd wait outside in the big corral until the taller, heavier quarter horses chowed down and wandered away. Then he'd come in and eat in peace.

Mary Kate was fascinated by Apache. "Do you think I could ride him?" she asked.

"I should ask Danny. He knows more about him than I do."

"Danny's up in Phoenix. He won't mind. When I got here, he said I had the 'run of the place,' I think the phrase was. Besides, you'll be with me, Mr. Protector." She grinned wickedly. "Think of this as facing a new challenge. Conquering my fears."

"Why do I get the feeling I'm being hung by my own rope?"

"Because you are, of course."

She smiled her sweet million-dollar smile and batted her eyes like a silent movie heroine. Where did that come from?

"Please."

Twenty minutes later, Mary Kate was sitting on top of a sulking Apache. He was not a happy horse.

Mary Kate was looking supremely confident, ready to start her very own "can do" generation.

I was holding on to Apache's halter as he pranced and hopped, trying to circle around me. I started walking him. He tried to bite my leg. I slapped his nose. He tried to rear up. I twisted his head down.

"I have a feeling he hasn't been ridden for a while," I said.

"He's got spirit. Perhaps if we offer him money."

I talked quietly to him. "Easy does it. Steady now. Play nice."

Mary Kate laughed. "Tell him you love him. That always works."

Apache started pitching his head up and down. My arm felt like it was being pulled out of its socket. We wrestled for another five minutes. Apache and I were sweaty and dusty and foam was forming around his mouth.

"Do you know what's happened, Billy Boy? This has become a war between the two of you. I'm just along for the ride. A battle of wills and won'ts. Just take your hand off his halter. You'll see. He'll calm down."

"I agree. But if we're wrong, you may enjoy your first flying lesson."

"I'll take my chances. Take your hand off the halter."

"OK. Here goes."

I let go and stepped away. Apache stood there, trembling. He took a few steps backward and, head down, ears back, stared at me. I turned and walked to the stable, Mary Kate clucked twice and Apache walked quietly, sedately, forward.

Mary Kate hooted. "He's just a little pussy cat."

Fifteen minutes in the August heat was enough for Mary Kate. We hosed Apache down and then opened the gate to the big corral. He trotted out and rolled on the ground like a dog after a bath.

* * *

We were sitting under the pavilion, sipping ice cold Cokes.

"How did you enjoy your time on Apache?"

"I loved it. Horses are so human, aren't they? Almost like a twelve-year-old."

"Temperamental. I bet you could buy him from Danny and take him to college with you."

"No, no, I had enough trouble in high school."

"You must have had some good times there."

She shook her head. "Not that you'd notice. I'm still trying to come to grips with graduation."

"You forgot to change the tassel on your mortarboard?"

She ignored me.

"I was supposed to give the valedictory speech. I had four years of straight A's. Well, just the thought of it made me sick to my stomach. I refused the honor. The principal, Mr. Landers was very upset. He came over to the house. Within ten minutes, he was shouting. You see, Mother and Father felt it was my decision to make, and since I'd already said no, there was nothing to discuss. I think they felt that way because he was such an obnoxious little grunt. They really disliked him. Finally, my father asked him to leave. He left. Shouting all the way to his car, while I was vomiting in the bathroom.

"By Monday, it was all over school. Mr. Landers decided there would be no Valedictorian this year. I told my parents I wouldn't attend the graduation. They said it was my choice, but I shouldn't let Mr. Landers intimidate me."

"Good for them."

"They said I should walk proudly across the stage and accept the diploma with a gracious smile. Not only that, but, Father had already invited four of his colleagues to the ceremony, with a party afterwards, at the house. I was caught.

"As I stood in the wings, I was trembling like Apache this afternoon. All I had to do was walk across the stage, about fifty feet, and accept the diploma, smile and walk off. I expected to be booed. I steeled myself for it. I heard my name called. 'Mary Katherine Hanson.' I froze. Couldn't move."

"My God. What happened then?"

"Someone pushed me from behind. I stumbled out of the wings to complete silence. I walked across to Mr. Landers. It was so quiet you could clearly hear my footsteps. He handed me the diploma without a word. I forgot to smile.

"As I walked toward the stage exit, I took off my mortarboard and threw it as far as I could into the audience. I don't know why I did it. If I'd thought about it ahead of time, I probably wouldn't have. Now, the people were booing and shouting. Suddenly, I didn't care. I held up my head and walked into the wings. The rest of the day was mostly silent.

Father cancelled the party. We never talked about it." Looking down at her hands, a tear ran down her cheek. "Perhaps it didn't happen."

I reached over and took her hand. "It not only happened, but it proved that underneath this timid little girl is the heart of a lion. That courage is the platform for all the changes you've made here. Columbus may have discovered America, but you're discovering Mary Kate Hanson."

She giggled. "Am I going to break out into thirteen little states?"

Chapter Forty-one

The horses were jittery. They wheeled and pranced and got into fights, biting and kicking and squealing like tired children. I wondered what had happened last night. Coyotes don't bother them. Horses are way out of a coyote's weight class. Mountain lions were exterminated long ago. I walked out into the big corral. Nothing had changed that I could see. Oh, well, they invented the word skittish for horses. I shrugged and trudged up the hill for breakfast. Shallah was making popovers this morning. I'd never had them, but I had been looking forward to it. They seemed much ado about little.

After breakfast I walked past the pool and stood on the rise. I closed my eyes and vacated my mind. No thoughts, just open to whatever was floating on the breeze.

Then, I knew what the horses knew. It was coming. Whatever sixth sense I had felt it. The earth knew it, feared it and welcomed it. I brushed away the dust and lay my hand flat on the caliche. It was there. A faint but steady vibration. Adrenalin poured through my veins. Time to get ready. All across the desert, people soon would be heading for shelter. Somewhere protected, safe, where it couldn't get at them. You didn't want to be caught too far away from home.

It would come. Bringing life and death. God's great freight train, scouring and cleansing the land. I stood on the rise behind the pool. The sun was hot under seemingly endless blue, but the sky had a surprise in store. I looked way beyond Sabino Canyon Road. A black curtain had formed above the horizon. A thin line, but it had plans for bigger things. Let it come.

A great thunderstorm was coming to the desert. Even then, the thunder was mumbling and cursing under its breath, like an elephant with a nightmare. A gentleman rattlesnake giving fair warning.

The great black curtain grew larger, taller, wider, as it ate more and more sky. A sickly yellow green pallor took over the light. Snaps of lightning and towering black and gray clouds boiled and roiled and churned in the distance. We could hear it distinctly now. It said, "I'm coming. Be ready. You want to see pure energy? Wait. I'll be there in a minute."

I ran to Mary Kate's room. Pounded on her door. She opened it, but before she could say a word, I asked, "Do you trust me?"

"I...think...yes. I trust you."

"Then come with me. I promise you an experience you'll never forget. Trust me, you'll be safe." I grabbed her hand and we ran out to the rise then turned and faced the storm galloping toward us.

"Oh my God!" she shouted, as she saw the seething, surging, monster. "It's alive!"

"Yes!" I gripped her hand tighter. "Don't blink an eye. Watch every second of it and don't be afraid of fear. It's all part of it. Here it comes. Hold tight!" It suddenly darkened as if the wind had blown out the sun.

Then it was towering above the ranch, swallowing the sky, bellowing like a huge black dog, snarling and snapping its jaws as it rushed toward us, filling the sky with rain, pouring down on us like cold syrup, drenching us. Lightning tore at the black clouds, making cracks in the walls of hell. Wind shoved us like a celestial bully, almost knocking us to the ground.

I looked up to the sky. "Blow! Damn you!" I cried. "Show us what you've got. You think you can beat us? You can't, Come on. Rage."

And it did. It screamed with fury and gnashed it huge teeth, throwing its monster tantrum. Over and over again, lightning stabbed the desert floor like electric snakes attacking the earth. We could almost hear it laughing at the puny humans. But we stood. Hand in hand.

Then it was over. It was gone as quickly as waking from a nightmare, and we hugged each other and laughed like the silly people we were.

"We did it!" Mary Kate cried. "We really did it."

"Yes, we did it." I looked at her intently. "You were terrific, I mean it. I thought you'd try to run back to your room, But you trusted yourself, and trust defeats fear. You'll remember that the next time you're caught in a storm. And you'll survive, just as you did today."

"I don't know if I'll go out into a storm again."

"Oh, there are all kinds of storms. Not all thunder and lightning, but still pretty scary. Always remember, storms don't stay. You'll still be around when they're gone."

"How do you know?"

"I've been doing this since I was a kid. And you know, it's just as frightening now as it was the first time. I always want it to go on forever, growing larger and more powerful, as if it's a glimpse of God. But then the storm loses its fury and I feel sad. Cheated somehow."

"That's amazing. I felt the same way."

"I guess sometimes God comes downstairs to clean."

She laughed. I stood back and surveyed my sopping wet friend.

"You'd better get back to your room. Take a nice hot shower, hop into dry clothes. I'll see you at dinner." I stood there watching as she disappeared into her room.

The sun returned and the blue sky quietly took back its home. The world smelled clean and fresh. The air, crystal clear. The plants would soon be fat and green. The desert was ready to live and grow again, with renewed energy and vigor, all left by the storm as a going away present. The only sound, water, seeking passage into the earth.

* * *

It was two days later. I was down at the stable, feeding and watering the stock, when Wally came by.

"Hey, Bill. Danny wants to see you when you're finished here. No hurry."

"Right. I know what he wants."

"He said he'd be here till eleven. He's taking Jan out for lunch."

I knocked on Danny's door.

"Come on in."

I did. Sat in the blood red chair, thought of how apropos that seemed. Danny didn't waste time.

"What's this about you taking Mary Kate into the damned thunderstorm the other day?"

"It's true."

He threw his pen on the desk. "Why the hell would you do a stupid thing like that?" He leaned toward me, chin jutting, teeth showing, eyes squinting. Biting his words as if they were my throat. "You could have gotten her killed."

"I did what I thought was best for Mary. The storm was a teaching tool. Did she complain?"

"Hell no. She thought it was great. What the hell would she know? She's an eighteen-year-old kid!"

"OK" I said evenly. "As soon as you've finished venting. I'll explain."

"Listen, I trusted you. I put her in your hands and what do you do? You take her out dancing in the lightning. What am I supposed to think?"

"I'm willing to explain when you're ready. I think you still have some anger you need to get rid of."

Silence. More silence. Danny sat down. I could sense his body relaxing, his color losing the red of rage. He unclenched his hands. Leaned back in his chair.

"OK," he said quietly. "Tell me."

"In front of my bunk house is a ten-foot water tank made of galvanized steel. The tank alone must weigh eight hundred pounds. Has it ever been hit by lightning?"

"No."

"Fifty feet away is the main house. Maybe seventeen feet tall, with a weight of what? Twenty tons? Ever been hit?"

"No."

"If you put up a steel tower two hundred feet tall, you'll be hit. On a regular basis. But, a five-foot, ninety-pound girl, with no metal except a few silver fillings in her teeth is not a target for lightning. Honest.

"I've been standing out in thunderstorms since I was a teenager. It's liable to give you a tremendous perspective. I recommend it."

"OK, so you're odd. Fine. You like to put yourself at risk, but what gives you the right to do that to Mary Kate?"

"I believe Mary Kate's personality is largely grounded on a lack of trust that leads to fear. Eventually, that affects every aspect of her life. Some of the problems she carries with her every day are anger, lack of spontaneity, and a lot of functional difficulties. She has problems trusting others. Meeting new people. Judging them. Simply interacting with them."

"I understand," he said.

"Her world consists of Mary Kate and everyone else. That's the definition of isolation. Oh, she may marry some day, have kids, but she'll never feel completely immersed in her own life. She'll always feel the most important part of Mary Kate is a secret. She deserves better. She's a wonderful girl. She needs to address her fears. Bring them out in the open and embrace them. The fears she faced during the thunderstorm were mostly instinctive, but they were very strong. That's why I took her out there. She couldn't deny them the way she does the fears buried in her subconscious. As she stood in the middle of the storm, her brain was screaming, 'Run! Find shelter! Save yourself! Run!' She didn't. She stood firm and felt the exhilaration that comes from facing up to her fears, acknowledging them and moving on with them as a sad part of her life, not a major piece of her identity. I know it's only one step, but it's a beginning.

"Mary Kate is so bright—brilliant really—she'll begin to understand one of these days, and when she does, a door will open. There's a chance she'll pass through it and discover a strong, healthy Mary Kate she never knew existed."

Silence. Danny looked up at me. "Don't you have work to do?"

Chapter Forty-two

After morning chores, I asked Shallah if she could put together a picnic basket for lunch. She stared at me.

"I don't know you that well."

"Of course, you do. I'm that terrific co-worker you dream about."

"I know you too well."

"Come on, Shallah, it's going to be a treat for Mary Kate."

Silence.

"OK," I said. "What if I give you a nickel?"

"Well, that's different. A professional catering job. The start of my very own catering empire. But it's not enough money. I've got expenses."

"A quarter?"

"No checks. Cash."

"Done."

Mary Kate was wearing the same outfit she arrived in, blue checkered shirt, jeans, boots and white cowboy hat. We were standing outside the main house.

"You'd better take a sweater or a light jacket, just in case. We'll be at nine thousand feet. There may still be snow in the shaded areas."

Mary Kate squealed. "Sounds too good to be true."

"Oh," I said, sounding highly offended, "Then I'm lying, is that it?"

"Aren't you the silliest thing?"

"I'll get the picnic basket; you'd better grab that sweater. We'll meet at the truck. I'll be the one with the white carnation. You'll be the one with the sweater."

I walked into the kitchen. The brown woven basket was sitting on the counter.

"Thanks, Shallah. I really appreciate this."

She turned toward me. "Don't you want to know what's in it?"

"No. Let it be a surprise."

"But what if you don't like it?"

"Shallah, you've never ever disappointed me. I'm in your debt. I'll have to do something for you some day. You'll find it very unpleasant of course, but..." That was when she threw a towel at me.

"Where's my quarter?" she shouted as I walked out the door.

We packed up and headed toward the Santa Catalina foothills. "We'd better hurry," I said. "I notified the ants we'd start the picnic at one thirty. They're booked for another picnic at two. They almost declined but I said, 'It won't be a picnic without ants.' They agreed, but can only stay for a bite. After their two o'clock, they have a lavish wedding to spoil at three."

The higher we went, the greener the landscape. At five thousand feet, the mountains broke out in a bad case of pine trees.

At one-thirty, we decided the five-thousand-foot mark was the most comfortable, upper seventies, slight breeze, giant pine trees and the scent of wild flowers thick enough to make us sneezy. Mary Kate picked out a little clearing covered with soft green moss and warm sunshine. We spread the rust-colored blanket Miss Emily lent us and settled in. Mary Kate unpacked the basket of surprises from Shallah: crisp southern fried chicken, potato salad, three cokes, a container of sour cream and finally, cheese enchiladas covered with extra thick cheese and sliced black olives, which just happened to be Mary Kate's favorite, still warm in a covered casserole dish.

"I can't believe it," she said.

"What?"

"Shallah. She tries to be so tough, but absolutely no one buys it. She's just a softie."

"Yeah, I love her too. She came to the ranch a month before I did and Maxine arrived two months before."

"Sounds like a gathering. I can't imagine the ranch without you three."

"Well, we had to show up to keep you company."

"You know what?" She popped a slice of black olive into her mouth. "I've never been so...relaxed, in my life. It's like a different planet. It's wonderful knowing it's possible to live with people who genuinely care for each other. No one's nasty or temperamental or stupid or any of the usual negative traits that show up when people work closely with each other. It's wonderful. You're wonderful."

"It's magic," I said. "Everything is exactly as you think. But, as soon as you leave, a dense mist will form in the valley, and when it lifts, the ranch and everyone in it will be gone. No longer needed. There'll be nothing left but an empty valley with a mound in the middle.

"Then, one day, a fifteen-year-old boy in Philadelphia with a good heart and a wounded soul, will run away from home and find himself at the Catalina Horse Ranch with Danny and Miss Emily and the whole gang. He'll be mad as hell. Everyone he meets will be stupid. It will mirror his feelings about himself. We'll like him, just as we like each other, just as we like you. We'll feed him fresh air and horses and hard work; we'll good food and laughter and finally the gift of belief."

"Belief in what?"

"Whatever he's lost along the way."

Mary Kate sat with a half-eaten drumstick. Tears coursed down her face. Dripped into the sour cream.

"Mary Kate, what's the matter? It was just a story."

"I know. It brought back a memory I haven't visited in years.

"I was five, living at the orphanage. It was the only home I ever had, but I dreamed of someday having a real mother and father. We all did.

"A young couple came looking for a little girl to take in as a foster child. When I was brought into the interviewing room, the husband took one look at me, stood up, held out is arms, smiled and said 'Mary Kate, you're the one we want.'

"I was so happy. I ran to him. He swept me up in his arms and twirled me around. 'You're perfect, Mary Kate, the little girl we've always dreamed of.' Their names were Mr. and Mrs. Sparks, and they took me out to dinner and bought me a big beautiful doll. Two weeks later they picked me up and brought me home. There were two other children there, girls. Dirty, skinny, with ragged clothes. They stared at me.

"My new mommy and daddy never looked at any of us again. Not really. Never talked to us. Fed us mostly oatmeal or cold cereal. We had to stay in one small room all the time and sleep in one bed. They even took away my doll.

"Finally, after four months, a social worker came by to check on me. The three of us ended up back in the orphanage. The Starks had received money from the state for taking care of us. It was all a trick, an illusion."

"I'm sorry, Mary Kate. I never should have told you that fantasy. You were saying such nice things and I can't handle compliments. I had to divert the conversation away from me. That's a personality fault I'm working on. So, my little story ended in tears for Mary Kate. I'm truly sorry."

She smiled. "Let's eat before my enchiladas get cold."

"First a toast. To a wonderful happy four years at Colorado State." We clicked coke bottles and ate the warm enchiladas right out of the casserole dish.

"Have you given any thought to what you want to do for the rest of your life?" I asked her.

"Yes. I really enjoy math. Two and two are four. Always have been, always will be. You can depend on math."

I nodded. "Absolutely. No tricks, no surprises," I said. "No humans to make a fool of you. Therefore, no pain."

"Is that so awful?"

"No, of course not. If math fulfills your needs, that's where you'll be happy. We all have basic needs. The elemental genetic arrangement makes us immediately recognizable as human. We also have needs created by our environment. These are the needs that develop individuality. They're not to be dismissed."

"So, I'm drawn to the security of math." She took a bite from a chicken wing and swung it like a baton. "There's another part of me that finds the predictability to be passive. Do you know what I mean?"

She took another bite and continued. "Look what happened with the thunderstorm."

A chipmunk stepped out of a nearby pine tree and sat on a low hanging branch snapping his tail, watching intently.

"If I were a mathematician, I'd put instruments at the top of a tower that would measure every aspect of the storm, from wind speed to the internal temperature of a lightning bolt.

"Instead, you and I ran out to meet the storm head on," said Mary Kate. "In a way, we challenged it and ourselves. Though we didn't walk away with a boatload of statistics, we left the storm with knowledge of our capacity to control our fears and be the better for it. A lesson we'll use our entire life."

"You were open to learning, otherwise you would have merely gotten wet and frightened."

"I've never felt so empowered by anything I've done in the past. I can see that sort of excitement being very addictive. Facing new challenges, whatever they may be. It just seems much more positive, what do you think?"

"I think what you think. And I also think we should finish the potato salad before the ants do."

Chapter Forty-three

After dinner, Mary Kate and I were sitting across from each other in front of the fireplace. There was a bit of a chill in the air. Since the rain had cleansed the atmosphere of the dust particles we lost more heat at night, and I'd made a fire. Flames were happily snapping and popping, sending flickering fingers running across the floor.

Mary Kate and I were now comfortable without constantly talking. Silence was no longer a negative. It was a good place to be. I decided to break it.

"Danny called me into his office today. He was pretty upset with me for taking you into the thunderstorm." We stared at the flames for a minute.

"I had a hint of that," she said. "When he asked me whose idea it was."

"What did you say?"

"I told him not to be upset. That it just happened. We were out walking in the desert. The sun was so hot, the thought of the cool rain was...irresistible. I admitted it got pretty noisy at the end. Kind of scary, but exciting."

"That's not exactly the way it happened, and anyway, he didn't buy your story. Why didn't you just tell him I dragged you into it?"

"OK," she paused to collect her thoughts. "You know how close he is to Mother and Father. He's sort of their stand-in at the ranch, so he feels responsible for my safety. I understand that. He knew me when I was a little girl. We haven't been close for a few years. I think he stills sees me as his little friend. To make matters worse, my mother was against this visit from the beginning. She always worries about me. She thinks I'm fragile.

She and Father argued about it for half the summer. I could hear them after I went to bed. Actual shouting. It was the first time I'd heard that and it made me very sad. I didn't want them to fight, especially over me."

"Of course, you didn't."

"My mother didn't realize I was in the room when she called Danny. She told him he had no right encouraging this misadventure, as she called it. She said that I wasn't ready yet. That...that I may never be ready. Then she hung up on him. That's why she wouldn't come with us."

"That explains a lot of things. Why you were so stressed coming down here. I'm sorry you had to go through all that emotional turmoil. It also explains why Danny got so mad. Wow. I suppose I should be grateful he didn't set me on fire. I hope I haven't made the situation worse for you. You're a good person and you deserve the best."

"Thank you. I just wish Mother would believe in me a little. It's like she's trapped in an emotional whirlpool and can't see it. She never lets me forget how I arrived on this planet. She's so overly protective, it makes me feel abnormal. I'm always aware that I'm different. Damaged somehow. That's why I love the ranch. I feel normal here and for the first time in my life I feel good about myself."

"I know it was a pretty awful way to start out life, but the chance you'll ever go through that again, is slim."

She laughed.

"Did she warn you when you left, 'And remember, stay out of dresser drawers'? I'm sorry; I shouldn't make light of the situation, but all I know is what you are now." Mary Kate looked at me with this lovely smile.

"And what exactly am I, now?"

"Well, as you know, I've been watching you since you arrived. Danny told me you were coming and asked me if I'd be your friend. Sort of your guide in the big bad desert. Keep you safe. I've enjoyed every minute of it, because of who you are, not what you were.

"You're beautiful, funny and quick, insightful, intelligent, and at times, brilliant. You have depth uncommon in one so young. Even two so young, and you're caring to the point of kindness. A very special trait at any age. You have a strong sense of beauty and more courage than you'll ever need. You don't trust easily, but when you do trust someone, you do that person a great honor. It's a trust composed of strength and insight not often found on planet earth." He paused a moment gazing at her before continuing. "You're unusually sneaky and devious. You have the cunning of a serial killer—"

"Hey! What happened to the good stuff?"

"Well, I could see your head expanding and I feared for your safety. I mean, if it suddenly explodes, I could lose my job."

"And my mother would be vindicated. Seriously, she means well, she just can't..." she stopped. "She just can't..."

"What? What can't she do?"

Oh my God. I'm doing my math again. Mary Kate's face dissolved into sadness. She hugged herself and rocked back and forth. A tear escaped and ran down her cheek. Then another. She stared at the ceiling.

We sat in silence. We had all evening and wherever she was going, I'd go with her.

She took a deep breath then, said in an almost whimpering voice, "My mother can't control her fears." Mary Kate thought a bit more, working it out step by halting step. "As much as Mother wants to help, she hurts, by transferring her fears to me." Mary Kate stared at the dying flames. "That allows fears no longer necessary to live on. Distorting life, hers and mine," Her voice reverberated from the now haunted hallways of her mind.

"My father and mother were in a concentration camp during the war," she said in a measured monotone. "Surrounded by death and the constant threat of death. Death was an ever-present weight on their lives from the moment they stepped foot in that awful place. Squeezing out the light. And when the light was finally gone, leaving only darkness, what was left was fear. Every hour. Every minute, every second. It became a permanent part of who they were and are. It's like breathing—you grow unaware of it. Soon it's no longer an emotion, it becomes the way you translate your experiences. Their whole world became a place of fear. They mistrusted every corner to be turned. Even the simplest change contained disaster lurking in the shadows.

"When they came to America, they packed their meager belongings. They didn't have to pack their fear. It was as much a part of them as the numbers tattooed on their arms."

Mary Kate clutched her face in her hands. She let out an *ooh*. Her voice caught in a sob. "My poor mother. What a horrible inhuman thing for the Nazis to do." Mary Kate sobbed and sobbed, and like the beating heart, she couldn't stop. I stood up and held out my arms and she came to me and we enveloped each other and we cried.

From the great sadness of it.

MAXINE
Chapter forty-four

The spirits called me. I needed to be up, waiting. For what? I didn't know...yet.

It was three o'clock deep into the star-studded night, as I stood staring out the window of my bunkhouse. Across the yard, a white figure appeared. It paused, as if making sure the ranch was asleep, then moved across the front of the units and turned toward the road.

I stepped out of my door and peeked from behind the water tank. The figure reached the road and stood gazing at the valley below, then began to walk toward the stables.

Ah, Mary Kate. This evening at dinner, I'd sensed her turmoil. Her last talk with Bill had caused the many emotions racing around in her head, chasing quicksilver thoughts. *She'll work it out*, but just to be on the safe side I walked after her. The spirits, after all, had me up for a reason.

We were two figures in long white chemises, floating through the desert night. An observer might think we were ghosts. They might be right.

"I couldn't sleep, either," I said.

Mary Kate turned. "Maxine. You startled me." She paused a moment. "The nights are so beautiful. When I can't sleep, I come down here," she said and leaned against the corral fence. "I look at the horses, sleeping on their feet, and I tell myself, if they can sleep standing up, I have no excuse lying in a nice, soft bed."

"Are you worried about something in particular?" I asked.

"Not really. Bill and I talked about some heavy subjects tonight, and I couldn't seem to stop my brain from working overtime."

"Did Bill say something to hurt you?" I said, frowning. I'm sure I had an edge to my voice.

She turned sharply toward me. "Bill? Are you serious? You must not know him very well. He has to be the sweetest boy in the world. He has this silly side, but it's harmless. Why, he's the brother I never had and never wanted. Now, he's an important part of my life."

Exactly what I wanted to hear.

"Come with me," I said. I walked into the tack room, grabbed a chair, a stool, and a saddle blanket and walked out to the middle of the road, Mary Kate following.

"This is what I do when I can't sleep. Go get your stuff."

We laid the blankets on the chairs and extended them out over the stools. "Our own easy chairs," I said. "Now, sit back and watch the stars. Soon, in the face of a trillion--no, a hundred trillion stars, you'll find peace. Just to be part of the vast universe calms the worried soul." We were quiet for a while.

"How did you find your way to the ranch, Maxine?"

"Serendipity."

"Really? A random accident?"

"I was raised in the bayous of south Louisiana, then Maman and I moved to New Orleans. It is fast and noisy there. The city is a hungry animal that would swallow little Maxine whole if I'd let it.

"We sit here watching a huge piece of the universe. But if you live in New Orleans, you'll never see this. It's never dark enough. The sky is lit by the lights of the city, not by stars. The city has its own allure, of course. Every place does, when you look for it. But one of the beauties of this place is above and around us. It's up to us to look at it.

"How about you, Mary Kate? Do you like it here?"

"I love it, but I count the days when I'll have to leave, and each time I feel an ache in my heart. The thought of leaving all my friends makes me very sad. Then, the next day I'll experience eagerness, a slight impatience to move on to whatever is next. Changes in my life have always frightened me. Not any more. I guess I feel more self-confident. It's really a good thing. Don't you agree?"

"Yes, I do. We've all watched you grow from cloistered to open, from timid to courageous, and we've been silently applauding every step of the way."

She reached for my hand, and we two friends sat in glorious peace, watching the sky. The morning sun found us asleep in the middle of the road, still holding hands.

Chapter Forty-five

I was at the pool, scrubbing the side tiles with a long-handled brush. It suddenly occurred to me I'd been on the ranch for three months and I'd never gone for a swim. I love water. Why didn't the thought cross my mind in the desert heat? I filed that news flash away for future exploration. It fit neatly right beside my favorite mystery: why haven't I talked about the "happenings" here at the ranch? That's not like me. I love to analyze, explore, poke into dark places. Find the why and share my theories with anyone I can hold down long enough to make them cross-eyed with boredom.

Miss Emily was sitting with her knitting in the pavilion. She called me over. "Bill, would you please take me back to my room?"

"Of course, I've always wanted to travel."

Miss Emily offered me a cup of tea. I declined. She poured one for herself and sat opposite me in her green velour wing back chair. She took a sip of tea, then mentioned casually, "I had a nice visit from Mary Kate this morning. Want to hear about it?"

"You bet I do. I'll trade you. She and I had a long talk last night," I said. "By the way how's your therapy going?"

"Just fine. Maxine seems to be in a good mood these days."

"So, do you want me to go first?"

"Not really, Mary Kate gave me a word for word accounting of the evening. It sounded pretty intense."

"For both of us. In the end, we stood there hugging and crying like characters in a bad movie. Did she mention that?"

She looked at me oddly. "No. She did say she was crying."

"It was pretty rough, but we made some discoveries that moved us closer to completing the picture. It's at least one solid step in the journey."

We sat and played with our mental food for a moment.

"She's beginning to trust you, Bill."

"I know, and I take that seriously. She's so intelligent; all I have to do is point the way and she runs toward it, even when she runs straight into pain. The sort of bone deep pain, most people would do anything to avoid. I have to be extra careful not to overdo it. Last night she realized things about her mother that will, I hope, help their relationship. That came with a steep price."

Miss Emily peered into her cup as though she were reading the tealeaves. "It seems to me pain is built into the situation. Do you know where Mary Kate is this afternoon?"

I shook my head.

"She, Maxine and Shallah are shopping in town. Mary Kate wants to buy clothes for college. She's never bought clothes without her mother."

"That's terrific. God bless those two. Girl stuff."

"Yes, she's developing relationships here that for some reason she hasn't been able to in Colorado. Not only with Maxine, Shallah and me."

She paused, looking worried. I sensed I was soon going to feel uncomfortable.

"I'm afraid Mary Kate is falling in love with you. It's understandable. You two are dealing with strong basic emotions. The very trust that's needed to pull those emotions out is also the basis for love. You don't want to resolve one set of problems and create a whole new set. That would betray the trust you've worked so hard to build."

"You're preaching to the preacher. Look, Miss Emily, everything you've said, I've said to myself, over and over again, from the day Danny gave me this assignment. When I met her, I felt an emotional magnet pulling me toward her. I was aware of it, so I dealt with it. I'm her mentor and her friend, and we're not going to have an affair. Period."

"What about the hugging last night?"

"If you'd been there, you would have seen the pain she was feeling for her mother, heard the primal sobbing, and you would have done exactly what I did. One human being to another. We weren't crying because we were about to make love. It's important for her to know simple human kindness. She's well aware of the cruelty. She needs to experience the God in all of us."

We sat across from each other, absorbing the implications of what had been said, aware of the relationship Miss Emily and I have built together.

"Am I being a foolish old lady?"

As gently as I could, I reached over and took her hand. "No, you'd never be that. You're being the sweet caring friend I've always known and loved."

I grinned. "By the way, we're not going to have an affair either."

* * *

That night at dinner, Maxine announced there would be a fashion show in the rec room when we'd finished eating. All the talk concerned the trip to town and the shopping spree. Hocabies, an old, well-established department store, had been the hub of the activity, but the girls had been all over town. They looked a bit weather beaten. The temperature had hit one hundred eighteen in downtown Tucson.

After dinner, we all gathered in the rec room. Mary Kate and Shallah brought out a dozen or so boxes. One by one they'd hold up a skirt or a blouse or whatever for our approval. We'd applaud and whistle and try to think of inappropriate remarks to brighten the evening. At one point, Mary Kate held up a red velvet hat with a veil, which Wally put on his head, then pranced around the room.

"Looks a lot better than that old lamp shade you usually wear," I shouted.

He laughed. "I'll have you know, my mother gave me that lamp shade on her death bed." He affected a wavering old lady's voice. "Wally, my son, wear this at every party. Naturally, you'll make a complete fool of yourself. However, everyone else will feel so superior, they'll think kindly of you forever."

Danny jumped in. "I've always felt superior to you, Wally. With or without the lampshade."

227

And so it went through the evening. When the last piece was shown we were all exhausted.

Mary Kate came over and plopped down next to me. "Whew, that's hard work. You know, I've never done anything remotely like this in my life."

"I thought you handled it very well, especially putting up with us blockheads."

"I was doing it in front of all the friends I have in the world, otherwise I could have never gotten through it."

She realized she had gone a step too far. A teenager with no friends, no buddies. I tried to think of some way to turn a negative into a positive. Nothing came to me that wouldn't be obvious.

"Why is it so much hotter in town than here?" she asked.

"Heat radiates off the concrete and there's less wind to carry it away. Did it bother you?"

"Bother me? I thought I was going to die, and at times, I was looking forward to it. I figured even, if I went to hell, it would be cooler than this."

"Don't even think of going to hell. For you, hell would be a dresser drawer."

She laughed. "A locked dresser drawer."

Chapter Forty-six

The days were winding down too quickly. I rushed through my chores, ever mindful of the hours, minutes, and seconds bleeding away. It was Thursday. Dr. Hanson would be picking up Mary Kate on Saturday.

Why had I thought I had so much time? Did I say enough? Too much? I wanted to show her a glimpse of a full life, filled with discoveries, challenges. A true journey, rewarding and rich. At least I knew one goal was met. We had become friends.

Why did I feel empty at the thought of losing her? I knew what my job was from the beginning, to get her ready for school.

I wondered if I should address her atheism. It's an intellectual concept. A negative. It offers little help making your way. You can't build your life on "there isn't any." When you surround yourself with a negative, anger is a short step away. Even when I didn't believe in God, I never wanted to be an atheist.

The next day we were having a going away party for Mary Kate, and Shallah had planned a special dinner. It would be one of those happy sad affairs, not a good time for conversation. We had to talk that night.

After dinner, Mary Kate and I walked slowly down to the rec room. We both knew this dance was at an end. Oh, we would write each other. Chatty letters. Friendly and casual. But there would always be the elephant in the closet—our future together. We would ignore it nicely. She would write of tests aced and football games. I would describe parts I almost had and theater parties. Two planes forever circling the field. Soon, two hearts would wither from lack of nourishment. Emotion would fade. The chatty letters would come less often, then stop. The closet would be empty, the elephant having wandered off.

"What's the matter, Bill? You look as though the Jolly Green Giant just stepped on your puppy. Are you OK?"

"No. I loved that puppy. Seriously, it's an actor's job to dramatize life. I was rehearsing for Hamlet and I kept dropping Yorick's skull."

"To be here or not to be here." she replied, with that damned twinkle in her eyes.

"Look, Mary Kate, I need to tell you something. Do you know why I went on the road after college?"

"Because you lost your faith."

"Through every fault of my own, I no longer believed in the God I'd spent my life embracing. You said that you'd never seen God's hand in your world. That you'd believe, if you did. In a way, we've both been on the same journey. You feel the search is over. The verdict is in. Am I right?"

"Yes."

"Well, I went on the same quest, hoping to find God in his creations. If God exists, there's a little bit of God in all of us. That bit of God would take the shape of kindness. But it had to be pure, with no hope of reward. Kindness for kindness sake. Which means I'd have to be the perfect nobody. No money, no land, no power. Completely vulnerable."

"I see. Throw yourself on the mercy of the masses."

"I came to the ranch in exactly that way, a simple working person. Something happened the first night. I was contacted by entities, described to me as "The Spirits.' All I can tell you is, the encounter was direct, unmistakable and beautifully executed. No. I was not drunk, hysterical or hallucinating."

"I'd never accuse you of that."

"When it was over, there was only one logical conclusion. There is life after death. Sentient, intelligent life, capable of constructing a complex, multilayered plan, going back decades. This force is benevolent and—"

Mary Kate held up her hand. "Wait! You're describing guardian angels."

"What?"

"You're talking about guardian angels." She shook her head. "Didn't that occur to you?"

"No."

"I can't believe it." She looked at me wide-eyed. "With your mind, it never dawned on you that a concept taught to every six-year-old in Sunday school, was at work here?"

"No. Not for a second. I saw the idea of guardian angels as pap for the little kids. You know, like Santa Claus and the Easter Bunny."

"Yet, they've given you back your God."

"Yes. God. If there's a spiritual world, there's a God. A God who is not knowable by me. Not a bigger, smarter, all-knowing friend and benefactor. Not a companion, so I'll never be lonely, God."

"Fine. You're an agnostic."

"Guilty."

"Then, what do you want from God?"

"Just his existence. Why would I need any more than that?"

We sat in cozy silence.

"Why did you wait this long to tell me?" she asked.

"I thought you'd see it as an attempt to manipulate you."

"Manipulation can be a synonym for teaching. I knew you were trying to give me a crash course in Living 101. But, from the very beginning, I also knew you sincerely cared for me." She gently touched my arm, "You wanted to serve me a large portion of happiness. It was touching in a way. You did it all for me. It felt good. Like being pampered. I'll miss it. And you. And Maxine, Shallah and dear Miss Emily. My friends. I've spent my life looking for a friend, a real friend, just one. I never dreamed someday I'd use the plural form."

* * *

It was Friday. That morning, while taking a shower, I disconnected the thinking part of my brain. I didn't want to slip into the pity pit I had visited the night before. I felt embarrassed.

Shallah made a Tex-Mex meal for Mary Kate, including a tripe soup Shallah had dared me to try. We had all donated money to buy a going away present for Mary Kate. Maxine and Shallah had gone into town and brought back an eight-inch statue of a crystal eagle perched in a tree leaning forward as if it was about to take flight. The tree was an actual piece of wood and engraved in the bronze base were the words, "Now, Fly." I hoped she would like it. I thought it was perfect.

Dinner was the usual blur, with a lot of talk and laughter and a few tears quickly dried. Wonderful food, which I was ashamed to say we had come to expect. Toasts and mini-speeches. Predictions and promises. Oaths of friendship and plans for, "the next time you come down." All of it honest and real. Thank God we didn't have to feign affection.

Wally started a chant. "Speech, speech, speech" and immediately switched to "short speech, short speech, short speech."

Mary Kate was still laughing when she stood up and the chanting stopped. Now, she was serious, and she said quietly, "I don't know how I can say goodbye. You've so quickly become my world. All I ever dared to hope my world could be. Just by being yourselves, you've taught me more than you'll ever know.

"For the first time in my life, I know the difference between want and need. I didn't want the ranch, but I needed it. I didn't want to stand up to a thunderstorm, but I needed to. Some day, my wants and my needs will be the same, and I'll be a fully balanced human being. Because of you.

"Bill used the phrase 'kindness for kindness' sake. And you're guilty. All of you. Unconditional kindness. Where did you learn that? Not in the world I grew up in. At least not until I was adopted by two wonderful people. And now you. Believe it or not, you have adopted daughter, sister, friend, who will carry you with her every day of her life. A life she would never have dared without you. Wherever life leads me, I'll never be alone. I'll always have you, each of you."

Then, casually, almost nonchalantly, she said, "I love you, all of you."

We all rose as one and gathered around her and gave her a hug and a kiss, and it was over. Done. Quietly and without pretense.

I was sitting behind the piano, my hidey place, when Mary Kate came, clutching the crystal eagle to her chest. Her face was lit by a broad smile for no particular reason. She sat next to me.

"If I refuse to leave, do I have to give back my eagle?"

"Yes. It goes to the first runner-up. If they won't go, the second runner-up and on down the line, till we find someone willing to leave the ranch."

She didn't answer, simply sat with her eagle and a smile.

"Was it as good for you as it was for us?" I asked.

"Yes. Right now, everyone at the ranch is lighting a cigarette and staring at the ceiling."

I laughed. "Such a silly lady. I'm proud of you."

"So, you've discovered God. Want to know what I've discovered?"

"Sure."

"I've found the secret to happiness. It's being with lovable people who love you."

"You already have your lovables. They're called, family."

"Yes, and thanks to you and the rest of my friends, I understand who they are and why. I know now, they love me as much as they can in the only way they can. I've always wanted them to be like other parents. Now, I understand they're the sum total of all they've experienced."

"That's very wise of you."

"If they're a little guarded and fearful, they've earned that right. We always assume the next thing to happen to us will be under our control. They know it's not always that way. I'm amazed they never gave up. They kept on, building a life for themselves and me. I'm lucky. I never thought I'd say that."

"There's a very nice man coming to take you home, tomorrow. I'll introduce you to him."

"I can hardly wait. Do you know what I'm going to do? I'm going to run up to him and give him a big hug and a kiss."

"He'll be embarrassed."

"Of course, he will and he might even be angry, but I won't stop. Eventually, he'll get used to it and then he'll grow to love it like any other dad."

"I hope so."

"I'm not afraid of his coldness anymore. That's something else I've learned here, never be afraid of fear. Especially someone else's.

"I've always tiptoed quietly around my parents. I was careful not to upset them in any way. Afraid of invading their inner sanctum. Afraid of testing their love, because I was never sure of the outcome. I don't think I did them any favors. We lived in an artificial world. Now, I'm simply going to love them."

"Mary Kate, most people would never look at love as an intrusion. I'm sure, in time, they won't either."

"I want to do for them what you did for me; give them a chance to open themselves up to a fuller, richer life. It may be too late and if it is, well, at least I loved them enough to try. You know, all my life, I've had trouble saying that word, love. Now, it's as easy to say as...ham salad."

"Funny you should say that, all my life I've had trouble saying ham salad. Now, because of you I..."

That's when she gave me the usual arm swat.

* * *

I lay awake Friday night, trying to think of something funny about the next morning. Nothing came to mind. At two, the tank over flowed. I slipped into my jeans, boots and jacket, stepped out of the bunkhouse and turned off the spigot. The moon was hanging over the dark silent ranch like a porcelain dish. I happened to glance over to Mary Kate's room across the yard. Her lights were on. For the next ten minutes I went through all the reasons why I should rush over there and make sure she's OK. But I wasn't smart enough to fool myself. I'd make a rotten salesman. I couldn't do anything but laugh at myself. Then I was conscious of laughing a bit too loudly. Was I doing that so Mary would hear and come out of her room to see what I'm laughing at? I dove back into my bunkhouse before I drove myself mad. The human mind is a dangerous place to spend your life. No wonder we never make it out alive.

MAXINE
Chapter Forty-seven

Miss Emily asked me, as we and Shallah sat at the pool, "Bill swears there is nothing romantic going on between them, and I tend to agree. I was concerned when I saw them hugging. I thought my instincts had gone awry. What do you two think?"

"I don't think, I know. There's nothing romantic going on. That doesn't mean Bill couldn't easily fall in love with her if he let himself. He'll mourn her leaving."

I paused, pondering the question. "Mary Kate has at last found someone she can tell everything. She's never had a friend like that before, someone to whom she can spill her inner thoughts without any censorship. In her situation, with her parents having lived through hell on earth, as has Mary Kate, she couldn't talk to them like that. She didn't want to upset them."

"You don't have to have come through hell to be unable to tell your parents your thoughts," Shallah said.

"That's true," Miss Emily said. "Few teen-agers tell their parents everything." She looked directly at me and smiled.

"Tell me about your shopping trip," she said, turning toward Shallah.

"It was fun. Mary Kate was a completely different person than the one who arrived here. We giggled and poked fun and joked the whole afternoon. When something looked hideous on her, we told her it was perfect and she ought to buy it. So she started trying on clothes that were more and more bizarre, and we became more and more enthusiastic about what she had on."

I grinned, thinking about the afternoon.

"Finally, when she couldn't get a straight answer out of either one of us, she was forced to start making her own choices or come back with nothing." Shallah laughed at the memory.

"Well, she made good choices," Miss Emily replied.

"Yes. We finally convinced her that even if she got back home and decided she didn't like something, after all, it's just a dress, or hat, or whatever. Hardly life-altering. Just put it in the closet and don't wear it."

"I imagine those were the first choices of that kind she'd ever made." Miss Emily wheeled her chair back slightly to avoid a shaft of sunlight that had fallen in her eyes. "I think the only other things she had ever decided was what book to read next or which item already in her closet to wear that day. She'd never been the lone purchaser of anything in her life."

The three of us sat in silence, thinking about the last few weeks with Mary Kate.

"We'll miss her when she leaves," said Miss Emily. "It won't be the same around here."

I still couldn't tell how much Miss Emily knew and understood about Spirit Ranch, about who we were and why we were here. I didn't even know if she realized who *she* was. We had many talks since I arrived here, and she knew about my gift of knowing, but did she know about her own gift of healing?

"Bill will be leaving, too," I said.

"Oh? I hadn't heard."

"He hasn't told anyone yet."

"But how can we help anyone else if he leaves? Isn't he supposed to be one of the helping spirits?" Shallah asked.

Miss Emily looked from one of us to the other, then a look of understanding came over her face, as if she were remembering why she was here. "I imagine it will all come together just as the spirits order when the time comes. Divine order, you know. And maybe next time I will be able to play a part with my gift. I can heal, you know."

I smiled at her. "Yes, Grandmother, I know."

BILL
Chapter Forty-eight

Saturday morning finally arrived after what felt like three weeks worth of tossing and turning with strong stomach cramps. I was exhausted. Numb. And after all that self-torture, I was forced to face the truth. There was Bill and Mary Kate and only one of them was in love, and it wasn't Mary Kate.

I trudged through my chores and struggled up the hill to breakfast. Ordered two eggs over easy, two pancakes, bacon and black coffee. I stared at my plate till I fell asleep.

"Hey." Someone tapped me on my shoulder. It was Wally.

"You were about to dive into your bacon and eggs."

"Damn. I was aiming for the pancakes."

"Long night?"

"Someone has to count the ceiling tiles."

He nodded. "I keep putting it off in favor of sleep."

I took my food back to the kitchen. "Shallah, could you throw this in the garbage? I'll eat it later."

"We'll all miss her," she said.

I walked slowly back to the bunkhouse, stepped in, went over to the bed and fell into it. I was asleep immediately.

There was a knock at the door. It caught me mid-dream. I struggled to get back to the bunkhouse. More knocks. I opened my eyes and staggered to the door. When I opened it, Mary Kate was standing there, frowning.

"Are you OK?" she asked. "I was worried about you. I couldn't find you anywhere. Dad's about to leave."

I stared at her so earnest face.

"Did you give him a hug and a kiss?"

"Yes, I did."

"And?"

"He was sort of flustered, but he wasn't angry. When we went to say goodbye to Danny, he held my hand. Isn't that sweet?"

"I think your mother may be a tougher nut to crack."

She grinned. "I'll crack her."

There was a long pause. I shifted from one foot to another. "So...you're going. Glad you woke me. If you can give your dad a hug and a kiss, why not me?"

She lunged forward and we hugged. A world class hug. At least a nine and a half. Then I kissed her cheek and she kissed mine. One of us was crying. Maybe both. She pulled away and we looked into each other's eyes. We knew this is the way it must end.

I smiled. She smiled. It was OK.

"Look, I'll be heading for LA, then New York. Since I'll be going through Colorado, I could stop by and we could get together. You can show me Fort Collins, and I'll buy you a coke for old times."

"I've already thought of that." She pulled a piece of paper from her jeans. "Address and phone number."

She touched my cheek, turned and ran back to the main house. I walked over to the pool, at peace for the first time in weeks. No turmoil. No regrets. The Mary Kate that arrived at the ranch last month would never have run. This Mary Kate was now free to run and laugh and feel pain and joy and best of all, some day, love. First for her mother and father, and then the world and finally, somewhere down the line, one extremely lucky fellow.

I began cleaning the bottom of the pool, enjoying the temporary gift of mindlessness. Back and forth. Back and forth.

Dr. Hanson and Mary Kate came out of the main house, looked up and waved goodbye. I waved back. After they drove away, Danny and Wally left in the truck, towing the big, four-horse trailer. They were going to Taos to pick up three new horses.

The ranch felt empty and gutted—like a ghost town. I needed to stay occupied, so I walked down to the stable. I collected five horses and tethered them in the small corral, each with a bucket of water and a small pile of hay. After cleaning them off, I watered them down, and combed out their manes and tails. When they were dry, I went over them with the brush. I took Braddock out and did the same, then walked him. He was nineteen and needed to be exercised and ridden, but he was Danny's personal pet and no one else was allowed to ride him. So, he stood in his stall until Danny had time, and most days, Braddock stood and waited.

Somber was probably the best word for dinner. Maxine, Shallah, Miss Emily and I were the only diners that night.

Miss Emily looked at me and smiled sadly. "What are your plans, Bill?"

"L.A., probably."

She nodded at the girls. "How about you two?"

"We're planning to head back to Orleans and open a Tex-Mex restaurant. There are very few there now. We think it's about to happen," said Max.

"Hey, that sounds exciting. You two work well together," I said. "You should do OK."

"I knew this was going to happen." Miss Emily said, as she poked her mashed potatoes with her fork.

"What?" I asked.

"That you three would be leaving the ranch."

"How would you know that?" asks Shallah.

"I'm not sure. Perhaps, because you three are not what we usually get for help. At least a cut above, I'd say. It's been wonderful having you. I mean that. But this isn't your life's goal...to work in a small horse ranch in Arizona. I keep thinking it's tied into Mary Kate's stay here. But I don't see how that could be. None of you knew about her when you came here. I didn't know she was coming till mid-July. Why, if my feelings are so strong, don't they make any sense? There's something I'm missing. Or I'm one senile old lady."

My heart jumped in my chest. I reached across the table and put my hand on hers.

"Sometimes, we know so much more than we realize. The knowledge is in our subconscious, so we can't access it, but that doesn't mean it's invalid."

Why can't I tell her about the "happenings"?

"I have a feeling the three of us being here is not coincidental," I said. "I think it was about Mary Kate. We tried to help her and I'm sure we did. I know we all cared for her and I'm proud of us for that. I think that helped her more than anything we said. She felt loved here. It was clean and clear and kind. Kindness for kindness' sake."

Two days later, I walked into Danny's office. "Hey, Danny. You got a minute?"

"Sure. What's up?"

"My stay here, as soon as you can replace me."

"Sorry to hear that. I didn't get a chance to thank you for what you did for Mary Kate. I could actually see her blossom. The whole crew did a great job. Even Dr. Hanson could see the difference. So, what's your next stop?"

"L.A., I think. At least, I'll give it a try."

I went back to my bunkhouse, put twenty-five dollars, wrapped in plastic wrap, in each tennis shoe, put them into my duffle, and walked down to the stable. I could feel the Catalina Horse Ranch slipping away, taking its place in the past. My step lightened. Looking up into that big blue cavernous sky, I started planning my future; the packing, the cab ride to the freight yard. L.A. and whatever adventures that would bring.

As I walked toward the stable, I saw a cloud of dust and smoke, moving along the road into the valley. Leading the parade was a 1948 Ford pickup, painted a flat rust color. As it rattled and clattered up the hill, I could see it wasn't paint; it was the real thing. It had been through too many sandstorms. It parked at the house and shuddered to an exhausted silence. A tall, middle-aged man stepped out of the truck. His long face was red and covered with sweat, dripping off his chin onto his worn work shirt. Obviously, he'd had a hard, bone-numbing ride. His entire body seemed to vibrate, as if he were still on the road.

I walked up to him, smiled my very best smile, and said, "Don't worry, you'll get the job."

Epilogue

The two women stood on the rise as the mist formed over the ranch. They watched as it grew thicker, enveloping the buildings in pearly splendor, spreading until the valley floor and the mound disappeared into the whiteness.

"A job well-done," said one.

"It was that," replied the other. "She'll be all right now. She'll live a good life."

"That Bill did good, for an amateur. I'm glad the spirits sent him to help."

"Yes. He's one of those who knows without knowing he knows."

"Yes."

"And all this will start his mind to working, puzzling over the things that happened on the ranch."

"Already is."

"And he will explore his lost faith, begin to gain back what he lost along the way."

"His faith was too limited, too small, for the truth that is the whole truth."

"And will he ever learn the whole?"

"If he questions enough. If he doesn't let traditions and beliefs of the past blind him."

"Will we see him again?"

"Perhaps."

"When the fifteen-year-old boy from Philadelphia runs away and ends up here?"

"Maybe."

"And when will that be?"

"Let's see. In about five years. He still has some things to go through first."

"Will I ever be as good as you in knowing?"

"Someday." She turned and put her arm around the other one's shoulders. "Now, let's go open that Tex-Mex restaurant."

"Can we? Really?"

"Sure. The spirits will tell us when to be back. Others, though, will find the ranch before that boy ends up here."

The two women stood as the mist reached and cloaked them. A breeze kicked up and blew wisps of cloud here and there, until they were all gone, and the vacant desert valley stood waiting.

* * *

BILL

Mary Kate entered Colorado State in September of '57. She left four years later, with a degree in English Literature and a minor in Psychology. We wrote back and forth during that time. Short letters. Chatty letters, sharing the triumphs and failures that are normal life on planet Earth. After graduation in June, Dr. and Mrs. Hanson took her on a two-month grand tour of Europe. Meanwhile, I was in New York working on my acting career. In mid-August, I received a telegram; "Returning August 17th on Ile De France. Docking: Pier 19, 12:10 P.M. You must meet my new husband, Jean Pierre."

I didn't.